The Light of the Oracle

Also available by Victoria Hanley:

THE SEER AND THE SWORD

THE HEALER'S KEEP

The Light of the Oracle

VICTORIA HANLEY

David Fickling Books

OXFORD · NEW YORK

A DAVID FICKLING BOOK

Published by David Fickling Books
an imprint of Random House Children's Books
a division of Random House, Inc.
New York

Published simultaneously in Canada by Random House of Canada Limited, Toronto, and in Great Britain by David Fickling Books, an imprint of Random House Children's Books.

www.randomhouse.com/teens

Library of Congress Cataloging-in-Publication Data
Hanley, Victoria.
The Light of the Oracle / by Victoria Hanley.—1st American ed.
p.   cm.
SUMMARY: Bryn, the daughter of a humble stone-cutter, is chosen to become a student at the famous Temple of the Oracle, a training school for future priests and priestesses.
ISBN 0-385-75086-2 (trade)—ISBN 0-385-75087-0 (lib. bdg.)
[1. Fantasy.] I. Title.
PZ7.H196358Li 2005
[Fic]—dc22
2004010732

Printed in the United States of America
May 2005
10 9 8 7 6 5 4 3 2 1
First American Edition

To Emrys and Rose

To Phoenix

And to Readers everywhere

Acknowledgments

Grateful thanks to the following people:

My dear children, Emrys and Rose, both of whom read various drafts of this book and then gave suggestions both astute and heartening. Special thanks to Rose for never wavering in her encouragement, and to Emrys for his extremely entertaining comments.

My husband, Tim, for his loving ways, which sustain and nourish me every day.

My parents. Dad gave me valuable criticism, Mom gave kind support. My sisters, Bridget and Peggy, and brothers, Brian and Quentin, and brother-in-law, Jonathan, for being avid readers and for extending good wishes during the process of writing. My sister-in-law, Cathrin, for graciously helping to translate German e-mails!

My friend Bonnie Callison, wonderful writing buddy, for egging me on, helping me laugh, and contributing her precious perspective and know-how. Other dear friends (Cliff M, Rhonda M, Rowan M, Carl S, Nancy R, Joan B, Brooke A, Erin M, Charli O, Van W, John R, Jeanne MC, Carol B, Cynthia T, Karen H, Jon G, and Brenda M), for keeping me company over tea and coffee and online. You are so worth knowing that you make life worth living. And thank you, Sophie Hicks, for representing me.

Thanks also to Bella Pearson for reading several drafts of this book and providing helpful comments each time, and to Sophie Nelson for expert copyediting. Thank you, Erin Clarke and the Random House team, for your excellent work publishing this book in America.

Greg Spalenka painted the wonderful artwork on the cover! Jason Zamajtuk is the cover designer, and Melissa Nelson designed the interior. Maps by Neil Gower.

Thank you, Readers around the world, some of whom I've had the pleasure of hearing from.

And joyful thanks to David Fickling, who really is the most fantastic editor, for your magnificently perceptive insight.

Victoria Hanley

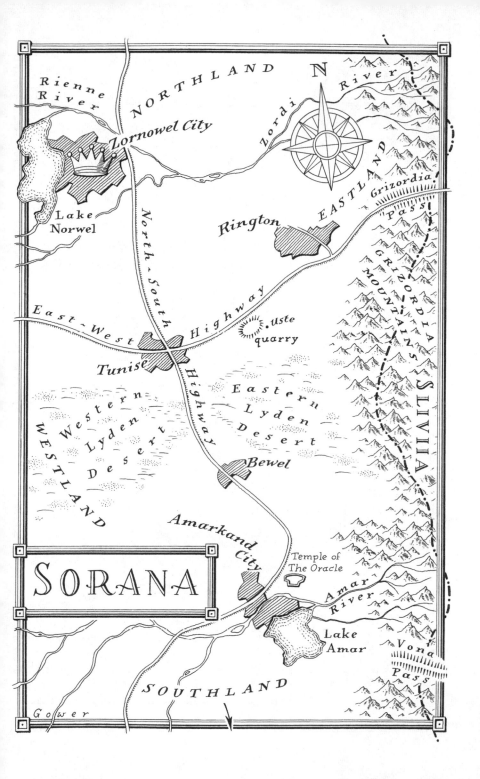

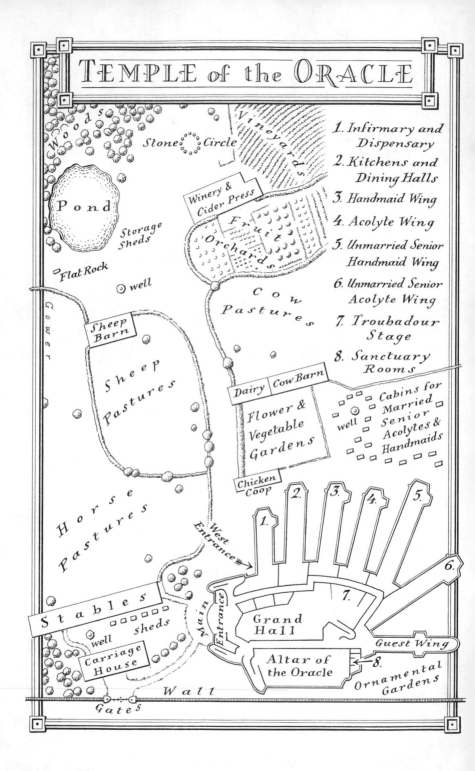

TEMPLE of the ORACLE

1. Infirmary and Dispensary
2. Kitchens and Dining Halls
3. Handmaid Wing
4. Acolyte Wing
5. Unmarried Senior Handmaid Wing
6. Unmarried Senior Acolyte Wing
7. Troubadour Stage
8. Sanctuary Rooms

Woods

Stone Circle

Vineyards

Pond

Storage Sheds

Winery & Cider Press

Fruit Orchards

Flat Rock

well

Cow Pastures

Tower

Sheep Barn

Sheep Pastures

Dairy | Cow Barn

Flower & Vegetable Gardens

Cabins for Married Senior Acolytes & Handmaids

well

Horse Pastures

Chicken Coop

West Entrance

Stables

well   sheds

Carriage House

Main Entrance

Grand Hall

Altar of the Oracle

Guest Wing

Ornamental Gardens

Wall

Gates

SPRING

One

Bryn knew that others would consider it childish for a girl of fifteen to chase through fields after a plume of thistledown. If her mother had been watching, she would have thrown up her hands and berated the gods for sending her a good-for-nothing daughter. Her brothers would sneer; even her father would look troubled. But Bryn wasn't thinking of her disapproving relations; to her, the web of sunlight caught in the threads of thistledown seemed brighter than anything else in the world.

The silky down brushed against Bryn's forehead before whirling away again, borne on the breeze. She tried to catch it, but it kept moving out of reach, spinning and leading her on. How had it come to be there, dancing in the winds of spring? Normally, thistles didn't shed their seeds until full summer.

A loud neigh brought Bryn up short. A spray of pebbles stung her bare ankles, and shouts filled her ears. Falling backward, she landed hard in the dust of the village road. The thistledown had led her straight across the path of a horse! She picked herself up, backing away

3

from the great hooves that had nearly crushed her head. Across the road in the field beyond, her thistledown was hurrying away with the wind.

"Who are you?" asked the man whose horse had nearly trampled her. His red robes, embroidered with gold, moved stiffly in the breeze. Behind him rode a line of soldiers; gold and red insignia blazed upon the breastplates of their armor. Beyond the soldiers, Bryn glimpsed more travelers.

She gazed, speechless. This vision was more real than any of the others that had glimmered before her eyes over the years. She blinked and waited for it to disappear.

"Who *are* you?" A large ring on the rider's hand flashed in her eyes.

Bryn was accustomed to being tagged the odd one, the strange girl, the silly dreamer. Only Dai, the village priest, seemed to think well of her. She had often been mocked for talking to her visions, but this one seemed to demand an answer. "Bryn, sir."

"Bryn, is it?" His lean face showed no expression. "Why did you run in front of my horse?"

Bryn looked again at the ornate embroidery on his robes. He didn't disappear; his form was just as solid as the pebbles digging into the soles of her feet. She bent into the deep bow Dai had taught her for greeting an important priest.

When she straightened, he was still staring. "I asked why you ran in front of my horse."

"I don't know, sir." How could she tell him that the thistledown had led her?

"Tell me. No harm shall come to you."

Bryn pointed across the field, though the wind was empty now. "The thistledown," she said. "It wanted me to follow."

He didn't laugh at her. "Where do you live, Bryn?"

"By the quarry."

"Does your father cut stone?"

"Yes, sir. My brothers, too."

"Can you ride a horse?"

Bryn nodded, somewhat guiltily. She and Aaron, the blacksmith's son, had made free with every horse in the village—at night when their stalls were left unguarded. Aaron had even dared her to ride a spirited stallion that had once been stabled with his father's horses. Bryn had taken the dare, and she would never forget the sensation of flying across the moonlit fields.

"Bolivar," the priest said to a soldier just behind him. "Fetch the white mare."

Bolivar, a large man with a short mustache, led forward a snowy horse, saddled and bridled with a blue harness. The soldier's armor creaked as he lifted Bryn into the saddle, the muscles of his arms bigger than a blacksmith's.

Bryn wasn't used to the sidesaddle position. She felt awkward. When she rode with Aaron, both of them simply flung themselves bareback on whatever horses they could find.

"Which way to your home?" the priest asked her.

"That way, sir." She pointed. To get to the quarry by way of the road, they would have to pass through her village, which was called Uste after the first rock miner to settle there. How Bryn wished she could ride this splendid horse through all her favorite places by herself. At home, this important man would tell her mother how foolish she had been; how she had run heedlessly in front of him.

"Come then," the priest ordered, and urged his horse to a trot.

Bryn rode behind him. She wished Dai were there to explain who this grand priest might be—but Dai would be alone in the rectory at this time of day. He called it his time of prayer, though Bryn knew he contemplated bottles of wine instead of focusing on devotion to the gods.

The villagers were calling one another out of their shops, bowing to the red-robed priest who led the procession of riders. When he lifted his shining ring, they bowed lower. Bryn eyed the ring uneasily. It was wrought into the shape of a golden *keltice,* the knot sacred to the gods. Dai had told her that the Master Priest of the Oracle had such a ring. *And no one but the Master Priest may wear it,* he had said, his filmy eyes crinkling at the corners.

Could it be the Master Priest himself visiting the meager village of Uste? It hardly seemed possible. The Temple of the Oracle was far away, past the Lyden Desert to the south. Besides, important people rarely passed through Uste. The stone quarried here was unremarkable; those who used such stone for making lowly walls and cottages would send laborers to transport it, not renowned priests.

The procession passed the baker's shop at the end of the village. As it approached the quarry, the road ahead began to fill with men and boys, rock hammers in hand. And from their midst, a woman hurried forward; it was Bryn's mother, Nora. Someone must have carried news to the quarry.

Nora pushed her way to the front of the crowd of stonecutters. When she saw who rode near her daughter, her face turned chalky. She bowed deeply. Bryn's father, Simon, shouldered through to stand next to his wife. He too bowed low.

"You are this girl's parents?" The priest's voice cut through all the murmurs around him.

"Yes, sir." Nora's face hardened. "Whatever she's done, please forgive her. She doesn't know what she's about."

"She has done nothing to offend. I have come to visit her parents. If you would be so good as to receive me into your home, I will speak with you and your daughter. Alone." He gave the last word only a small emphasis, but the knot of men and boys began to unravel and move back toward the quarry. Astonishing. Bryn had never seen a man with such power.

"Our house is close by, Your Honor, but we have no stables, only one stall," said Simon, looking anxiously at the mounted soldiers grouped behind the priest.

"I understand." The priest dismounted. He nodded to Bolivar, who leaped from his own horse and then lifted Bryn down from the mare.

Bryn walked with Bolivar after the priest, who

followed her parents down the path worn smooth by generations of stonecutters. The rest of the procession stayed silently behind. She looked up only when they came near the cottage where she lived. It had been her home for fifteen years, but now she imagined seeing it for the first time, and the sagging porch and patched walls stood out glaringly.

The priest stooped to go through the door. Bolivar remained outside, glaring vigilantly across the scarred land.

Inside, Simon dragged forth the good chair for their guest. Nora prepared tea while Bryn stood watching. Nora set forth the white porcelain cup decorated with painted violets that had belonged to her grandmother; the cup Bryn and her brothers were never allowed to touch.

"Sorry I have no sugar, Your Honor," Nora said.

"No need. I never take sugar in my tea." The priest gestured with his ring for them to sit. Bryn sank onto the bench beside the old wooden table, across from her parents. "You know who I am?" he asked.

"Master Priest?" Simon breathed, bowing again from where he sat.

The priest inclined his head. "Yes. You may call me Renchald."

Renchald. Bryn heard Dai's voice in her mind, cracked and thin with age and wine, telling her that name. "*I was long gone from the Temple, my dear, when Renchald rose to be Master Priest.*" Bryn stared at the tall, clean-shaven man sitting so upright in her family's one good chair, his robes gleaming with gold, his green eyes inscrutable. His shoulders weren't as broad as her father's nor his chest as deep, but somehow he exuded great strength. Strands of silver threaded the dark hair at his brow; his long fingers gripped the porcelain cup firmly. The Master Priest of the Temple of the Oracle sitting in a stonecutter's cottage, drinking ordinary tea? *Why?*

"This journey I'm on," he said, "includes the purpose of finding new handmaids to serve in the Temple of the Oracle. As you may know, these handmaids and the male acolytes who also study there receive the best education in Sorana. Some handmaids progress to the rank of priestess." He paused. "Your daughter would be suitable to become a handmaid."

Bryn nearly choked on her tea. Sweat ran over Simon's face, as if he labored in the sun instead of sitting in the cool of a stone cottage. The skin around Nora's eyes jumped as though bitten by unseen insects.

"I don't see how that can be, sir," Nora protested. "The girl is nothing but a dreamer. Not good for anything but talking with the air, idling about in the woods with nothing to show for her hours away."

Bryn opened her mouth to say she knew better than to talk with the air, but Renchald spoke first. "Come now, madam. I have been Master Priest for more than a decade. Do you believe that I am mistaken?"

Bryn's mother shook her head, her narrow face whitening as she looked at the floor.

"Those who serve the Oracle see what others miss," the Master Priest went on. "A child born to such a calling is often thought to be a dreamer."

Bryn swallowed more tea, gulping back a hundred questions.

"Can she read or write?" Renchald asked.

"Why would the daughter of a stonecutter learn to read?" Simon answered mildly.

"The daughter of a stonecutter," Renchald answered, "might have no reason to learn. But a priestess of the Oracle must be able to read the messages of kings and queens." He turned to Bryn. "Would you like to study such things?"

Bryn swished the dregs of her tea and then set down her cup. "I *can* read and write," she said. She met her mother's outraged eyes. "Dai taught me." Without the Master Priest's presence, Nora would surely have shouted in anger. Bryn addressed Renchald, explaining, "The village priest. Dai."

"Ah." If he knew of Dai, he didn't say. "How long has he been teaching you?"

"For many years. I've read all his books several times over."

"Ah," he said again, and a spark of unreadable feeling flickered in his eyes.

"I don't understand." Simon sounded as if someone had told him the quarry where he'd worked all his life was not a place to cut stone after all.

"The gods keep their ways hidden," Renchald answered.

The gods. Ever since Bryn could remember, her

mother had called upon the gods, asking why they had made her bear five sons, then finally given her the daughter she had prayed for, but such a daughter! A girl who burned the supper if asked to mind it, who flitted about the fields and woods, coming home with sap stains on her threadbare clothes and foolish lies on her lips—lies about people she had never met and places she had never been. Why, Nora had demanded, would the gods send her such a child?

Her father asked the gods for their blessing every morning and evening, his prayers a tumbling mutter that meant little to Bryn. And though Dai had taught her the rudiments of the pantheon, most often he spoke of the gods as if they were malicious tricksters who would trip a man on his path for the pleasure of seeing him stumble. *"Winjessen is a sly one, but it's Keldes you must look out for—Keldes wants more subjects for his kingdom of the dead. . . ."*

Bryn wanted to ask Renchald what made him think she could be a handmaid in the Temple. But he was speaking to her parents, his ring glinting as he raised a hand. "Do you give your consent for Bryn to travel to Amarkand? There she will be with others of her kind. She will serve the gods."

Others of her kind! Bryn's heart swelled. Were there others in the world like her? Perhaps they, too, had mothers whose faces never softened when they were near. The Master Priest had said that sometimes handmaids became priestesses of the Oracle. Could anything on earth be more wonderful?

Simon wiped the sweat from his face with his dusty

11

sleeve, leaving tracks of grime on his forehead. "She is our only daughter."

"She will bring you honor," Renchald said.

Nora shrugged. "When would she go?"

"If you are willing to part with her today, I will take her with me now," said the Master Priest. "If we leave soon, my companions and I will have time to reach Tunise by evening. The journey to the Temple will take two more days."

Bryn looked at the lines on her father's face, lines like grooves in a beloved carving. He held out his hand. "Come here to me, girl." He put a finger under her chin. "It's a chance for you. Shall you go?" And she knew that if she said no, he would not give his consent.

Looking past her father through the open doorway, Bryn nodded. When Simon folded her into his arms, she hoped her tight embrace would tell him how much she would miss him.

"You have my blessing, Bryn," he said.

She faced her mother next. "My blessing, daughter." Nora's kiss was cold as sleet on Bryn's cheek. She spoke to Renchald. "What should she take with her?"

The Master Priest stood. "The Temple will supply her with everything she needs." He looked down at Bryn. "Unless there is something you particularly wish to bring?"

In her mind the girl counted over her belongings. She had one other dress, but it was even more stained than the one she wore. No shoes, and she had outgrown her old coat; she was supposed to make herself another but she'd put it off, for the weather was warm. She kept some pretty rocks near her bed, but somehow when she looked at the Master Priest's stern eyes, she couldn't bring herself to mention them. She shook her head.

Renchald gave a formal bow. Her parents bent nearly to the floor.

At the threshold, Bryn turned back. "Tell my brothers goodbye," she said.

Two

Outside in the glare stood Nirene, Sendrata of Handmaids. As Sendrata, it was her job to oversee all the handmaids within the Temple of the Oracle; to make certain they obeyed the rules of the Temple, from rising at the gong to snuffing candles at the end of the day.

Nirene regretted being part of this expedition. She'd much rather be attending to her duties back at the Temple, where her authority was firm, than be here, suffering in the sun, a distant shadow to the Master Priest. The only reason she'd been obliged to travel with him was because of Clea Errington.

Clea. Sixteen-year-old daughter of Lord Bartol Errington, the most powerful man in Sorana's Eastland and distant cousin to the queen. Brought up in royal splendor, now Clea would have to adjust to being only one more handmaid in the Temple. Instead of lacy gowns, she'd be expected to wear blue student robes. The spacious bedchamber that had been hers in her father's castle would give way to a small cell separated from her sister handmaids by nothing more than a curtain. No longer would she be waited on hand and foot; she'd have chores assigned to her.

Traveling with the Sendrata of Handmaids was supposed to help the girl reconcile herself to such changes, but Clea had done nothing but complain: Why must she ride at the rear of the procession? Why were she and Nirene given second-rate rooms at the inns where they stayed? How dare she be made to wait for food when she was hungry? The wine was no better than vinegar. . . .

Now she stood beside Nirene at the end of the procession, wrinkling her pretty nose. "How long must we wait in this sinkhole?"

"Patience," Nirene answered sourly. She watched as the Master Priest led the scrawny stonecutter's daughter toward her. Bolivar, captain of the Temple guards, marched close behind them, his hand on the bridle of the white mare the girl had been riding.

"Nirene, meet Bryn," Renchald said when he drew near. "She will become a handmaid in the Temple. I put her into your care."

Nirene bowed: Sendrata of Handmaids to Master Priest. Renchald bowed quickly in return. "Bryn, meet Nirene, Sendrata of Handmaids to the Oracle."

The girl's eyebrows were strongly arched like birds in flight; she had odd teak-colored eyes, which she lowered properly when she bowed. Her bow itself was appallingly inept, however. Her palms hardly met before flopping open as her back hunched and straightened, but if Renchald was offended by her ignorance, he concealed it. He spoke to her politely. "I believe we passed a rectory?" he asked.

Bryn nodded, biting her lip.

"We will stop there on our way out of the village so you can say farewell to this priest who taught you," he said. Before she could reply, he turned away, walking to his horse.

Bryn's glance fell across Nirene and then went to Clea.

Lord Errington's daughter had hair the color of dandelion flowers; she wore a dainty bonnet trimmed with yellow ribbons. Lace adorned the collar and cuffs of her dress, silky flounces her skirt. Soft leather boots fit her feet so well they had obviously been made just for her. It would have been hard to find a greater contrast to the stonecutter's daughter, with her tangled brown hair hanging loose down her back, stained smock so skimpy it was almost indecent, and bare feet covered with scratches and calluses.

Nirene touched Clea's shoulder. "Meet Clea," she told Bryn. "Like you, she will study in the Temple."

Bryn smiled with surprising warmth. She bowed to Clea.

Lord Errington's daughter flinched. "He can't mean it," she said disgustedly to Nirene. "*She* is going to Amarkand?"

A wary look passed over Bryn's face.

"The Master Priest has chosen her," Nirene answered.

Clea's eyes glittered spitefully. "But she's so . . . dirty. Rather like a rat."

Under Clea's stare, Bryn's cheeks began to burn red beneath the smudges on her face.

"In the Temple, you will be sisters to one another," Nirene promised, not believing her own words. "Now, mount up. We are moving."

Clea mounted expertly, her foot light on the stirrup, springing to sit sidesaddle. Bryn grasped her mare's neck, pulling herself astride the horse like an untaught boy, the hem of her smock riding up to her knees in the process. Once mounted, she threw both legs awkwardly over one side of the saddle.

Clea laughed unpleasantly. "I spoke out of turn," she said. "What rat could ride with such grace as that?" She guided her horse to one side of Nirene while Bryn rode on the other, and they followed the Temple procession.

Bryn turned to Nirene. "Are you a priestess?"

Nirene gritted her teeth.

Clea gave a loud sniff. "Can't you see she's not wearing the robes of a priestess? She may be Sendrata of Handmaids, but she's still a *handmaid*—and she'll never be a priestess." She smirked. "The gods did not find her worthy."

Stung by Clea's words—however true they might be—Nirene seethed. She'd have liked to throw Clea from her horse and see her dragged in the dust. It was something the Sendrata of Handmaids could order. But Clea's father was too important a patron of the Temple to risk his disfavor. Nirene contained her anger with silence.

Bryn too kept quiet as they passed through the

village of Uste once more. The people stood in front of their wretched little shops, bowing. A grubby lad with a tuft of sooty hair waved wildly at Bryn, and when she waved back, a grin split his face.

On the edge of town the Master Priest halted in front of a dilapidated rectory. The building had once been painted red, as was suitable, but only peeling strips of dull color remained. The keltice knot carved in the door was nearly invisible in the weathered wood.

Bryn almost fell as she slid from her horse. She bit her lip again, looking anxiously at the rectory.

The Master Priest approached on foot. "Come, Bryn," he said. "You too, Nirene."

They mounted broken steps. The door opened to a musty entryway. The unmistakable smell of sour wine greeted them as they passed into the rectory itself, where a few crumbling pews faced an altar. A single candle, set upon a dingy altar cloth, burned before a woefully faded image of the god Solz. An old man in tattered robes lay sprawled beneath shelves stuffed with books. Several empty wine bottles were strewn beside him.

Bryn rushed forward. She bent to the man, shaking his shoulder gently. The reek of wine was overpowering.

"Dai," Bryn whispered. "Dai, wake up!"

He stirred, but didn't open his eyes. "Bryn?" he mumbled. "G'on—take any book."

"Dai!"

"Step away from him," said the Master Priest.

18

The girl stumbled as she took hasty steps backward.

Renchald's deep voice sounded eerie in the impoverished rectory. "Won't you pay your respects to the Master Priest, Dai?" His gold keltice ring shone in a band of light where dust motes danced.

The man's lids fluttered. He gazed up at Renchald through bloodshot eyes, then began a fruitless scramble to get to his feet. He kept tumbling over. "Szorry," he muttered.

Nirene could barely contain her disgust. Stinking drunk under the very nose of the gods! Well, this so-called priest wouldn't live much longer. Nirene's practiced eye sized him up: *Not only very old. Sick enough to be near death's door.*

Dai stopped trying to stand. He sat, gray head swinging slowly from side to side. His bleary glance found Bryn, and he began to laugh in a strange despairing cackle. "G'bye," he said. "Always knew . . . they'd come for you, Bryn." His hand flapped toward the door as he looked up at the Master Priest.

"You knew?" She seemed puzzled.

"Remember—" Dai began, but then groaned heavily, clutching his chest. The sound of his breathing filled the rectory as he struggled for air.

"Dai?" Bryn flung herself to the floor beside him. "Dai?"

"No," he gasped out. He pitched backward, his body twitching like a tired fish, eyes wide and popping. His skin began turning blue.

Bryn caught one of his flailing arms, but he pulled

19

it away. He didn't seem to see her, gazing fixedly at the wall beyond. She looked around wildly. "Help him!" she cried.

The Master Priest kneeled next to her. He cradled Dai's head in his large hands as the old man thrashed about. Dai went rigid. A long deep sigh escaped him and then he was still.

Bryn tugged at his shoulder. "Dai, please, please." When he didn't move, she sank back on her heels, panting like a winded animal.

"Don't grieve," Renchald said softly. "He probably lived with pain for many years." He looked up at Nirene. "Take Bryn outside. I will administer the final blessing."

The girl's stare was blank. Her large eyes filled with tears, and she looked even more of a waif than she had before. The simpleton obviously didn't comprehend Dai's good fortune. Why, the Master Priest himself would give the final blessing! It was what every priest hoped for.

"Come," Nirene said briskly, snapping her fingers.

Bryn wiped her eyes with grubby hands, leaving more dirt streaks on her face. She got to her feet, and Nirene put a firm hand on her elbow. At the doorway she paused to look back at the Master Priest bending over the dead man, but Nirene didn't let her linger.

The sunlight outside stabbed their eyes sharply. From the back of her horse, Clea sneered down at Bryn. "Why are you crying? Is that the only way to wash your face?"

"Hush," Nirene said. "Her priest is dead."

Clea gave a disdainful sniff. "What did he die of? Shame?"

Bryn glared. "He was more than you'll ever be," she said.

"Quite a eulogy," Clea answered. "More than me? Undoubtedly he was—more ignorant."

Bryn didn't answer, turning her back. Clea smiled knowingly.

During the ride to Tunise, the Master Priest halted the procession each time they came to a crossroads; there he would pour libations of wine and lead prayers to Winjessen, the god who presided over travel as well as learning.

After several crossroads, Bryn, drooping in her saddle, surprised Nirene by asking, "Why must Winjessen be reminded again and again to watch over our journey? Isn't he fleet of thought and quick of memory?"

"Hush," Nirene said, glad they were too far from the Master Priest to be heard. "Don't speak of things about which you know nothing." How abominably backward the girl was. Well, judging by the state of his rectory, her village priest had likely forgotten everything he'd learned in the Temple as a youth.

Clea was snickering. "She doesn't know *anything*. Why don't you throw her back in that sinkhole she crawled from?"

Bryn was quiet, patting her horse.

When they reached the city of Tunise, Bryn's head waved like a weed in the wind, her eyes wide, taking in the streets. Vendors, colorfully dressed beneath flimsy awnings of orange, yellow, and blue cloth, called out to passersby; mobs of children, circling the vendors, looked for treats they might steal; merchants haggled with their customers.

At last, the Temple procession arrived at the inn where they would stay. After dinner, Nirene and her two charges were given a small, dank chamber with three narrow cots.

Clea stood in the middle of the room, sputtering her rage. "This place is no better than a cottager's shed. Order a bath for me, Nirene, and a better room."

Nirene took a firm grip on her patience. "Tunise is not a wealthy city. The accommodations are scant, as you can well see. I cannot better them. When you arrive in the Temple, your quarters will be as small. You may as well get used to it." She pointed to a basin in the corner. "We'll wash there."

Clea whirled upon Bryn. "I'm descended from King Zor. I'll not sleep anywhere near this rat, nor share a basin with the likes of her. She looks as if she's never bathed in her life."

"I bathe in the quarry," Bryn flared in answer, "where the water is deep."

Clea lifted her nose. "And in the winter? What do you do then—wait for spring thaw?" She clenched her fists. "Get her out, Nirene."

"You can't dismiss a sister handmaid, Clea. If you don't wish to sleep here, you may stand in the corridor."

Clea threw herself onto the cot closest to the wall, turning her face away.

As Bryn splashed water on her skin, she imagined she was washing away her sadness over Dai's death along with the dust of the road. She wished she'd known the day before that he was close to the end of his life. She would have told him what it had meant to her to know him, to be taught by him.

I would have said goodbye.

What had they talked about instead? She remembered him saying that he'd pondered the riddles of life, and that his own fate was known all too well. *"The only possible mystery to be found in Uste is that of a glorious girl named Bryn. Why was she born in such a sinkhole?"* He'd chuckled and raised his glass to her.

Had he really known that "they" would come for her? And what had he meant to remind her of when he said "Remember"?

Bryn slid onto her cot, lying quite still as Nirene snuffed the candles.

Listening to Nirene's quiet breathing, Bryn missed the sounds of her brothers tossing and turning, of her father's gentle snores. Her thoughts swirled like the thistledown she had followed earlier. It hardly seemed possible that in the morning she had been running through the fields like a heedless child. Now the old man who had opened the world to her by teaching her and lending her his books was dead. She was lying on a cot in a city she'd never seen before between two near strangers, both of whom seemed to dislike her.

On my way to the Temple of the Oracle to meet with others of my kind, she thought wistfully.

At that moment Clea hissed at her. "Psst."

Bryn turned. She couldn't see Clea through the dark. "What is it?"

"When the Temple holds the Ceremony of Birds," Clea whispered, "I know which bird will choose me."

Ceremony of Birds? Had Dai ever mentioned that? Bryn had a good memory, but all she could recall was his wheezing laughter as he told her that he was "bird-chosen." *"I couldn't be a priest without being chosen. Every priest and priestess in the land was once given a feather in the Ceremony of Birds."* He had tapped his wizened chest. *"I was chosen by the common robin. Not a bird of power, I assure you."* Bryn had dismissed his talk as rambling. Most of what he said about the Temple made little sense, his words and his thoughts fuzzy with wine.

"Do you mean you'll be bird-chosen?" she asked Clea hesitantly.

"Are you really as stupid as you seem? Yes, bird-chosen. I'll be chosen by the vulture, the most respected bird of all. Then the curses I cast will be forged by Keldes, Lord of Death."

Curses? Bryn wondered if she'd heard right. "But how do you know which bird will choose you?"

Clea laughed, a hissing trill in the darkness. "I know which bird will choose *you*."

"Which one?" Bryn blurted out before thinking.

A small, satisfied snicker. "None of them," Clea answered, and said nothing more.

Three

In the morning, Bryn couldn't forget what Clea had whispered. *"Once I'm chosen by the vulture, the curses I cast will be forged by Keldes, Lord of Death."*

Outside after breakfast, Nirene gave Bryn a wide-brimmed hat and long white gloves. "You'll need these for getting through the Lyden Desert."

With good horses and water supplies, the Lyden could be crossed in a single day by following the road that had been built through its narrowest stretch. Straying from the road would lead to death, for the desert ranged a long way to the east and west.

The travelers set out with Bolivar and two other soldiers at the forefront just behind the Master Priest. The rest followed, riding three abreast. Again, Nirene rode between Clea and Bryn at the end of the line. The road seemed deserted except for the Temple procession. Soldiers of the rear guard rode so far back that Bryn seldom glimpsed them.

They'd been traveling awhile before Bryn asked Nirene to explain the Ceremony of Birds.

Clea sneered. Nirene stared straight ahead as she

answered: "It's the ceremony held on the Temple grounds at the summer solstice to determine whether the gods have chosen any of the handmaids or acolytes."

"How do the gods choose?" Bryn asked.

"If you're chosen, a bird will fly to your feet and give you a feather. After that, you begin studying to be a priestess. If you were a boy, it would be the same, but you would become a priest." Nirene spoke curtly. Bryn remembered that Nirene had never become a priestess. It must be that no bird had ever chosen her. *What if Clea's right, and none of the birds choose me, either?*

Clea had called the vulture the most respected bird. Why would a vulture be well respected? Bryn had seen vultures—great, ugly, staring things, feeding on carcasses.

As they rode, the rocky hills, fields, and forests gave way to a shiny, bare surface, reminding Bryn of a cake she had once burned. The precious sugar Nora had given her to glaze its top had melted into a brown crust that tasted bitter. "Where are the trees?" she said.

Nirene adjusted her hat. "You won't see any more trees until we've passed through the desert."

The sun glared hot and bright. Bryn felt glad of her hat and the full water bottle hanging on her saddle horn. Her eyes roved about curiously.

"Nirene, what's that?" She pointed ahead. A dun-colored heap lay at the side of the road, too far away to be clearly seen yet.

Nirene, riding on Bryn's left, maneuvered to see what the girl pointed to. She shook her head, moving back into formation. But as Renchald's horse drew even with the mysterious object, it moved—revealing itself to be a young woman kneeling beside the road. Her clothes were ragged; tags of her sleeves fluttered in the desert breeze as she raised her arms. "Stop!" she called, her voice gritty.

But Renchald did not stop, did not slow his horse. Bryn caught her breath, wondering if once again she was seeing something invisible to others. No one else seemed to hear the poor creature as she began to scream hoarsely, "You pretend not to see me? Ellerth will bury you, Renchald. I have seen it!" Bryn gasped to hear Ellerth's name spoken against the Master Priest. Ellerth, goddess of the earth and its creatures, was supposed to bring life, not death.

Not one horse slowed; not a single head turned. This must be an apparition, visible only to Bryn. She expected it to go the way of other visions, to shimmer and vanish. But as her mare came closer to the young woman, she looked even more real. Disheveled brown hair hung about a sunburned face. Her lips had cracked and bled; the blood had dried. Maddened hazel eyes looked directly at Bryn.

"Turn back while you can," she cried, her strained voice rising to a screech. "You don't know what they are. You don't belong to them."

Bryn pulled on the mare's reins, slowing, but beside her Nirene seized the bridle, pulling her forward. As they began to pass her by, the young woman lifted her hands. "Please. Water."

Bryn grabbed the leather bottle from her saddle

horn and flung it, nearly unseating herself. The pleading figure caught it. Bryn looked back and saw her pull out the stopper, saw her drink.

When her neck wouldn't twist anymore, Bryn faced forward again. Nirene thrust the mare's reins into her hands.

"Who was that?" Bryn asked.

Nirene didn't answer.

Bryn knew then, with a certainty that tingled through her bones, that Nirene had seen and heard everything and was only pretending she had not; that everyone in Renchald's company, including the Master Priest himself, had purposely bypassed the desperate soul beside the road and left her to die.

Why? Weren't these people pledged to serve the gods? Dai had said many times that the gods would look with favor upon kindness to those in need. Why then had the parched young woman been treated so callously?

She must have committed some terrible crime.

"Turn back while you can. You don't know what they are."

But Bryn couldn't turn back. She would never be able to walk to Uste alone. Besides, she wanted to study in the Temple, become a priestess of the Oracle if she could. Uste already seemed a bleak and graceless place, nowhere she wanted to be.

Gazing at the harsh landscape, Bryn rode in silence until she began to burn with sickening thirst. When she felt she couldn't bear it anymore, she asked Nirene for a drink of water.

Nirene's face was all hard angles as she turned to Bryn. "What have you done with your water bottle?"

"You saw—I gave it. She would have died."

Nirene shook her head, frown lines deepening. "You must learn to take better care of what you are given."

"But how could I just leave her? Please."

"No. I can't reward your carelessness."

Bryn met Nirene's narrowed eyes and understood that she must say nothing more now. She must act as if what she had seen had been a specter. Fear raised goose bumps on her hot skin. How long would she have to endure the desert without water? What sort of people were these, and what would be her fate among them?

When the group halted briefly for midday prayers and food, Nirene gave Bryn a biscuit and a handful of dates. Bryn had trouble swallowing, for the biscuit was dry and the dates fibrous. Clea lifted her water bottle to her lips and made gloating, gurgling sounds while Bryn waited for someone to offer her even a few drops. No one did. The mare was watered but not Bryn.

Should she go to the Master Priest, tell him of her thirst? But Renchald had ridden past the nameless woman, unmoved by her cries. If he learned that Bryn had given away her water, he might order her to be left behind.

She pulled her legs into the circle of her arms, trying to gather her whole body into the shade of her hat. *I'm glad I gave her my water,* she told herself stubbornly.

They rode all afternoon. As the heat wore on,

Bryn's sore lips cracked. At every crossroads, she wanted to run to where Renchald poured the wine, wanted to catch it on her tongue. Visions of water streamed through her mind, brooks and ponds and the deep side of the quarry. She imagined the desert as a fresh and sparkling lake. How she wanted to close her burning eyes, slip down onto the road. But if she did that, she doubted anyone would pick her up.

As the sun sank lower, tufts of green began to dot the sand; Bryn thought at first that she dreamed. But no, the air began to smell different; a hint of water caressed her nose, an inkling of coolness. She saw clumps of hardy grass, then wispy bushes, finally trees. Odd, twisty trees, with needles rather than leaves, but trees nonetheless. As the travelers crested a hill, a city was laid out not half a mile away.

"Bewel," Nirene said. "We'll stop there for the night." To Bryn, her words sounded garbled and distant.

Just when Bryn was sure she would tumble onto the road, the procession halted. She dropped from the saddle, landing in a heap on hard-packed dirt. As she floundered on the ground, a fine boot trod on her hand and she heard Clea's spiteful laugh. How she would love to trip King Zor's descendant into a pile of steaming manure.

Nirene stood over her. "Get up."

Bryn got slowly to her knees, looking about for a prop, but there was nothing at hand. The horses had been led away. She reached for Nirene, but the Sendrata folded her arms. Setting her jaw, Bryn forced herself to stand, but the inn yard wavered. She toppled, falling.

"Very well," Nirene said. "Sleep here." She stomped away, the last to enter the inn where everyone else had gone.

Bryn tried to call after her but no word came out, only a dry sound, like a rock scraping against another rock. She closed her eyes.

In the best room the inn had to offer, Nirene faced the Master Priest, who was flanked by Bolivar.

"You're telling me the stonecutter's daughter threw her water bottle to Selid?" For an instant, Renchald's calm seemed shaken.

"Yes, Your Honor. For punishment, I deprived her of water. She wasn't able to stand when we arrived, and I left her outside. What do you wish me to do now?"

He tapped his index fingers together. He looked at Bolivar. "Post a discreet guard to watch over the girl. See to it she is not harmed. Allow her to help herself as she can, but give her no aid." The soldier nodded. Renchald turned to Nirene. "Bryn may rejoin us in the morning if she is able to do so under her own power. Allow her water at breakfast, but give her none on the journey tomorrow."

"And Selid?" Bolivar asked. "Do you wish action taken?"

Renchald clicked his tongue lightly. "Selid's sentence decreed she be left in the desert without water. That was done. The goddess Monzapel must still favor her, but she cannot live for long, consecrated to the Lord of Death as she is. Let Keldes work his own way with her. We need not intervene."

Bryn awoke shivering, with the sensation of something crawling over her neck. Giving her head a violent shake, she scowled at the distant stars that glimmered upon the deserted inn yard. "You're all right," she whispered grimly to herself. Her tongue felt swollen and dull. She gave a croaking laugh. "Among your own kind."

No one seemed to be around. Bryn didn't see the soldier who watched her from the shadows. A few lights shone in the windows of the inn, but it looked too far to get to. The stable was closer. She began to crawl toward it.

Panting, she found the horse trough. With the last of her strength she heaved herself bodily into it, dunking her head to wash away the bitter sand of the desert. She pumped the cistern, her face under the spigot. When she felt the water singing in her veins, she hauled herself from the trough, and went to find a bed of hay near the white mare.

Selid, former handmaid of the Temple of the Oracle, bird-chosen by the red cardinal, clutched the precious water bottle that had been thrown to her by an unknown girl, as she walked alone down the path of the moon. Monzapel's light had never appeared more lovely—it touched Selid's shoulders with soft silver fingers, guiding her forward. The pain of the previous two days was gone, days spent under Solz's unremitting heat. Selid knew her raw and blistered feet should hurt; her burned skin should be on fire. But instead, protected and guided by Solz's gentle sister Monzapel, Goddess of the Moon, she seemed to float within a web of comfort.

By the time the sun's shimmering rim began to rise, eclipsing the moon's cooler light, Selid saw a city ahead. Grateful tears filled her eyes. "Thank you, Monzapel," she told the moon as it faded. "Thank you, and watch over the one who gave me her water."

Bryn crept into the inn as the sun rose, gnawed by dizzying hunger. When she joined the others, no one welcomed her, but she wasn't turned away and was given breakfast along with the rest of the Temple travelers. She ate ravenously.

"Where did you learn manners?" Clea asked. "In a sty?"

Gulping milk, Bryn longed to break a plate over Clea's head.

When they rode out of the inn yard, Bryn noticed there was no water bottle hanging from her saddle horn, and her mouth went dry. But the agony she felt watching Clea drink freely when they stopped to rest was more bearable than it had been the day before. She told herself that by holding up her head without complaining, she was proving herself worthy to the

gods; she wanted them to send her a feather. Not a
vulture's feather, though. A lovely one.

Bryn was too tired even to exclaim in wonder when the
Temple of the Oracle came into view. The road had
climbed steadily for much of the day, until mountains
were visible in the distance and the air was somewhat
cooler.

At first Bryn believed she must be dreaming, for
surely it was impossible for a building to be bigger
than the entire village of Uste.

Stern guards wearing red and gold insignia waved
the line of travelers through a wrought-iron gate in a
thick, high wall. Red and gold banners flew proudly
from the Temple's turrets; turrets higher than the
tallest trees back home. The stonecutter's daughter
marveled at the way the Temple walls were set. She'd
heard her father speak of masons so skilled that they
could make walls like these, with corners smooth as
glass, the mortar mixed so well that it appeared to be
only an artful addition to the stone. Marble stairs wide
enough for fifty people to stand abreast led up to great
doors embossed with brass, the metal cast into symbols
twined around a silver-inlaid keltice. The great silver
knot was delicately worked, yet it looked strong
enough to bind the world.

Bryn dismounted along with the others beside
long stables. Eager for water, she took a step toward
the Temple. A firm hand fell on her shoulder. "Come
along," Nirene said sharply, waving both her and Clea
down a path away from the broad stairs.

"Where are we going now?" Clea asked irritably.

Nirene rounded on her. "Royalty or not, Clea, I will tell you only once: When anyone here in the Temple, whether priest, priestess, guard, or Sendrata of Handmaids, gives you—a *student*—a direction, do as you're told." She took in both girls with her furious glance.

Faint and nauseated, Bryn nodded, very glad that she would not have to walk up all those stairs just now. Clea nodded too, resentfully, and Nirene led on past a corner of the Temple, along a wall, and around another corner where soldiers guarded a studded door. Nodding to the guards, Nirene opened the door, pushing Bryn and Clea into a wide hallway lit by flaring torches.

Four

Dawn was the tallest handmaid in the Temple of the Oracle. Her morning was beginning badly, and she believed her height was to blame. She'd already bumped her shins on the edge of her bed—*twice*—and had nearly upset the basin while washing, though she'd purposely risen before the gong to give herself extra time. At seventeen, she should be done with growing taller—would she ever stop? Her student robe was getting short. Again.

She hurried back to the long room she shared with dozens of other handmaids. She would make her bed, straighten her desk, and draw her curtain so that it hung evenly as it should, all before the gong sounded and woke the others.

As she wrestled with the stiff loops of the heavy beige curtain that separated her bed from those of the handmaids on either side, Nirene approached her. Dawn sighed, expecting to be reprimanded for something, but the Sendrata of Handmaids bade her sit on her rumpled bed, and then abruptly told her that it was time she became a duenna. Duennas looked after new handmaids for their first year at the Temple, guiding them, helping them study and learn.

"Ohh!" Dawn cried, excitement vying with surprise within her; she'd been doing well in her studies and not causing too much trouble, but she wasn't bird-chosen yet and might never be.

"For pity's sake, don't squeal," Nirene said, frowning.

"I'll be the best duenna you have, Sendrata," Dawn whispered fervently. "But which handmaid will be my ward? You brought in two last night." Dawn hoped she'd be assigned to the ragged peasant girl, who'd been so tired when she arrived that she'd fallen onto the bed assigned her. Nirene, lips pursed in irritation, had drawn the curtain around the sleeping girl herself. The other new handmaid, the yellow-haired one with a false smile who put on airs, was rumored to be a cousin to the queen.

Nirene pointed across the room. "Her name is Bryn. A stonecutter's daughter. You may begin by getting her out of bed and explaining what is expected of her."

The one she'd hoped for! Dawn grinned, even as nervous fear rose in her chest. Bryn was sleeping in the bed formerly belonging to Selid, the handmaid who had disappeared a week or more ago. "Won't Selid be coming back?" Dawn asked.

"No," Nirene snapped. "You'd best forget her, and there's no need to gabble about her to Bryn."

"Yes, ma'am." Dawn wanted to ask where and why Selid had gone, but it would be useless.

"Remember, duennas are responsible for the actions of their wards. As you know, Queen Alessandra will be visiting the Temple in a few weeks." Nirene's lips tightened. "You must teach Bryn protocol, so she doesn't disgrace you."

Dawn sucked in her breath. Yes, of course she knew about the impending visit by Sorana's queen. "I'll teach her everything she needs to know, Sendrata."

"See that you do. Today, you'll show her the work areas and grounds; you're excused from your studies. And try to divine any abilities Bryn may have so that when I assign her chores I won't be too gravely disappointed."

"Me? Divine her abilities?"

The Sendrata frowned. "Haven't you been studying the stars for more than two years? Ishaan tells me your progress is adequate."

Adequate? Dawn didn't know what to make of Nirene's comment. Ishaan was teaching her about the heavens: the stars and planets, led by the gods, influenced people and events. She'd been chosen to study the stars because she was head of the class in mathematics and she could calculate planetary positions in the skies. But Ishaan had never given Dawn the least indication that she was making "adequate" progress. In fact, he frequently scowled at her, bemoaning her lack of understanding.

Fortunately, Nirene didn't wait for a reply. She marched away. Dawn saw her approach Alyce's curtain and pitied Alyce, guessing she was to be duenna for the other handmaid, the conceited one. Strangely enough, Alyce wasn't bird-chosen either. Ah well, who knew why the Sendrata did what she did? Her orders could not be questioned, only obeyed.

Pulling aside the curtain around the bed that had been Selid's for so many years, Dawn wondered again what had become of Selid. Chosen by the red cardinal and said to be the most talented prophetess in the Temple, Selid had treated everyone with the same distant kindness. She'd been close to becoming a priestess when she left. *Will I ever find out what happened?*

The wake-up gong was still several minutes away. Dawn kneeled by Bryn's bedside. She would wake her now and show her where to wash before the other handmaids rose.

Untidy strands of chestnut-brown hair spilled over Bryn's pillow, and her face was streaked with grime. Her dress was stained and threadbare, torn at the hem and one of the shoulders. Lifting one of her hands, Dawn felt calluses on the palm and fingers.

Bryn opened alert golden-brown eyes. "Water," she whispered.

"Sorry about the old robes and scuffed shoes," Dawn said after she'd given Bryn water and taken her to the dispensary for clothes. "It's the penance for being poor. Wealthy handmaids get their robes sent from home—more fancy every year." She snorted. "So much for being 'sisters' here at the Temple."

"These are finery to me," Bryn said, but Dawn thought she looked very shabby. When they reached

39

the dining hall, Bryn stared about her with great eyes, awed by the length of the room, the deep windows on two sides, the well-varnished tables, the senior handmaids who served those who were eating. She handled the dishes as if they might break at her touch. Dawn, a weaver's daughter, remembered her own first day in the Temple, and how elegant the glazed pottery had appeared to her, how soft the linen napkins, how clean and smooth the granite floors.

Once the grace had been spoken, Dawn introduced Bryn to the other young women who often shared an eating table. "This is Jacinta. She's dove-chosen." Jacinta's glossy braid was wound with blue ribbons. Her robe fell in elegant lines, and her skin glowed. She greeted Bryn with gentle friendliness.

"And here's Alyce," Dawn said, pointing to the young woman sitting across from her. Alyce had straw-colored hair and darting blue eyes. "Did Nirene make you duenna to the other new handmaid?" Dawn asked her friend.

Alyce tossed her braid behind her shoulder. "Oh yes. Clea. *Lord* Errington's daughter, as she made plain within seconds."

"Descended from King Zor," Bryn put in.

Alyce laughed. "Pity me. I'm her duenna, but she can't bear to be seen with me; she must have smelled out that I'm nothing but a baker's daughter. How will I endure a year with her as my ward?" She pointed with her fork at the table behind Dawn. "Look. The Feathers have accepted Clea before she's even set foot in the Ceremony of Birds."

40

Turning, Dawn saw Clea seated next to Eloise in the group of bird-chosen handmaids known as the Feathers. "Naturally," Dawn said acidly. "She probably met Eloise when they were both little nibbies crawling through their papas' castles, long before they wanted to be Feathers."

"Feathers?" Bryn asked, puzzled.

"Bird-chosen snobs," Dawn explained. "The girls who keep sneering in your direction. They call themselves the Feathers." She hefted her mug to her friends. "How we'll laugh if no bird chooses Clea."

"She thinks the vulture will choose her," Bryn said.

Dawn had just taken a drink of milk. "Vulture?" she spluttered. Across the table, Jacinta and Alyce froze. "May the gods forbid," Dawn said.

Bryn watched as the others laid their napkins on the table to signal completion of the meal. She copied them.

"Trying to teach the quarry rat manners, Dawn?" said a voice at her shoulder. Turning, Bryn saw one of the young women who had been sitting with Clea. Wispy eyebrows lifted into the girl's high forehead, and her full lips were gathered into a sneer. The satiny sleeves of her blue robe looked as if they hadn't seen a day's wear.

Dawn didn't look up. "Find someone to teach *you* manners, Eloise."

"How touching that you would stick up for your rat. But for gods' sake, give her a bath!" And Eloise moved away, surrounded by a group of sniggering handmaids, all of them dressed in fine robes.

"Don't listen to her," Dawn said. "She's chosen by the woodpecker, which means she has a tireless beak." She smiled grimly. "I'll show you the grounds now."

Her long legs set a rapid pace through the hallways as she led the way to an outside door. She bowed to a guard standing by. He wore a helmet of beaten brass; red cloth was embroidered with gold over his breast-plate in the insignia of the Temple soldiers; a sword and dagger hung at his hip, a bow at his back.

"What do they guard against?" Bryn asked as she followed Dawn out into the sunlight.

"Didn't anyone tell you that the word of the Oracle is very valuable? What if prophecies meant for Queen Alessandra or Lord Errington fell into another's hands? The Temple has some of the most skilled warriors in the world. They pledge their lives to safe-guard the prophecies and protect the priesthood."

"Oh." Bryn felt ignorant again. She looked over her shoulder at the guard's bristling weapons.

Dawn led her past immense gardens where young vegetable plants climbed upon trellises and poles. Broad beds of flowers patched the garden like a color-ful quilt. Several acolytes and handmaids tended the plants.

Dawn explained that the Temple grew produce and kept flocks of sheep, chickens, and geese to pro-vide for its members. A vineyard and dairy were at-tached to the grounds as well. "Come on," Dawn motioned.

Scurrying a little to keep up, Bryn began asking questions. "You said Jacinta was chosen by a dove? Why isn't she one of the Feathers, then?"

Dawn snorted and waved her slender hands. "Jacinta's a poor tailor's daughter. Feathers call her 'Pigeon' and coo in a nasty way when she walks by. You need more than a choosing bird to become a Feather—you must have a wealthy family. Clea's the first one they've accepted *before* she's been chosen by a bird."

"How does Clea know she'll be chosen by the vulture?" Bryn asked.

Dawn shrugged. "Some claim to know their choosing birds beforehand, but most are wise enough to keep quiet about it. Nothing more humiliating than saying a certain bird will choose you and then being chosen by a different bird or by none at all." Dawn's black hair set off startling azure eyes as she peered at Bryn. "I've always admired the heron, but people are seldom chosen after they are sixteen. I'm nearly eighteen, so this year will be my last chance."

Bryn thought the heron would suit Dawn precisely and hoped the elegant bird would choose her.

Chickens squawked as they approached a large coop. Dawn jumped when a big wolfish dog suddenly appeared round the corner of the coop, but Bryn dropped to her knees beside the dog, stroking his speckled black and white coat. He looked at her through mismatched eyes, one bluish white, the other nearly yellow, then put his muddy paw on her shoulder.

"You'll have to wash your robe," Dawn said,

hanging back. "Jack isn't normally so friendly with strangers."

"Jack?" Bryn was fascinated by the dog's intelligent expression. "Hello, Jack."

The dog whuffed at her and pawed her shoulder gently, giving her a strangely human grin.

Just then a young man strode out from behind the coop. Slightly taller than Dawn, he had shaggy reddish hair. Freckles sprinkled his skin as if someone had thrown baker's cinnamon powder over him. He looked at Jack. Bryn had the odd feeling that he and the dog were silently talking. About her.

"Kiran, this is Bryn," Dawn said, "a new hand-maid—and I'm her duenna."

Jack lowered his paw and Bryn got to her feet, her robe mussed. Kiran gave her a long glance; the shade of his eyes matched his hair. He murmured a gruff hello.

"Hello," she answered, feeling flustered and not knowing why.

Kiran began moving away, whistling a short call to Jack, who paused to lick Bryn's hand before following the tall young man.

Bryn twisted to look after them. Dawn left the foot-path to walk through the grass that bordered a pasture fence. Bryn trailed after her, the long grass dragging at her robe. "But who *is* Kiran?" she asked.

"He's from the Eastland. The Master Priest found him there," Dawn answered. "He keeps to himself, but he's good with animals. Everyone says he should be swan-chosen."

"Should be?" Bryn asked in confusion.

Dawn climbed the fence that divided a flock of sheep from a herd of horses. "A swan's feather means spirit-talk with the animals, though don't tell anyone I said so."

Bryn perched beside her, watching the colts gallop. "Why not tell anyone?"

Dawn frowned. "We're not supposed to speak of the bird gifts. They're secret."

"Bird gifts?"

"Gifts," Dawn answered firmly. "All the bird-chosen can prophesy, of course, though some are *much* better than others—"

"Prophesy?" Bryn interrupted.

Dawn squinted at her. "Surely you know what prophecy is? Seeing visions sent by the Oracle. Visions of the future."

"Oh." Bryn chewed her lip. "All the bird-chosen see visions, then?"

"Yes. While they're young. Prophecy dwindles with age," Dawn explained. "I don't know how quickly it's lost—handmaids aren't told about such things. But beyond prophecy, all bird-chosen people have one other talent that's secret, a talent given to them along with their feathers. A few of the talents are so famous they're no longer secret. For instance, everyone knows that being chosen by the vulture means being able to cast curses. But the gifts are *supposed* to be hidden." She leaned nearer. "At any rate, most of the bird-chosen are unable to use their gifts—except for prophecy—until they join the

45

priesthood. After that, they guard the secrets of their gifts very closely."

"Oh." Bryn thought of the way Kiran had looked at the dog Jack. "Is the swan feather famous too? Is that how you know it means spirit-talk with animals?"

Dawn nodded. She lowered her voice. "A swan was winging for Kiran in the Ceremony of Birds when he was thirteen but he spoke to it—mind to mind—to make it leave without choosing him. He's sent it away every year since; I've seen him do it four years running. The Master Priest wants honored feathers such as the swan to be part of the Temple, of course. No doubt he's enraged by Kiran, though who can tell what the Master Priest is thinking?"

Not I, thought Bryn. Just then a black colt dashed up to the fence. Dawn leaped down, but Bryn stayed where she was. The colt nudged her with his downy nose. She put a hand on his forehead and set her cheek against his face for a moment.

"The colts won't be trained until fall," Dawn cried. "He's wild."

Bryn patted the young stallion's neck before jumping off the fence. He pranced along the greensward, and something about the proud tilt of his head reminded her of Kiran.

That evening, Dawn sat at her scarred desk with a worn Star Atlas, using her abacus to calculate the positions of Bryn's stars. Bryn had been born one minute past midnight on the day upon which the winter solstice fell.

Dawn carefully drew the full star chart. She studied it closely to glean understanding from the symbols arranged in a circle on her parchment.

Many unusual placements, with Ellerth foremost. According to the stars, Bryn is stronger than she seems. If I'm interpreting correctly, she'll need every bit of her strength to get through the next two years. Dawn cocked her head, wondering what sort of dire hardship could possibly overtake Bryn within the Temple. Would she fail to be chosen by a bird, and made to serve the likes of Clea and Eloise? Many men and women who came to the Temple as youngsters were never chosen by birds. They grew old within the Temple, wearing handmaid or acolyte robes throughout their lives, performing whatever tasks they were assigned. Would that be Bryn's fate?

Dawn shook her head. She didn't think so. Bryn's chart held not one but three powerful aspects for prophecy. She'd surely get to be bird-chosen. No, her horizon showed portents of something much more menacing than being denied a feather.

What could it be? *If I only had Ishaan's knowledge, I'd comprehend better. Maybe I'm wrong. After all, what danger could come to her here in the Temple?*

Dawn thought of Selid, and shivered. A tap on her shoulder almost made her spill her ink. She hadn't heard Alyce draw her curtain.

"We're summoned to the Sendrata of Handmaids," Alyce told her, sounding disgruntled.

Light from wall sconces bounced off the floor of the hallway as they hurried from the handmaids' hall to Nirene's office. Alyce tapped on the polished door, and Nirene called them in.

"Be seated." The Sendrata hardly noticed their bows, waving them toward chairs. "I must arrange chores for the new handmaids. Tell me what they'd be suited for."

Alyce slumped into her chair. "Cleaning latrines," she muttered darkly.

"Come now. That's reserved for punishment." Nirene frowned. "Has Clea disregarded the rules?"

"She looks down her nose at me constantly, but there's no rule against that, is there?" Alyce answered.

"Look to yourself, Alyce, or you'll be the one cleaning latrines. What work would she be suited for?"

Fiddling with her blond braid, Alyce sighed. "She fancies herself a great reader."

Nirene nodded. "I'll put her in the library." She turned sourly to Dawn. "And Bryn?"

"But I've only just finished drawing her chart, Sendrata—"

"Never mind the stars."

"But I thought you wanted—"

"You spent the day with her." Nirene flapped a hand impatiently. "What is she good for?"

Feeling muddled, Dawn tried to recall the time with Bryn. The girl had asked a hundred questions. She'd been much more interested in the outdoors than in the classrooms. They had needed to wash her robe because of all the dirt that clung to it, not to mention Jack's paw prints.

"If nothing strikes you, Dawn," Nirene said, breaking into her thoughts, "I will assign her—"

"Kiran!" Dawn yelped. Then she caught herself and spoke quietly. "Bryn could help Kiran to care for the horses. She sometimes tended them back in her village." She swallowed, hoping Nirene wouldn't find out that Bryn hadn't mentioned that she'd ever "tended" horses. *But Ellerth, Goddess of the Earth and its creatures, is foremost in her chart. She's sure to be good with animals. The young stallion liked her, didn't he?*

"You're recommending she help Kiran in the stables?" Nirene looked doubtful. "The girl is frightfully backward, and assisting an oaf like Kiran would hardly improve her manners." Dawn said nothing, afraid that if she pressed, Bryn would end up working side by side with Clea or Eloise.

Nirene drummed her fingers. "Very well," she said at last. "Clea shall have her chores in the library and, if the Sendral of Horses approves, Bryn shall assist Kiran in the stables."

Five

Bryn followed Dawn through cool stone corridors on her way to her first class in Temple protocol. She and Dawn entered a stream of blue-robed handmaids and acolytes flowing through the halls. Bryn's robe, which had looked lovely to her when she received it, seemed terribly worn now. Many students were draped in embroidered silk.

Out beside the pond the day before, Dawn had told Bryn that the protocol instructor, Alamar, would expect her to know the correct bow for greeting him. "Show me your bow of respectful greeting," she'd said.

Bryn had reluctantly stopped watching the ripples of water where fish were splashing. She'd bowed as Dai had taught her, eyes cast down, hands meeting, body bending at the waist.

Dawn clicked her tongue. "Might pass in the outer world but not here in the Temple. You aren't holding the bow long enough. And when you hope to receive knowledge, curl your thumbs toward your palms like this." Dawn pulled her thumb joints back and pointed her thumbs inward. "Turn in your toes to show you have no status."

They had practiced until Dawn was satisfied. Now Bryn's bow would be put to the test.

Once inside the classroom, she and Dawn stood at the back of the room. Alyce and Clea were there, bowing to the instructor, a thin, dry-looking man in gold-embroidered robes, who wore crystal spectacles.

Clea's shimmering robe accentuated her graceful bow. The instructor pointed her to a seat in the front row of chairs.

Dawn stepped forward and bowed: duenna introducing her ward to the instructor of protocol. "Sir, meet Bryn Stonecutter. Bryn, meet Alamar, a priest of the Oracle."

Bryn bowed. She knew as she straightened that she had been too hasty, had not shown full respect.

Alamar's face remained impassive. "Sit in the tenth row, beside Willow," he said.

Dawn looked annoyed. She guided Bryn to a seat and left her to go to her own place several rows away. Willow, a girl near Bryn's age with olive skin and mild eyes, gave her a shy smile, but Bryn's cheeks burned. It seemed she could hardly take a step in the Temple without treading on her own ignorance.

She stared about her, feeling small. The windows at the front of the room were taller than the baker's shop in Uste. Crystal chandeliers hung from the ceiling—unlit because the sun shone—and Bryn saw not a single cobweb or mote of dust upon their shining surfaces.

The rows holding student chairs were tiered, looking down on a circle at the head of the room where Alamar stood. "We will begin today with the gestures that express disdain or respect when bowing," he announced.

Bryn blinked. Had she heard him correctly?

"I need two students to demonstrate the bows," Alamar said. His eyes searched the room. "Kiran," he called out.

Kiran rose from a chair in the back. His acolyte's robe was shabbier than Bryn's—the cuffs badly frayed, the collar sagging, both sleeves stained. As he moved to the front of the room, his large hands bunched into fists at his sides.

"And our new handmaid, Clea Errington," Alamar said.

Clea glided up to join Alamar and Kiran. Everything about her seemed to glow: her light hair, her silk robe, her satiny slippers. She bowed to the instructor—Bryn didn't recognize the bow but knew at once that it was expert—and to Kiran. Muffled laughter rippled through the room. Kiran glowered, the freckles on his face standing out like burnt crumbs.

"Clever," Alamar said. "Who can tell me what Clea's bow to Kiran meant?" He pointed. "Eloise?"

Eloise rose. "That he might be her equal if he wore a new robe."

"Indeed," Alamar answered. "However, Kiran would need to do far more to be the equal of this young lady." Bryn's stomach turned as she watched Clea preening. "Now tell me, class, the meaning of this bow." Alamar bowed to Kiran, and as he came out of the bow, he waved his right hand so that his palm faced backward and his index finger pointed up. At the same time, he lifted his right foot, scraping it slightly against the floor.

This time he called on one of the young men. "Gridley."

Bryn saw only the back of Gridley's head. Neatly trimmed brown hair touched his neck; his rich robe draped his shoulders smoothly as he rose. "You said Kiran walks in manure because he can't learn to be civilized," he answered in a strong voice, enunciating every syllable.

Bryn heard snickering.

Alamar held up a hand, and the snickers died. "Not quite, Gridley. I said Kiran doesn't trouble himself with civilization, which keeps him close to manure."

Loud laughter. Bryn clutched her robe where it lay over her heart, all her sympathies with Kiran. What would he do? What could he say?

Kiran gestured with both hands over his head, as though receiving something from above. He bowed quickly, his two fists meeting over his chest. He opened his hands as if flinging something down. Straightening, he stamped his foot against the floor with a ringing thud. He finished with one hand pointing at Alamar, palm up.

Silence fell as Alamar glared at Kiran. "Leave at once," the instructor said. "I will consult the Master Priest about your punishment."

Kiran held his shaggy head high as he left.

*　*　*

When Dawn guided Bryn out through the Temple doors in midafternoon, Bryn was so glad to be outside she nearly broke into a mad run.

"I'll never, ever be able to understand what Ishaan is talking about." She felt as if someone had been pounding numbers into her skull with a rock hammer. She looked up at Dawn with awe. "How do you understand everything?"

"My first day I wanted to go home and never come back," Dawn answered, waving her hands sympathetically. "If Ishaan had prophesied that I'd get to be head of the math class, I would have thrown my abacus at his head and called him a liar—except I wouldn't insult an instructor, of course; only Kiran would dare such a thing." Dawn was walking so fast Bryn had to skip to keep up with her. "Promise me you'll never insult a teacher, Bryn?" The door to the stables was open and Dawn led the way in without waiting for an answer. "Kiran!" she called.

Bryn stood in the wide entry, breathing the reassuring scents of horses and sweet hay. Slits cut high in the walls let in shafts of sunlight.

"Up here," said a voice. Kiran, holding a pitchfork, looked down at them from a loft. He'd changed out of his student robes into pants and a shirt. Muscular forearms bulged out of his unbuttoned cuffs. "Look out," he said, and tossed a bale of hay from the loft to the dirt floor. It landed with a thump, sending out puffs of dust as it burst its binding.

"Did the Sendral tell you Bryn will be doing chores with you?" Dawn called up to him.

Kiran nodded. He climbed down the loft ladder to stand in front of them.

"Good, I'll leave you here. See you at dinner, Bryn, and I'll help you study in the evening." Dawn rushed away.

Bryn gazed about, hoping to see Jack. For no reason, a blush began burning her face. "Is your dog here?" she asked.

"He's off exploring the far side of the pond. Likes to roam now and again." Kiran was looking at her with the same unnerving keenness he'd shown when they met. Bryn had the feeling he could tell just how little work she was accustomed to and exactly how much she'd be capable of. She hoped he wasn't thinking she'd be more trouble than help.

She gestured at the stalls, most of which were empty. The horses must be outside. "What needs to be done?"

"The water trough filled. Grain measures made ready."

Bryn nodded. "I'm glad you stood up to Alamar," she said impulsively.

He raised cinnamon-colored eyebrows. "It was foolish. I expect a summons from the Master Priest any moment."

"What did it mean, the bow you gave?"

He was silent a minute, and she wondered if she'd offended him. Maybe he wouldn't answer. Then he said, "It meant that although there is wisdom in the world, he doesn't have any, and the subject he teaches is less than manure."

"You said *that* with a bow?" Bryn's eyes widened.

"Yes." He bowed to her, one arm tucked behind his back, raising a foot as he straightened, putting the foot down gently while lifting both arms up. He finished with one hand pointing to himself and one to her. "Welcome to the stables, Bryn. May we both be wiser than manure and not step in it too often."

Kiran met Renchald's opaque gaze, trying not to show how uncomfortable he felt in the Master Priest's sanctum. From the wall, a tapestry of a gyrfalcon glared at him. To his left, on a pedestal, stood a heavy statue of a vulture wrought in black marble. *Temple of the Oracle, where the bird of curses is second only to the gods.* Kiran knew that the Temple's vulture-chosen priest had died without a replacement. *Who will perform the Master Priest's curses now?* he thought grimly.

Renchald did not invite him to sit. Instead, the Master Priest sat unmoving, his green eyes boring into Kiran's. When at last he spoke, he wasted no time on pleasantries. "Alamar showed me the bow you performed today," he said. "Ironic, isn't it, Kiran, that you would use what you learned from him to insult him as a teacher?"

Kiran didn't answer.

"If you had a grain of wisdom," the Master Priest went on, "you would know that unspoken words are even more important than words said aloud."

Kiran folded his arms.

"Protocol can be a siege or a sanctuary, a weapon or a peace offering, depending upon how you use it." Renchald's voice became louder, yet he didn't change expression. "The role you've been playing—that of un-teachable oaf—cannot continue. I didn't take you from the slums of the Eastland to allow you to flout the customs of the Temple. Don't forget, I can easily drop you back in the gutter where I found you."

Kiran's fingers curled within his palms, tension spreading from his arms into his back and down his legs.

The slums of the Eastland. Why did it bother him to hear such words? They were true. When the Master Priest had discovered him at the age of twelve, he *had* been living in the slums. With his father, Eston, a man overly fond of whisky. Kiran had too many memories of his father—unable to stand, being kicked aside by lords who might have given him a place training fine horses if he had only been sober.

Eston had eagerly accepted Renchald's offer to take Kiran off his hands. Kiran's beloved mother had died years earlier in a riding accident, so there was no one else to consult.

"To atone for your disrespect," continued the Master Priest, "you will make a bow of perfect apology to Alamar during every protocol class until he releases you from the punishment."

It doesn't matter, Kiran told himself, squeezing his fists behind his back. *It's only a gesture. Means nothing to me.*

He bowed, and the red threads of the carpet matched the color of his anger.

Six

Alessandra, Queen of Sorana, and Princess Zorienne, heir to the throne, arrived at the Temple of the Oracle and were installed in a sumptuous suite of rooms in the guest wing. During the previous weeks the senior handmaids and acolytes had been cleaning and trimming and cooking in a frenzied bustle of preparation.

Not only for the queen. Another suite had been made ready for Lord Bartol Errington and his son, Raynor, a remarkably handsome youth eighteen years old.

"Why has the queen come here?" Bryn asked Kiran as they filled feed buckets.

She couldn't quite read the look he gave her; it almost appeared that he pitied her. "Prophecies," he said. He put a hand on her shoulder. Bryn was so distracted by his warmth she had trouble listening to his words. "You know the Princess Zorienne is ill?" he asked.

"I heard the rumor, yes."

Kiran took his hand away. "Perhaps the queen hopes to learn of a cure for her daughter."

Bryn shook oat flakes into a bucket. "Dawn says that if Princess Zorienne dies, the succession will pass to Raynor Errington." She looked up to see him nod. "I don't understand why. Even Clea only claims to be a *distant* cousin to the queen."

"True. No close cousins, though, you see."

How did he know? "Why wouldn't Lord Errington be the king, then?"

Kiran shrugged. "Errington enjoys the position he has now, ruling over the Eastland. He stepped aside in favor of his son."

"So Clea's brother could become King of all Sorana?" A shudder passed over Bryn, causing some oats to pour onto the floor.

Kiran helped her scoop them up. She could feel his breath on her neck. "Yes, and the gods help us all if that should happen."

She would have asked him a hundred questions, but just then the Sendral of Horses appeared, to discuss caring for the train of mares the queen had brought with her, and their conversation was cut short.

Bryn entered the great room of the Oracle's central altar for the first time, trailing Dawn closely. Every member of the Temple had been ordered to assemble in formal welcome to Queen Alessandra.

The domed ceiling alone took Bryn's breath away, so high it seemed to rival the heavens. It had been plated with gold, its centerpiece a ruby-colored design of stained glass laid in the shape of the keltice. Seven stained-glass windows reached from the floor midway up the gently sloping walls. Above each window hung a tapestry, intricately woven, depicting the face of a god or goddess.

The detailed weavings were uncanny. Bryn hadn't realized a tapestry could show the chill of Keldes, Lord of Death, so well. The face of Solz, Lord of Light, looked radiant as the sun, the heavenly body he ruled. Opposite Solz, across the vast chamber of the Temple, was Monzapel, Goddess of the Moon, her distant smile cool and silver. Ellerth's tapestry showed the Earth Goddess among flowers that seemed to wave as if a breeze blew upon them. Winjessen, winged Lord of Thought, appeared ready to fly. Ayel, Lord of Battle, lifted a gleaming sword. Beside him, Vernelda, Goddess of Justice and Love, smiled compassionately.

"Stop gawking, rat." A sharp finger jabbed Bryn's ribs; she turned to catch Clea's spiteful glance. She quickened her pace, following Dawn into one of the tiered rows of pews. To her relief, Clea continued past, all the way down to the front. *Of course. She's descended from King Zor.*

The Temple filled with hundreds of people. Everyone continued to stand. There were a few hushed words, quickly swallowed by silence. Bryn gazed at the great altar: a tall, wide slab of pearly marble shaped into an oval. Upon it stood seven large round silver bowls filled with clear water, and seven burning candles set in finely worked silver holders. Each holder was adorned with a silver keltice.

The Master Priest stood on the dais to one side of

the altar, his robes looking as if they'd been sculpted of stone, the gray streak in his hair standing out starkly. Bryn could no longer fathom that this same man had been in a stonecutter's cottage.

On the other side of the altar stood the First Priestess of the Oracle. Her red robe had gold embroidery at the collar and cuffs; nearly as much gold as Renchald wore, and she was close to the same height as the Master Priest. Her skin was a rich olive hue; her face, beneath a stately crown of dark braids, showed a powerful calm.

Then, from a door in the side wall near the altar, the Queen of Sorana emerged. Brocade robes swathed her and she wore a ruby-studded crown. Though not as tall as the First Priestess, she moved with grace and dignity as she came up the steps of the dais alone.

The Master Priest received her with a deep welcoming bow. "The Oracle is pleased that Your Majesty was able to journey safely to the Temple," he intoned. "We are proud to continue our history of serving rulers with the Oracle's prophecies."

Queen Alessandra inclined her head. She turned to face the assemblage. "I greet you, my good people."

And there in that sacred place, before the altar of the Oracle, a spontaneous cheer rose up. Dignified priests and priestesses allowed their affection for Alessandra to burst forth along with that of the youngest handmaids and acolytes. Hundreds of joyful voices united in homage from the people to their beloved queen.

She bowed to them, at which their cheers swelled even more.

The queen extended a hand toward the door left open by the altar. A tall young woman wearing a light, shining crown stepped forth to join her on the dais. "My daughter, Princess Zorienne, here to pay her respects to the Oracle," Alessandra said, smiling regally.

Zorienne was too pale, her figure too thin, but her eyes were bright, her bow graceful. She too received the adulation of the gathering.

Close on her heels, disdaining to wait for the queen to summon him, strode Raynor Errington, dressed like a prince in gold and purple satin. He bounded up the steps. His father hastened behind him.

Cheers died away almost instantly. Silence fell.

The Master Priest hurried to fill the void. "We are honored by your presence here," he said, bowing very formally.

He called for prayers then, to support long life for Her Majesty, Queen of Sorana, and for Zorienne, the crown princess. The members of the Temple stood with clasped hands, lips moving to join his entreaty to the gods. Voices lapped over one another, muffling the meaning of the words.

Bryn's head ached, and she felt a little dizzy.

To steady herself, she focused on the embroidery that covered the First Priestess's robe. As she gazed, the golden threads seemed to float out of the fabric and come toward her. A soft wind was carrying them, a wind that had traveled the length of the world before coming to this place.

Whispers stirred in Bryn's ears. One word was clear, spoken in a voice that rang through her mind like a bell. *Prophecy.*

The wind increased, grew louder, whistling now, taking hold of her, bringing with it a storm of change. Oh yes, change would come, blowing sorrowfully across the land. Not only for Bryn, but for the Queen of Sorana.

Bryn's arm lifted, her finger pointing at Princess Zorienne. "Beware his death," she whispered. "His sleeping death."

Bryn felt a hand shake her arm. She snapped back to normal awareness and realized she was the only one standing and that Dawn was tugging at her frantically. She fell into the pew, gasping as if all her air had been taken.

What she had seen and heard bewildered her. *Sleeping death? His sleeping death? But who was* he*? And why was it Princess Zorienne who should beware?*

Dawn quailed when Nirene yanked her and Bryn aside after the long ceremony with the queen was finally over. The lines around Nirene's mouth were drawn taut. Her ire seemed to fill the alcove where they stood. "When I made you a duenna, Dawn, I assumed you knew the basic protocol for an important ceremony." She whirled upon Bryn. "Standing when all others were seated! What did you mean by such a display?"

"I'm truly sorry." Bryn was pale, her golden-brown eyes haunted.

"And did you speak as well?" Nirene demanded.

Bryn looked as if she would start gasping again.

"Did she speak?" Nirene asked Dawn.

Dawn shook her head vehemently. She'd been near enough to hear that Bryn *had* spoken—muttering something about death and pointing at Princess Zorienne. Dawn had grabbed her arm instantly, and hoped no one else had heard; she hated to lie, but if she told Nirene what had happened, there would be no living with it. "No, Sendrata. She was having trouble breathing. That's all."

"This is the most sacred ground in Sorana," Nirene hissed. "You are here to serve the gods, not to show your impertinence." She narrowed snapping eyes at Dawn. "A duenna is responsible for the conduct of her ward. To remind you of your duty, both of you will clean the handmaid latrines before the morning gong until the summer solstice." She frowned severely at Bryn. "I have my eye on you, girl. If you break the rules so shamelessly again, I'll find worse chores for you than cleaning latrines."

Dawn bowed apology. She had to nudge Bryn with an elbow before Bryn followed her lead.

Nirene ignored their bows, a deliberate insult. "See to her training" was all she said as she swept out of the alcove.

Bryn's cheeks were flushed now. "I'm so sorry," she said.

"It's plain you'll be a world of trouble to me," Dawn told her.

* * *

64

That evening, in one of the sanctuary rooms dedicated to the Oracle, the Master Priest met with Queen Alessandra and the First Priestess.

Temple guards and queen's soldiers stood outside the door, but inside they were alone. Alessandra stood upright beside the seven candles burning on the small altar to the gods. Her fingers trembled slightly as she received her scroll of prophecy from Renchald's hand.

"Please, Your Majesty," he said, "be seated." He guided her gently to a chair.

The queen looked up at him, dark eyes very alert. "You know, of course, what the prophecy says."

Renchald nodded. "If you wish to read it in private, we will leave you, my queen."

Alessandra held the scroll prayerfully. "Thank you, but you may stay." She unbound the scroll, broke the heavy Temple seal, held the message close to the candlelight.

Renchald had penned the message himself, as he did all important prophecies. Every word of it was engraved on his mind:

This prophecy proceeds from the Oracle's light.

Your Majesty's daughter, Zorienne, will not live to reign over Sorana. Your Highness is advised to prepare the way for the next in line to the throne.

Brought from my pen before the gods,

Renchald, Master Priest of the Temple of the Oracle.

Alessandra finished reading. Long, long, she gazed silently into the flames.

At last she rose.

"Thank you for consulting the Oracle on Zorienne's behalf," she said. She fixed them both with her intelligent eyes. "I depend upon the sacred trust of the Temple not to reveal what this prophecy contains."

"Our trust will never be broken, Your Majesty," the Master Priest assured her. The First Priestess murmured agreement.

"This message shall be burned," Alessandra told them. "I am still the queen. I will depart here tomorrow. And I shall fight for a different future than the one you have predicted."

A week later, Bryn woke from a dream of following a silvery plume of thistledown through unknown hallways in the Temple.

She sat up. She knew where she was—in her bed in the handmaids' hall with other girls sleeping nearby, each behind a separate curtain. Her own curtain should have made her bed very dark, but light hovered around her.

Even more peculiar, a bright wisp of thistledown above her head was at the center of the light. Bryn reached out to see if it was real or merely a remnant of her dream. The thistledown drifted away from her fingers toward the edge of the curtain.

In her cotton nightgown, she slipped from her bed, her bare feet gripping the stone floor. Sliding through the curtain, she saw, shimmering several yards in front of her, the thistledown.

"It wants me to follow," she whispered. When she took a few steps, the thistledown moved too. She followed it past the curtained row of beds to the door leading to the main hallway. When she pressed on the door, it opened. She expected to be stopped there, for Dawn had assured her that guards always stood by that door. However, the hallway beyond was empty except for torches flickering in sconces on the dark walls.

Bryn hesitated, watching the plume of thistledown, wondering how it could be brighter than fire and moonlight; it made the torches appear dim and the moonlight streaming in through the skylights seem pale and thin. She should go back to her bed. She could almost hear her mother's voice berating the gods: *"Why have you given me such an unnatural daughter?"*

The girl took a deep breath. Why should she doubt what was happening to her? She was in the Temple of the Oracle. Her mother did not rule here, Renchald did. She recalled his words the day they met: *"Those who serve the Oracle see what others miss."*

Bryn walked forward, pursuing the glow that drifted purposefully down the hallway. She thought it strange that she saw no one as she continued on, for the thistledown led through many corridors, deep into the Temple. Though she kept expecting to come across a guard or at least a senior acolyte, no one appeared. She crept down winding stairways of stone; as she gradually descended, the floors grew chillier. The thistledown glided in front of her, shedding light.

She came to yet another stairway; its narrow steps led straight down. At the bottom, a blind trench of stone ended in a silver door.

With the thistledown hovering close, Bryn examined the door. Its metal was wrought into twisting patterns around a large keltice at the center. Hesitantly, she touched the keltice. Her fingers pulsed.

The door swung open, silent as Bryn's feet on the smooth floor. She entered a warm chamber that seemed to be formed out of the same light that shone from her thistledown. Pure and bright, the light cascaded over hundreds of symbols she didn't recognize, and flowed across the softly domed ceiling and over the clean floor.

Bryn bent to the floor, wondering how stone could be so radiant. Her father and brothers had spoken of a stone known as alabaster. Was this floor made of alabaster? Was the entire chamber made of it?

Kneeling, she felt the chamber's brilliance pour through her, dazzling her mind. The longer she kneeled, the brighter the light shone in and around her.

When at last she stood, she felt as if her spirit had been altered by a power utterly beyond her understanding. *I'll never be the same again.*

She noticed a couch upholstered in gold velvet next to the wall, and wondered how she had missed seeing it before. She sidled up to it. The cushion felt softer than anything she had ever touched, as if spun from golden flower petals.

She was suddenly tired, terribly so. She knew she

should leave again now, find the thistledown, let it guide her back to the handmaids' hall. But how inviting the couch was; surely it wouldn't hurt to lie down for a little while, just until she felt able to climb the stairs again.

Bryn fell asleep almost instantly after lying on the golden couch, and began to dream vividly.

A roar filled her ears. A strong wind was tumbling her toward an enormous faceless rock. She couldn't stop her headlong rush or even guide her own direction in any way.

She sped toward the wall of rock, extending her arms to brace herself against the impact that would come. As her hands hit it, the rock dissolved into grains of sand. Her arms sank into the softening stone, and her body followed, driven by the forceful wind. Sand coated her as she passed through it.

When she staggered out into free air, she sensed she had landed in the future, and that she was in Sliviia, the empire beyond the Grizordia Mountains.

The only light in the great room where she stood came from one narrow window and a skylight. The newly dead bodies of at least fifty men were strewn on the floor. Beside her was a soldier; he wore a leather doublet, striped gray and black, and steel-banded gloves. A black axe hung at his hip, its wicked blade gleaming. A double line of evenly cut scars ran from his forehead to his jaw. Fresh blood spattered his cheek.

Bryn tried to jump away from him, but she

couldn't move. He paid her no attention, and she realized he couldn't see her.

Others like him were grouped nearby, all looking down at a man who lay bleeding from a cut in his throat. Though his position seemed helpless, the wounded man inspired fear. Who was he? Bryn wondered.

Lord Morlen, said a voice in her mind—the bell-like tone she'd heard only once before, in the great room that held the altar to the Oracle.

Morlen spoke in a rasping whisper. "I will seek you through death and beyond."

Bryn's heart pounded in terror. To whom did he speak?

Lord Morlen will die, killed by a young woman with a knife, said the voice of the Oracle.

Then the wind took hold of Bryn again, carrying her away from the dream of death in Sliviia, rushing her back through the wall of sand.

Stirring uneasily, she was vaguely aware of lying on the gold velvet couch. She struggled to waken fully, wanting to sit up, to get off the couch, leave the bright chamber. But she might as well have tried fighting all the gods at once; she could not even open her eyes.

The wind picked her up and threw her at the heavy wall again; the wall appeared as solid as it had the first time. Again it turned to sand, and she was borne through it to another place, another time, a different dream.

A room with walls decorated in wooden mosaic surrounded her; the colors and shapes had been cut and polished like fine stones and then laid to form patterns like ripples in a pond. Candles were grouped on a shelf beside a slanted writing desk, their light flickering warmly.

At the desk sat a woman, writing. Her head was bent in concentration, but as Bryn watched, she looked up, hazel eyes aware and staring.

There was no mistaking that face. Clean now, and the lips smooth rather than cracked, the skin healthy instead of burned, hair neatly combed, expression calm, but recognizable nevertheless: it was the one who had screamed at the Master Priest from the side of the road in the desert.

"You lived?" Bryn whispered. *This is a dream,* she thought. *She cannot hear me.*

But the woman nodded. "Don't tell him," she said, looking directly at Bryn. "She'll never read my words."

Tell whom? And what? Bryn took a step closer to ask.

Dawn went to wake Bryn. The two of them had been scrubbing latrines in the early mornings for a week, and still Bryn hadn't learned to wake herself before the gong. Drawing aside her curtain, Dawn was surprised to see that Bryn was up already. Where had she gone?

Rushing to the washroom that adjoined the handmaids' hall, Dawn saw an empty row of porcelain basins. She hurried to check the latrines, but they too were deserted. She tore back to the handmaids' hall. Still no Bryn.

Dawn gathered a water bucket and scrub brush.

71

"Ellerth give me patience; I'll have to scrub all the latrines myself," she muttered, shaking flakes of strong soap into the bucket.

Dawn finished the last latrine just as the wake-up gong sounded. She raced to stash her cleaning supplies and wash her hands and face. She threw on her student robe, not bothering to smooth its folds. Standing watch at the door to the main hallway, she quivered with anxiety as face after face passed, none of them Bryn.

"Did you have a nightmare, Dawn?" Eloise said. "Or are *you* the nightmare?"

Dawn barely heard her. She prayed to Vernelda, Goddess of Justice and Love: *Please, Vernelda, if I've offended you by asking so many times to stop growing taller, I'm sorry. If Bryn isn't here I'll have to report her missing, and what will the Sendrata of Handmaids do then? I'll be scrubbing latrines until the equinox.*

But once again Vernelda did not answer her prayers. Bryn did not appear.

Renchald enjoyed his silent hour of meditation each morning. He knew many of the priests and priestesses secretly looked upon it as a chore, but not he.

Today, however, something was wrong. He had performed the rituals flawlessly—lit seven tall white candles, one for each of the gods, and bowed to Keldes, Lord of Death, who looked after his choosing bird, the gyrfalcon. And yet, when he sat to meditate, instead of calm, a humming disquietude filled his mind.

Renchald breathed slowly, reaching out with his awareness, asking Keldes for a vision to help him discover what was wrong in the Temple.

He saw the keltice, the sacred knot, binding a silver thistle flower. The thistle grew out of a stone quarry, and the rocks of the quarry were carved with signs from the door to the deep chamber of the Oracle.

Even as the vision arose, Renchald knew its meaning: the Oracle's alabaster chamber was in use, though no one was scheduled to be in it, and the one who slept there was not a priest or priestess.

Stonecutter's daughter.

Renchald's eyes flew open. *Keldes give me strength.*

It seemed impossible. Perhaps he was mistaken. His powers of prophecy had been diminishing. But no, this vision was real. He felt the prickle of truth on his skin.

But how did she get there? Why did no one stop her?

He abandoned meditation. Clamping his jaw, he went to the door, opened it. Ilona, First Priestess, stood in the corridor beside a silent guard. She bowed instantly: First Priestess honoring the Master Priest. Renchald gave the return bow automatically.

"The Oracle is calling, sir," she said. "But she has drawn her veil. I cannot perceive to whom she speaks."

"The stonecutter's daughter sleeps in the alabaster chamber," he said into her ear. "Fetch her to me."

Seven

Bryn felt lost within a heavy chair. She gathered her thoughts, trying to comprehend that she was in the Master Priest's sanctum, led there by the First Priestess herself, who had woken her from sleeping on the golden couch.

Along the walls beside her chair ranged tapestries of the gods, each one framed by a border of thick red satin. She looked for Solz, God of Light, hoping for his shining countenance, but instead she saw Keldes, Lord of Death. And in the corner, standing on a tall white pedestal, a black marble statue of a hulking vulture, rendered in such detail that Bryn almost expected it to fly at her and begin tearing her throat.

From another chair the First Priestess gazed at Bryn with deep eyes. Up close, she seemed even more stately than she had looked standing at her place beside the Oracle's great altar; her dark braid wound about her head like a gleaming crown, her olive skin lustrous in the morning light streaming through windows, her high cheekbones and sculpted lips

74

remindful of the tapestry of Ellerth, Goddess of Earth.

The Master Priest faced them both, clenching his lean jaw. Bryn felt as if a belt squeezed her waist, but she wasn't wearing a belt; wasn't dressed yet, still in her plain cotton nightgown. When she tried to swallow, her mouth felt as dry as it had on the day she'd ridden through the desert. She wanted to ask for a drink, but what if they meant to deprive her of water again? For clearly, she had transgressed unknown rules.

"Tell us," Renchald said, "how you came to be in the deep chamber of the Oracle."

The arms of her chair were carved with designs. Bryn pressed her fingers into the grooves of the carving. "I followed—" But even as she spoke, she thought of how foolish she would sound. *Followed thistledown?* He would think her an imbecile.

"You followed?"

Bryn swallowed. "I followed a light." It was true, after all. She didn't need to say that the light came from thistledown. Besides, she realized then, she didn't want him to know about that. Ever.

"A light? Where did you see it?"

"In front of me, Your Honor. It led through the halls and down stairways."

"And no one stopped you?" His tone was icy.

"I didn't see anyone, sir."

"You followed a light from the handmaids' hall to the alabaster chamber?"

So she'd been right. An alabaster room. "Yes, sir. I

was going to lie on the couch for only a few minutes. I didn't mean to sleep."

"And did you dream?" At her nod, he said: "Tell us your dreams."

The pressure Bryn felt around her waist worsened, and her mouth felt so parched she wondered if she could form any more words.

"Speak," he ordered.

Bryn looked at the floor. "There was a man, full of darkness. A lord in Sliviia," she said croakingly.

"His name?"

"Morlen. I believe he died, killed by a girl with a knife."

"Only a knife? Nothing more?"

"Nothing more, Your Honor."

"What else?" His voice sharpened.

She didn't want to tell him the rest. How to phrase for the Master Priest what she had seen? *I dreamed of the one whom you rode past in the desert, the one who cried out that Ellerth would bury you.*

Her dream had been broken when the First Priestess shook her awake. There was more, she was sure, that she would have understood had she not been interrupted.

"Speak," the Master Priest urged again.

She opened her mouth to tell him about the woman who had sat so solemnly writing. But just then she saw a glimmering plume of thistledown bobbing beside the door. A breeze began to blow within her mind. The breeze whispered: *Don't tell him. She'll never read my words.*

Bryn clutched her belly, afraid she would be sick.

Don't tell him, the breeze repeated. *He'll find me and order me killed.*

Pain threaded through Bryn's joints, drawn tight by the knot in her stomach. She doubted she could walk. "I don't remember anything more," she mumbled.

When the pain mounted into her head, turning everything black, she felt grateful that she could no longer see the Master Priest's eyes. She fell forward onto the carpet.

Ilona, First Priestess of the Oracle, summoned senior handmaids to bear Bryn to the infirmary after the girl fainted. Then she sat across from the Master Priest and waited for him to speak.

Renchald was perfectly calm. "In all the annals of ancient lore, there is no mention of an unsanctioned member of the Temple being found in the Oracle's most sacred chamber," he said.

"It is indeed puzzling. The Oracle's hand must be guiding this stonecutter's daughter," Ilona said.

"Can we be certain it was the Oracle who led her?" he asked.

"Nothing is certain: the Oracle never reveals all of her mysteries," Ilona answered.

"Perhaps this vision of Lord Morlen's death is Bryn's prophetic test. Morlen is a skilled Shadow Sorcerer. What girl could approach him with a knife, let alone kill him with it? However, time will tell."

Time. Yes, time, as always, would tell. Time revealed the truth, whether it was wanted or not.

"Will you question the guards posted last evening to discover how Bryn went unnoticed?" Ilona asked.

The Master Priest shook his head slowly. "That would never do. Word of this must not become part of Temple gossip. Have you spoken with anyone?"

"No, sir. None but you."

"Let it remain so."

She nodded acquiescence. "I must confess to wondering which bird will choose Bryn."

"Perhaps no bird will choose her. Perhaps she'll be chosen by the wind." His eyes hardened almost imperceptibly. "Are you astonished that I should mention it? The chance is remote, yes, but the possibility exists nevertheless. After all, it was the wind who led her to me. She was chasing after some thistledown when my horse nearly trampled her."

The First Priestess did not know how to answer him. She prayed that if Bryn turned out to be wind-chosen, the Oracle would help her guide such a gift— a gift she'd never encountered before and could not claim to understand.

The infirmary smelled of lavender. Starched sheets crinkled around Bryn when she awoke, and the curtains on the windows looked like crisp shrouds. Emma, the Temple's apothecary, poked and prodded her, looked at her tongue, and then insisted she must spend the day in bed. "You'll stay here the night as well."

"May I send word to my duenna?" Bryn asked, anxious about Dawn.

"No, dear. The Sendrata of Handmaids knows of your illness, and that is as much as anyone needs to hear. The Master Priest has left word that you are to speak with no one at all about what occurred during the night—no one but him." Emma's brown eyes glinted with curiosity.

Bryn plucked at the sheet. "What will he do to me?"

"Nothing, child, if you follow his orders. As you're new to the Temple, I remind you that orders from the Master Priest must always be obeyed." She shrugged her plump shoulders. "Whatever you did, he has excused you."

Bryn nodded, and sank down on the pillow, but a leaden uneasiness lay in her stomach. She had the impression that she'd broken many rules, rules so important that perhaps they'd never been broken before. Would the Master Priest truly forgive her?

Next morning, she was allowed to leave the infirmary. She hoped to slip into the handmaids' hall unnoticed, but just as she arrived, handmaids began surging through the doors, Eloise and Clea in the lead.

"Ooh, look," Clea called, pointing at Bryn and widening her blue eyes. "A rat dressed up in a nightgown."

"Ooh!" Bryn answered, pointing at Clea. "A talking stinkweed dressed up as a handmaid."

Eloise lifted her eyebrows. "Rats should be exterminated."

They swept past Bryn. Charis, chosen by the hummingbird, and Narda, chosen by the crow, were close on their heels, tittering raucously.

Bryn edged her way through the door and hurried to Dawn's curtain. Dawn, looking tired, was arranging the bedclothes. She looked up and stood frowning, her black braid hanging over a shoulder. "You couldn't have *told* me you were feeling ill?" She tugged at her blanket, the knobs of her wrists poking from her sleeves. "Now *I* have to scrub latrines until the fall equinox, because of the stir I caused when I lost you."

"I'm so sorry, Dawn, please believe me. I'll help you until the equinox, every day faithfully, if you'll wake me."

Dawn scooped up her pillow. She hurled it at Bryn. "Get dressed so we don't miss breakfast. I'm hungry."

When Bryn went to join Kiran for chores, Jack greeted her enthusiastically before she got near the door, leaping up to put his paws on her. Obsidian, the black colt Bryn had met her first day at the Temple, nickered a greeting from the pasture fence. She'd named him Obsidian after the shiny glasslike stone fired in the depths of the earth.

Inside the stables, Kiran picked up a fifty-pound sack of oats, hefting it as easily as if it were filled with down. He set the sack on the stable floor to split the top with his knife, and asked Bryn why she hadn't been there to help him the previous morning.

"I couldn't be," she said. "I was with the Master Priest and First Priestess."

He leaned on his rake to look at her. "What did they want with you?"

Bryn hesitated. "They ordered me to keep it secret."

His cinnamon-brown eyes searched her face. "I'd no more spill your secrets than Jack would." He picked up a feed bucket.

Bryn believed him. She had learned to rely on Kiran's word: if he said he would fetch a skittish stallion from the far pasture, it was done; if he promised to put together a new teasel brush by tomorrow, he'd place it in her hand the following morning.

She wanted to tell him about the magical night and the frightening morning afterward; she didn't want to keep so many confusing events to herself.

So be it.

Bryn's tale burst out in choppy sentences, from the thistledown's appearance by her bed to the dreams that had taken her as she slept in the Oracle's chamber.

When she described Morlen's death, Kiran raised an eyebrow. "You saw it happen?" he asked.

"No. But I heard a voice saying he would die. It was a very vivid dream."

"That wasn't only a dream," he said gently. "That was a vision, and the voice you heard was the voice of the Oracle."

Did he mean prophecy? Bryn rubbed a foot through the straw uneasily, remembering what had happened during the queen's visit. *Beware his sleeping death.* She'd put the incomprehensible words out of her mind. What could they possibly mean?

"The Master Priest wanted me to give him all my . . . dreams."

"Naturally he did. Visions are the trade of the Temple." He sounded bitter. "Did you tell him what you saw?"

"About Morlen's death, yes," Bryn said. "But during our journey to the Temple something happened . . . so that I didn't trust him with the other dream I had."

She told him about the girl by the roadside in the desert, screeching at Renchald and begging for water.

Kiran leaned in toward her. He began to question her intently. When she finished answering him, his color was very high, making his freckles stand out darkly. "It could only have been Selid," he said.

"Selid?"

"Chosen by the red cardinal. Such a gifted prophetess that Renchald and the First Priestess were nearly swooning over her. But she let it be known she was keeping some of her visions back. They treat that as a crime here in the Temple. One day she was gone, and no one would speak of her." He shut his eyes for a moment. "I'm glad you gave her water." He shook his head. "I hope she survived."

Bryn nodded eagerly. "If it's true that those dreams

were prophecies, she *is* alive. I saw her again." She described the image of Selid writing at a slanted desk.

"She spoke to you?" He looked at her sharply.

"Yes. But before I could ask what she meant, the First Priestess woke me." Bryn took up a rake. She ran her hands up and down the handle. A splinter caught her palm. She dropped the rake and began probing for the sliver. Jack, who had been nosing about, came to put his head against her side.

Kiran extended a hand. "Splinter?"

She offered her palm. He brought it close to his face, blowing on the spot that hurt. Bryn's knees felt weak. She blushed, and hoped he was concentrating too hard to notice. Deftly, he plucked out the splinter, flicking it to the floor. "You're right to keep that vision from the Master Priest," he said grimly. "It may be that Selid was writing a prophecy when you saw her. If Renchald knew she was alive and practicing prophecy outside the Temple, he'd hunt her down with all his power."

Don't tell him. He'll find me and order me killed. Bryn shuddered, and Kiran gripped her hand tightly before letting it go.

"The lighted thistledown—you say it moved in front of you?"

"Yes."

"If you ever see that light again, you must follow it. No matter where it leads."

Goose bumps fanned over Bryn's back and down her arms. *I'm glad I didn't betray Selid to the Master Priest.*

But what if Renchald knew she had concealed a dream from him; what if he brought her before him again and ordered her to reveal it? If she refused, would he send her back to Uste? Or worse, leave her in the desert to die?

Don't tell him. She'll never read my words. Again the sorrowful whisper drifted through Bryn's mind.

SUMMER

Eight

On the morning of the summer solstice, the day of the Ceremony of Birds, Bryn woke as usual to Dawn shaking her shoulder. "Stars and luminaries, Bryn, get up—hurry!"

They had agreed to rise even earlier than normal, so they could finish scrubbing the latrines in time to take baths. Usually the bathing tubs would be filled only on Kelday afternoons. The Feathers would always take first turn; by the time the likes of Dawn and Bryn could bathe, the water was tepid and filmed with spent soap suds. But today, senior handmaids would draw the baths in the early morning. Several women were already busy filling large copper tubs with steaming water as Bryn and Dawn grabbed their scrub buckets and aprons.

Bryn began at one end of the line of latrines, Dawn at the other. They competed with each other to see who would reach the middle first. Bryn scrubbed as fast as she could, listening for the sounds of Dawn's brush scouring soapy boards.

They finished in good time to bathe before the

gong. They had the washroom to themselves; the senior handmaids had left full tubs steaming.

Bryn flung off her scrub-apron gleefully before washing her hands in a basin. She put aside her nightgown and stepped into a bath. A cake of soap lay in the small wire basket hanging from the tub. She rubbed suds through her hair, then dunked under the water's surface to rinse. When she popped her head out again, she and Dawn were no longer alone.

Clea stood at the side of her tub; Eloise beside Dawn's. Charis, Narda, and a few of the other Feathers gathered around.

"Eloise," Clea said, "a rat has nearly drowned in this tub."

"Rats should know enough not to spoil the baths for us," Eloise answered.

"There are other baths ready, Eloise," Dawn said, pointing. "And you've polluted more than your share," she muttered.

Eloise's fist shot out, knocking Dawn's head against the edge of the copper tub. The metal rang like an eerie bell. A cloud of blood burst through the bathwater.

Dawn lifted her head, gripping the sides of the tub. Blood ran down her face from a gash at her hairline.

Yelling Dawn's name, Bryn sprang out of her bath, bare feet slipping on slick tiles. Pushing Clea and Eloise backward, she tried to reach Dawn.

Someone seized her feet, tumbling her into the bath with Dawn. A hand pushed against her head.

Sputtering, she fought. Another hand added its weight to the first, pressing heavily, forcing her face into the water. Bryn twisted, legs flailing. The hands against her head slipped. She snatched a desperate breath before more arms grabbed her shoulders and neck, shoving her violently down.

Her lungs burned, but she could not escape. She tried to stand, pressing her feet against the tub with all her might, but her legs were tangled uselessly with Dawn's. A black haze crept close. Just before it swept her away, the hands let go. Bryn burst through the surface of the water with a great gasp. Next to her, she heard Dawn coughing.

"What's this?" Nirene stood over the tub.

Bryn heard the Feathers' cloying voices telling Nirene that Bryn and Dawn had fought over the tubs; that they had both nearly drowned. Bryn tried to speak, but all that came out was a cough. Dawn's wound streamed blood and she took long, rasping breaths.

Nirene folded her arms, scowling at Bryn and Dawn. "You have ruined one of the baths on the day of the solstice."

"It's not true," Bryn gasped. "We weren't fighting."

Dawn rose from the bath. She snatched a towel for herself and threw one to Bryn. Head down, she wrapped herself, covering her bony, shivering frame. She took up another towel and held it to her head, glaring at Eloise and Clea.

Bryn hated getting out of the bath with others looking on. She pulled the towel closely around herself.

"Come with me," Nirene ordered the two dripping handmaids.

"It isn't true," Bryn said again, following Nirene into the hallway leading to the handmaids' hall.

"Don't waste your breath." Dawn spoke grimly at her side. "Every Feather will swear to the same story." Nirene's back ahead of them remained rigid while Dawn's words poured out. "The Temple can't risk *their* fathers being displeased." Dawn slapped her long narrow feet against the stone floor. "If Clea or Eloise were to drown in a tub, it wouldn't be overlooked. But if Lord Errington's daughter takes a notion to drown *you*, well, you're nothing but a stonecutter's daughter."

Nirene rounded on Dawn. "You'd best watch your tongue. It seems you enjoy cleaning latrines. Very well, you will clean them until *next year's* fall equinox; Bryn will assist you. Now make yourselves ready for the Ceremony of Birds."

She left them, the hem of her robe swinging briskly. Bryn gaped at her retreating back. "She punishes *us* for what they did?"

Dawn's teeth chattered as she pressed the towel to her head. "I'm sorry, Bryn. I should have kept quiet."

Bryn put an arm around her. "I wouldn't know how to begin a day without scrubbing latrines. As for Clea, may she be chosen by a dung-beetle."

In the handmaids' hall, Alyce and Jacinta took Bryn and Dawn in hand.

"Feathers?" Alyce asked, exclaiming at Dawn's

bloody towel and the bruises showing on Bryn's shoulders.

"Who else?" Dawn replied.

"At least it wasn't the Wings," Bryn said, trying to cheer Dawn. The Wings were the male equivalent of the Feathers. Led by Gridley, they were just as insufferable as Clea and Eloise could be.

"Never mind," Jacinta soothed, cooing like her choosing bird, her soft eyes full of sympathy. "We must get you ready for the ceremony."

Jacinta's eye for beauty was respected. She knew how to arrange the folds of a ragged robe so that it somehow appeared more graceful; how to dress hair to bring out a handmaid's best features; how to walk with elegance even when wearing old shoes. Bryn sometimes wondered if the dove's secret gift might be involved in Jacinta's talent for bringing forth all that was lovely.

Alyce bound Dawn's head with cotton. Using lengths of white ribbon, Jacinta concealed the bandage. She braided Dawn's hair with more ribbons. "There. You look wonderful." Turning her attention to Bryn, Jacinta cocked her head. "I wish your robe weren't so frayed, but as it can't be helped, we must make the best of your hair." She wound blue ribbons through Bryn's hair, coiling it into a smooth knot at the back of her head. Just as she finished, a deep gong began to sound, its solemn tones reaching throughout the Temple.

"Your first Ceremony of Birds," Dawn said to Bryn. "May you be chosen by a swan."

A swan! Bryn smiled at the thought. She'd be satisfied with any feather. "May the heron choose you, Dawn," she whispered.

They emerged into a corridor thronged with hand-maids and acolytes. Feathers fluttered by in satin robes and shining shoes. Members of the Wings strutted; they wore vests sewn from tapestry over their robes. Each tapestry depicted a bird. Bryn saw Gridley, his vest showing the bird that had chosen him—a peacock—its tail glowing with blue-green threads.

Outside, the sky shone like a polished turquoise. Bryn searched the horizon quickly, wondering if birds would be hovering, waiting for the ceremony to begin. She saw nothing, not even a stray drifting seed, for there was no wind.

Dawn guided her out to a clearing east of the pond where everyone was going. There, great stones ringed a large circle of scythe-cut grass. On the north side of the circle, a platform stood, its polished wooden railing perhaps twelve feet above the ground. Red cloth, embroidered in gold with the sign of the keltice, hung from its sides.

Renchald stood alone on the platform, watching the confluence of Temple members. To the side of the Master Priest, a gong as tall as a man rested in a black lacquered frame, its burnished metal reflecting the sun. Across the circle was another platform where the First Priestess stood.

Behind the outline of stones along the western edge of the circle, a dais draped in red held a row of priests. Facing the priests on the eastern rim, another dais supported priestesses. The only break in the stone circle was a narrow space in front of Renchald's platform, near the gong.

Dawn led Bryn to stand with the other handmaids who had not yet been chosen by birds and were between the ages of thirteen and seventeen. Bryn saw Clea wearing a satin robe thickly embroidered in a pattern of feathers. The rich blue fabric set off her yellow hair, which was wreathed with bands of gold. Her glance stopped on Bryn's plain robe and shoes; she might as well have scoffed aloud. She smirked at the sight of Dawn's unusual headdress.

Group prayers began, led by the Master Priest. They seemed interminable, for every god and goddess must be enjoined to bless the ceremony. When all seven deities had been properly entreated, the sun was several degrees higher.

Renchald lifted his arms. Silence fell.

"Before the gods," the Master Priest declared, "we are assembled here for the Ceremony of Birds. We bow to the will of the gods, awaiting the choices they will make." He nodded to a priest who stood beside the gong. The man raised a padded golden stick, striking the gong three times. A deep note reverberated around the circle.

Acolytes were forming a line beside the gong, a line ordered according to their ages, with the oldest first—those whose last chance it was to be given a feather.

Marvin, an acolyte almost eighteen years old, hurried through the break in the circle of stones. The gong sounded once as he stepped inside the circle. He walked to the center and stood quietly, hands clasped, the air around him so still that his black hair appeared painted to his head. A minute passed. Bryn searched the sky. Another minute went by, but nothing moved anywhere on the horizon. The heat of the morning seemed to grow in the silence.

The gong sounded again. Marvin left the circle, unchosen.

Two more young men repeated the ritual. No birds appeared. Bryn wondered what would happen if a domestic chicken were to stray into the circle by mistake. The thought made her want to burst out laughing. She clapped a hand over her mouth, afraid of disgracing herself. Then her attention was riveted as Kiran strode past the gong.

He had taken no special care with his appearance. His faded acolyte's robe bunched across his shoulders; shaggy hair touched his collar. He clasped his big hands.

A minute passed. Kiran seemed unconcerned. He might have been at the stable door looking for clouds. Another minute. Were his lips moving?

The First Priestess lifted her arm, pointing north where a large speck drifted in the sky. The speck became a bird, winging steadily toward the circle of stones.

It didn't look like a normal swan. Swans were white, with black beaks. This bird's feathers were dark, and as it came closer Bryn could see that its beak was red. The biggest bird she had ever beheld, its wingspan wider than that of a golden eagle.

But it wasn't an eagle. Its eye didn't flash like a bird of prey's; its neck was too graceful to belong to anything but a swan. Black feathers glistening, it swept above the gong to land smoothly on the grass within the circle.

Black swan. Bryn wasn't surprised to see Kiran go down on his knees. The bird's red bill tugged out one of its feathers. The long neck extended toward Kiran, holding out the shining quill. He received the swan's feather and then bowed to the ground.

The black swan turned. It took a few steps on webbed feet, and lifted on majestic wings.

Bird choosings fascinated Dawn. Who would be chosen, and by which birds? Most of all, she wondered why the gods favored people like Gridley and Eloise.

The triumph she felt when Kiran's swan gave him a feather made her heart beat rapidly, causing her wounded head to throb. Not only a swan, but a black swan, rarest and most noble of birds. *That* would stick in the craw of the Feathers and Wings who liked to sneer at Kiran.

There was another shock in store for the arrogant Wings. Brock, a smith's son from the Southland, was chosen by the spotted owl, a bird of high status. New to the Temple, Brock had already shown such promise in math class that Dawn doubted she would be able to keep the title bestowed on her by her friends: Queen of Numbers. The other students didn't know what to make of Brock, with his dark skin and quick, musical way of speaking. He would rumple his black curls and quirk one eyebrow when Ishaan frowned on him, and then offhandedly give the right answer to the most perplexing problems. Dawn remembered the day he'd solved the Quarend Theorem, an achievement that had taken her hours; Brock had calculated the solution in minutes by strumming the beads of his abacus while looking up at the ceiling, his eyes darting back and forth, his head wagging.

And now he was owl-chosen.

None of the birds who gave feathers to other acolytes was as spectacular as the swan or the owl. After each of the waiting acolytes had passed the gong and spent his allotted time within the circle, it was the handmaids' turn. Dawn took her place behind Alyce to await her last chance for a feather.

Alyce entered the circle and left it unchosen. She would not participate in the Ceremony of Birds again. If she stayed in the Temple, she would be a handmaid all her life. But her face showed no disappointment. Alyce was fond of baking and had no ambition beyond being assigned to the Temple's bakery.

As Dawn passed the gong to enter the circle she was glad no breeze blew. A breeze might have disturbed the ribbons concealing her bandage. Her wounded head flared painfully with every beat of her heart, and she concentrated on staying upright, knowing everyone would be gawking at her height. Why, oh why didn't Vernelda listen to her prayers? She'd been taller than she wished to be for more than two years, and her bones kept lengthening.

But none of that would bother her anymore if only the heron would choose her.

As she stared at the blank sky, her moments within the circle seemed to last a long time. No bird appeared. Her waiting ended with the sound of the gong. Dawn tried hard not to show her hopeless disappointment. Now she would never be given a feather. At least she had her study of the stars. The heavens might be confusing, but learning to read star charts was better than drifting toward old age as a senior handmaid serving in the dairy, or worse yet, the dining hall.

The first handmaid to receive a feather was Willow, the quiet lord's daughter who sometimes shared an eating table with Dawn, Alyce, Jacinta, and Bryn. A rock wren hopped onto her hand, presenting her with a soft gray feather. Willow might be invited to be a member of the Feathers now, but she would not accept—she didn't truckle to Eloise.

Clea Errington's slippers twinkled with jewels beneath her glimmering robe as she walked to the center. She did not have to wait more than a minute before her bird appeared in the sky. Even from a distance Dawn recognized the brooding flight of a vulture. The bald bird alighted in front of Clea, its wrinkled neck and coarse quills a preposterous contrast to her satin and gold. Clea bowed low to receive her feather.

As the vulture winged away, Dawn thought she caught a whiff of carrion on the still air. She wanted to shake her fist at Keldes, the god who ruled vultures.

Why would the Lord of Death reward Clea's cruelty so? What had she ever done to deserve distinction, other than be heartless and haughty? With the power to cast unbreakable curses, what would she become?

Dawn watched disconsolately as Bryn passed into the circle, walking with her usual light step. Her robe looked terribly old and plain, but Jacinta's blue ribbons drew the eye to her piquant face.

A minute passed, while Bryn stood clasping her thin hands. Dawn's eager gaze saw nothing on the horizon. Another minute went by, but the sky didn't stir. Or did it? A small breeze sprang up, the first one of the day. It ruffled the grass in front of Bryn.

Now there was no mistaking it. A true wind rose, but only within the circle, blowing swiftly, flapping Bryn's robe against her legs. The wind mounted into a sudden gale, pulling the ribbons loose from Bryn's hair so that they streamed around her like blue zephyrs. The girl bowed to its force, and the soft knot of her hair came loose; the unbound strands whipped wildly about her head.

Dawn put her fist to her mouth to keep from shouting. Chosen by the *wind*? Was it possible?

The wind pushed against Bryn until she lay full length on the ground, face up, eyes shut. A gust slid underneath her, lifting her easily. Bryn didn't squeal or fuss; she lay in the arms of the wind as though dreaming on a fine bed. A few moments later, it set her gently down. A small whirlwind spun a shower of grass cuttings as it whistled to the edge of the solstice circle. It flew at the Master Priest, causing his stiff robe to flutter. Then it was gone.

The delight Dawn felt about Bryn being wind-chosen nearly choked her when she caught sight of Clea. In the excitement, Clea must have forgotten to hide her emotions beneath the pretty mask of her face. She stared at Bryn, blue eyes glazed with hatred, mouth flattened to a slit of fury.

Standing high on his platform, Renchald watched everything. A Master Priest might live and die without ever seeing the wind choose a handmaid or acolyte. But the gods had ordained that he, Renchald, would rule the Temple when a wind-chosen girl entered it.

His predecessor had warned him: the wind-chosen made exceptional prophets and prophetesses; they could enhance the reputation of the Oracle with their wondrously accurate predictions. But if they managed to align themselves with all the powers of the wind, they became dangerous, able to summon cyclones at will, quite impossible to control.

Except with a curse.

Master Priests of the past had made a practice of curbing the wind-chosen before they could develop the full powers of their gift. A vulture-chosen curse, secretly ordered and secretly carried out, would nullify any threat Bryn might pose in the future.

Renchald would not be hasty. Bryn might remain quiescent for years to come. He knew what to watch for; knew how the wind's latent power would show itself in the beginning. The smallest touch of a breeze would start to follow her wherever she went. It would not be enough to draw notice unless one were alert.

The Master Priest intended to be alert.

Nine

Bryn asked Dawn to explain the significance of being wind-chosen, but Dawn had little to tell her. "I haven't seen or heard much of any lore about it except that it's a terribly unusual gift, which is why so many people keep staring at you."

Bryn twisted her mouth. "I thought I must have a smudge on my nose."

Dawn shook her head vigorously. "People stare at anything strange. They stare at me because I'm tall. Being wind-chosen is *much* more unusual."

Bryn sighed. "But what does it *mean*?"

"I believe you'll be allowed to join the prophecy class just as if you'd been given a feather," Dawn answered. "And I know that Ellerth looks after your gift." She threw up her hands. "Beyond that, I'm sorry, I don't know."

Bryn searched for a book that would explain, but found to her irritation that the Temple library was staffed by Feathers each time she went in. She reluctantly approached Charis for help, but the hummingbird-chosen young woman led her to a shelf full of dusty volumes, none of which had anything to do with the wind, or gifts, or even Temple history. Bryn heard Charis tittering gleefully with Eloise, and left the library with nothing to show but the dust on her fingers.

However, Dawn had spoken truly as far as her knowledge went. The First Priestess included Bryn along with the newly bird-chosen handmaids and acolytes when she issued formal invitations to her prophecy class.

Overflowing with curiosity and awe, Bryn and Willow found their way to their first prophecy class together. The Sendrata of Handmaids stood at the door to greet students as they entered. She pointed them to their places.

Fluted pillars stood at the four corners of a wide room lit by high windows and filled with simple wooden desks. Each desk was supplied with a neat stack of parchments, an inkwell, and quills. A long marble table at the front of the room held rows of small red teapots and cups. Four large steaming kettles stood on an iron range. Tapestries graced the walls, showing handmaids and acolytes bowing to birds of every description; accepting feathers long, short, wide, and narrow.

Bryn took the seat indicated for her beside Willow and fidgeted as she waited for everyone to assemble. Kiran came in, and a few minutes later Brock, the owl-chosen acolyte; Nirene seated them next to each other on the opposite side of the room from Bryn. When all were present, Nirene left.

The First Priestess advanced to the front of the room. Her eyes shone in her bronze face like black olives as she silently regarded the students. She carried a slim ivory stick. She bowed formally: First Priestess of the Oracle greeting prophecy students. The class rose as one to bow in return: humble students of the Oracle greeting First Priestess.

Ilona motioned them to their seats. She waited until the rustles and whispers died away, and then allowed silence to grow until it took on power.

"We have a number of new students," she said at last. "You are welcome. Our class time is precious and will not be used for introductions.

"All of you are gifted with prophecy. You have a great deal to learn, not only about the fine points of how to interpret your visions, but also about how to treat your prophecies and those of others." Her gaze roved over them. "Some of you consider yourselves knowledgeable because you have attended this class in prior years. I expect you to listen as closely as the new students. Early lessons bear repeating."

She paused. "You must obey three basic laws if you wish to serve the Oracle. First: Never speak of your visions outside this class to anyone for any purpose. Second: Treat every other prophet's visions with the same sacred confidence as you do your own. Third: Neither conceal any vision from me and the Master Priest nor pretend to visions you do not have."

For a moment, Bryn saw the image of a golden eagle hovering behind Ilona; its wings overlaid her arms, its head was like a helmet. "If you break any one of these laws, the gods will know it," Ilona said. "They will not pardon you."

Bryn's heart began fluttering against her ribs as if it were a bird trapped in a cage. She clutched the edge of her desk. She had lied to the Master Priest, told him she remembered nothing more of her dreams when she had slept in the alabaster chamber.

But she did remember.

"The punishments for transgressing these laws are both secret and severe," Ilona was saying.

That was certainly true, Bryn knew. Hadn't Kiran said that Selid let it be known she was keeping back some of her visions? Why had she done so? Bryn had seen an entire procession follow the Master Priest's lead, bypassing Selid in the desert. It could only have been by his order that she was left in the Lyden without water. Very likely he now believed her dead.

Bryn felt the urge to run to the First Priestess, throw herself on her mercy, confess the lie, tell the vision, beg, in the name of the gods, to be forgiven. But then she heard Kiran's words echoing in her mind: *If Renchald knew Selid was practicing prophecy outside the Temple, he'd hunt her down. . . .*

She could not betray Selid. She could not.

Why had the thistledown guided Bryn to the alabaster chamber; why had the Oracle chosen her? She could not believe it was chancc. The same light that had shown her where to go for the vision of Selid had urged her not to reveal what she had seen.

Bryn stared at Ilona, cool and knowing and enigmatic. Would the First Priestess guess her mind?

Were the gods, perhaps, simply biding their time before striking?

Sweat stinging her skin, Bryn wiped her forehead with her frayed sleeve.

The First Priestess was speaking again. "Many, if not all, of those who begin learning to prophesy feel glad to be chosen. But serving the Oracle is painfully difficult. For every happiness she bestows, the Oracle gives a double measure of sorrow. She sends visions, yes. A few may be pleasant, but most are not." Ilona's dark eyes were serious.

"Consider what it means to see the future. Whereas sometimes dire events can be changed for the better by a timely prediction, just as often they cannot be altered and the best that may be done is to prepare for hardship and catastrophe."

She tapped her palm lightly with the ivory. "Sometimes you will perceive images that you do not understand until there is no time left to give warning of what they foretell. When you are unsure of the meaning of a vision, simply write an exact description of what you have seen. Do not attempt interpretation unless the meaning is clear to you."

She pointed her stick. "You have a question, Brock?"

The owl-chosen young man rose. "Why is the Oracle cryptic? Why not send either a clear vision or no vision?"

Ilona didn't change expression. "It is not the Oracle who is cryptic, but the acolyte who is inept." Her eyes swept the room. "My answer speaks to all of you, not only to the acolyte wise enough to ask the question. The Oracle never sleeps, but *you* sleep even when you seem to be awake. The remedy for your native blindness is to develop awareness—the quality of being truly awake. This is more difficult than you can imagine."

She tapped the stick sharply against the table that held the teapots. "You will learn to clear your minds of hopes and wishes, for your desire to see a particular future will blind you to what the Oracle shows. For instance, if you hope to see water, even if the Oracle sends a vision of fire you will not perceive fire; you will see mist or some other delusional mixture of your wishes and the Oracle's knowledge."

She pointed to the row of teapots. "Those who seek guidance from the Temple's prophets are directed to send us dried tea leaves from tea they have previously drunk. Some of the essence of the person who drank the tea remains in the leaves. The Oracle reveals the destiny contained within the essence." She lifted the stick. "Another question?"

Brock was still standing. "If destiny is contained in essence," he asked, "how could a prophetic warning lead to a different future?"

Ilona's eyes shone darkly. "All people can make choices," she answered. "For example, if a lord is warned about the opium he has been smoking, what choices might he make, Brock?"

Brock waggled his eyebrows. "He could quit his pipe?"

"If he were wise," Ilona answered. "Then again, he

might decide to hide his pipe, and continue smoking in secret. The decision he makes will cause his essence either to strengthen or to weaken." She spread her hands. "You will encounter thousands of examples during the course of your time serving the Oracle.

"A prophecy may be simple or confusing. The most straightforward prophecies foretell accidents, especially those involving children; most of these accidents can be averted. The most convoluted prophecies apply to powerful adults with many secrets."

She waved Brock into his seat. "The curiosity of the owl-chosen is legendary, but I must ask you to hold further questions. Now we'll proceed with drinking tea and seeking visions." She pointed to a row of handmaids. "Eloise, fill the teapots. Jacinta, Narda, and Charis, hand round the cups and pots. I will deliver the tea." Eloise began filling the small red and gold teapots with hot water from the kettles.

Jacinta set a cup and steaming teapot on Bryn's desk. The exquisite little cup had a scalloped rim glinting with gold leaf. Ilona added a dry drift of tea leaves to the bottom of it.

When everyone was supplied, Ilona rang a bell. "Pour the water," she directed. "We will say the invocation to the Oracle as the tea steeps."

Bryn poured, watching the heated water cover the tea leaves, plumping them. She murmured the invocation with the others. Ilona rang the bell again; its silver chime reverberated with an oddly piercing note.

"The tea leaves are from Lord Abernam of the

Southland. He expects a superior harvest of grapes this year. He asks for a vision concerning the quality of the wine that will be brewed in his new casks.

"Sip your tea. Await the vision. When it arrives, inscribe it on your parchment exactly as it appears to you."

Along with the other students, Bryn lifted the delicate red and gold cup, and took a drink; it was so small it held only a few sips.

She closed her eyes, wondering if the Oracle would grant her a vision. She didn't have long to wait before she felt a sensation reminiscent of the alabaster chamber, as if liquid light were pouring into her. Her forehead tingled.

A room full of wine casks appeared to her. The casks looked newly made, the workmanship fine, the wood carefully shaped and banded with metal struts. A man, frowning in concentration, poured deep red juice into one of the casks.

Bryn looked carefully at the man so that she might describe him. He had a small, jagged scar on his left cheek, and his hair was thinning. He must be important in some way, she thought. Why else would the Oracle show him to her?

But her attention was drawn away from the man and focused on the dull bands of metal circling the casks. Her vantage changed and she could see *inside* the casks, where more metal strips were nailed, reinforcing the bands on the outside.

A breeze rushed past her ear. *Lead has been beaten into the metal. Those who drink the wine will sicken.*

The words were spoken in the tone that Bryn recognized from her dream on the golden couch, the bell-like certainty of the voice of the Oracle.

Prophecy.

Bryn's eyes flew open. She dipped her quill and began to write.

The prophecy that named leaden strips as a poisoning agent in Lord Abernam's wine was the first of Bryn's predictions to be verified. She took to prophecy like seed to the wind. As summer ripened toward autumn and autumn grew cold, she outstripped more experienced students, rising to head of the prophecy class, with Clea a close second behind her. Furious over not being first, Lord Errington's daughter never missed an opportunity to insult or irritate Bryn outside class.

"Bryn," she would say sweetly, "the second privy from the right among the latrines didn't look clean this morning—see to it, won't you?" And then would come her mocking laughter.

Eloise always seemed to be nearby, and she would chime in: "Dawn, when you go out today, don't forget to bring your pet rat."

With the days growing shorter, Bryn and Dawn had to get up long before the sun to finish cleaning before the gong sounded. The scrub-water was icy. As they worked, they made up extravagant curses for Clea and Eloise. *May Clea live in a latrine. May Eloise meet with a woodpecker who mistakes her for a tree.*

Brock continued grinning and joking his way

through his studies. He questioned all the instructors past their patience, then laughed off the scowls and punishments he earned. He prophesied with vigor and flair, but he was always getting himself in trouble for having visions that strayed far afield from whatever assignment Ilona had given. The fact that his prophecies were unvaryingly true didn't sway the First Priestess from giving him low marks; she wanted Brock to follow instructions. But the curly-headed smith's son simply smiled and went his own way.

As for Kiran, he often remained silent throughout a class. His behavior was so different from Brock's that everyone but Bryn was surprised when the swan-chosen and owl-chosen young men became good friends.

FALL

Ten

A day's ride north of the Temple of the Oracle, in the city of Bewel on the edge of the Lyden Desert, Selid dipped her quill.

She had developed a reputation as a fine scribe, but it brought her no pleasure; she was afraid of drawing notice from the Temple. She never gave her true name to her customers, of course; everyone knew her as Zera.

More than half a year had passed since her ordeal in the desert, but Selid still sometimes awoke believing she heard the Temple gong. Then she'd open her eyes and realize that she was beside her new husband, Lance, a carpenter of Bewel—Lance, whom she loved with passionate tenderness, and from whom she hid the secret that she had been consecrated to Keldes, Lord of Death.

If an unknown handmaid had not given her water, her bones would be picked clean by now, sinking into the desert sand. She often thought of the girl's kindness and hoped she had not been punished too harshly.

Selid had tried, at first, to resist the carpenter's love. She knew that each day she lived was borrowed from Keldes by the mercy of Monzapel, Goddess of the Moon, who guided and protected her. It was unclear how long the goddess could intercede—the slender silver thread that kept Selid alive would snap one day. She didn't know when.

Lance had persisted in courting her. Perhaps he'd known from the beginning that she was only pretending she didn't care for him as he did for her, for who could not love the good carpenter? His love eased the agony Selid had felt over being cast out of the Temple.

Lately she had felt Keldes stalking her. The Lord of Death had begun walking through her dreams wearing Renchald's face. Was it premonition? Did the Master Priest seek her? Selid didn't know. Maybe he believed she had died. He had once thought she would become First Priestess. Did he remember that he had taught her how to conceal herself from other prophets who might be looking for her? He had called it "placing an etheric cloak." She practiced the technique daily without knowing whether it was working. The only thing she could be certain of was that despite being stripped of her feather, her powers of prophecy had not diminished.

Yes, prophecy had followed her—surviving the painful secret ceremony consecrating her to Keldes, and all that had come afterward. A red cardinal lived in the branches of the spruce tree outside. Since leaving the Temple, Selid had learned that she didn't need tea leaves to see visions—they would arise, unbidden, in the midst of the market or the middle of the night.

Now, she pulled the candle a little closer. She trimmed the nib of her pen. Lance had gone to bed hours ago while she scribed. He thought working by candlelight would strain her eyes, but she liked the quiet of night.

Lance would not like to know what she was writing now. It would worry him, and so she kept it to herself. Sitting alone, Selid defiantly practiced writing visions.

Practiced writing them in the style of the Master Priest.

South of where Selid lived, the handmaid who had saved her life ran along the Temple path toward the pond. It was Velday, day of freedom from classes.

When Bryn decided to slip away for a walk in the woods, she didn't have any idea that a curse was laying a trap for her.

She whistled for Jack, but the dog didn't appear. She knew Kiran was in the library; he had mentioned, grudgingly, that if he wanted to understand the math lessons, he'd need to get help from Brock.

Bryn followed the footpath that would pass the pond and veer into the trees. As she ran, a movement caught her eye. A collection of small outbuildings stood not far from the pond, and something had darted between two sheds.

Bryn stopped, peering ahead, thinking she'd glimpsed Eloise's cloak—a cloak with a distinctive pattern of cascading feathers woven into the fabric.

Hoping to gain the trees before being spotted, Bryn hurried on. Where Eloise was, Clea was generally close by. She didn't want to encounter the two of them if she could avoid it.

As she came close to the woods, some thistledown appeared in the air ahead of her.

It was much too late in the year for a real plume of thistledown to be floating about. Autumn had long since stripped the trees and turned the thistles to dry, shriveled husks.

This plume shone through the cold as though lit from within by silvery fire. It moved, leading away from the path to the woods, going toward those sheds by the pond where Eloise might be lurking.

Bryn hesitated. She wanted very much to go roaming through the peaceful trees. She looked hard at the sheds. Yes, that was definitely Eloise's cloak peeping out from a corner.

The thistledown floated lightly, as if beckoning toward the place where Eloise was hiding. Were she and Clea lying in wait? Bryn was in no mood to listen to the Feathers' taunts.

As she stood irresolute, the thistledown faded; its light winked out and its gossamer fibers disappeared. Whatever it was trying to tell her couldn't have been truly important, or it would have persisted, she thought. She turned and headed down the path toward the trees.

She hadn't gone far into the woods when she heard crying.

A rock formation higher than Bryn's head bordered the path on the left. As she approached it, the crying grew louder. Curious, she left the path to look round the side of the rock. Dead leaves matted the earth under her feet as she crept past thorny brambles.

Huddled against the rock face was a wailing handmaid. Yellow strands of her hair bunched against the rich collar of her cloak. Her eyes streamed tears, her nose was red and her body heaved with sobs.

Clea.

When she saw Bryn, she clapped one hand over her mouth.

"Are you hurt?" Bryn asked, wondering what could make Clea cry.

Clea shook her head. She put a dainty handkerchief over her nose and blew. Red-rimmed eyes looked up at Bryn. "You wouldn't understand." She waved dismissal. "Go away."

Bryn stopped, half turning, then squared her shoulders and faced Clea. "You're not hurt, then?"

Clea wiped more tears. "If you must know, I'm crying because my father wants me to be head of *every* class, and I can't be," she sobbed.

Her father? Astonished, Bryn watched the other girl compassionately. Was that the reason Clea always put herself forward, trying to outdo everyone else? Bryn thought of Simon, and the lines of patience in his face. She'd never considered what it would be like to have a different sort of father.

Clea jerked her head in the direction of the Temple.

"I can't tell anyone *there* that I'd rather not study so hard. They wouldn't understand."

Bryn thought of Eloise's harsh wit; of Charis's eager gossip; of Narda's hooting laugh. Such friends as those would certainly not understand.

Serves you right. You picked your friends.

Clea's sobs were subsiding. "No one expects anything of you," she said, sounding more like herself. "It's not fair. You could become First Priestess one day, and you don't even care if you do."

Bryn shook her head with certainty. "I won't become First Priestess."

"No? Have you *seen?*" Clea was speaking of prophecy.

"I haven't seen," Bryn said. "But I know it won't be me." *And I hope it won't be you.*

Clea mopped her face with the handkerchief. "My brother's the lucky one. Next in line to the throne, he spends *his* time learning how to behave when he becomes king, while *I'm* expected to become First Priestess."

"Becomes king? But I thought the Princess Zorienne's health was improving."

Clea tossed her head. "That sickly thing? She won't outlive the queen. Everyone knows it. My brother and I are all that's left of the descendants of Great King Zor."

Bryn shivered, remembering what Kiran had said about the possibility of Raynor Errington becoming king: *The gods help us all if that should happen.*

Clea interrupted her thoughts. "My father will be visiting the Temple for the Winter Solstice Festival. He won't be pleased to hear that a stonecutter's daughter is best at prophecy." She rubbed her eyes, fresh tears sliding down her cheeks.

Bryn felt the old anger start up. But Clea looked so miserable with her tear-streaked face. "Never mind," Bryn said kindly. "You leave me and everyone else behind in protocol, not to mention oration and ritual. And isn't Lord Errington pleased about your feather? You're happy with it, aren't you?"

Clea shifted a little, bracing herself against the rock behind her. "Yes. I wouldn't trade it for any other." She paused, then said in a friendlier tone, "Would you like to see it?"

Bryn drew back a little. Dawn had said that only close friends showed feathers to one another. Did Clea really want to be her friend? And she had no feather of her own to show; she didn't carry the wind with her.

But this was a chance. If Clea ceased to be her enemy, maybe Eloise would stop baiting Dawn and Jacinta. Maybe the other Feathers too would relent. "I suppose so," Bryn said.

Clea peered round the rock. "There's no one behind you, is there? I don't want anyone else to see me this way."

Bryn shook her head no.

"Sit here." Clea patted the ground. "You can show me the wind after you see my feather."

Bryn looked about. The chilly air was quite still. "The wind comes to me when it wishes to—it's not as if I can call it forth."

Clea smiled warmly. "Never mind. I still want to show you my feather."

Watching Clea's fingers reach inside the neckline of her robe, Bryn felt uneasy. She stood poised to run, not sitting as Clea had invited her to do.

Clea pulled out a long, narrow case attached to a fine gold chain. She unfastened the chain. She opened the red laces that topped the case and drew out a feather, dull black fringed with iridescent gray. "You see?" she said, putting aside the casing and getting to her feet. She waved the feather slowly; it carried the scent of carrion to Bryn's nose.

"I-it's lovely," Bryn said, nearly choking on the words.

"Isn't it?" Clea's voice was all friendliness now. "But I wonder *you* should think so." She waved the feather a little faster. "Eloise thought this would be difficult. She didn't believe you could be such a little fool."

Bryn gasped, inhaling the smell of decay. Her arms and legs felt suddenly dead; she dropped to the ground. What was wrong with her? What was Clea saying? She didn't know. Her ears buzzed. The only sense that seemed to be working was her eyesight; she saw the feather waving inexorably; saw Clea, her mouth curved in a triumphant sneer while she spoke words Bryn couldn't hear.

Curse. She's cursing me!

Bryn blew the vile air out of her nose and held her

breath to get away from the vulture's sickening scent. She closed her eyes so she wouldn't see the horrid feather weaving unknown patterns. Trying with all her might to get her feet to move, she tasted panic.

"You can breathe now." The words were quite clear. The buzzing in Bryn's ears stopped. Her eyes flew open. Clea was sliding the feather into its case.

Gulping air, Bryn thought of leaping on Clea, tearing the feather from her hands, stomping it into the earth. But her body was as useless as a picked carcass.

Clea bent close, her cornflower-blue eyes more scornful than ever. "In tomorrow's prophecy class you'll be *last.*" She slipped the long black case into her robe. "If you tell anyone, I shall put death curses on your friends." She stepped on Bryn's hand, grinding her fingers into the dead leaves. "Don't think I wouldn't."

Before she disappeared behind the rock, she flung something to the ground. It rolled near Bryn, stopping at her feet. A freshly cut onion. Bryn gazed at the translucent skin, the delicate white rings. So that was how Clea had made herself cry so convincingly.

Dawn watched the doorway to the handmaids' dining hall. "Has anyone seen Bryn?"

"You've asked us three times," Alyce told her.

"Something must be wrong. I'll go look for her." Dawn scrambled off the bench.

Just then Bryn came through the door. Her drab beige cloak, issued by the Temple as she had none of her own, hung off one shoulder to trail on the floor, but she didn't seem to notice. Dead leaves and dirt clung to her shoes; a twig lodged in her limp braids. Her features seemed to be fading into her skin, except for her eyes, which stared out, even larger than usual, but with a half-blind expression.

Dawn rushed to her side. "What is it?"

Bryn's mouth hung slack. She didn't answer.

Dawn heard a wave of giggles breaking behind her back. Whirling, she saw Clea and Eloise, their faces split with contorted grins. As always, they sat at the head of a long table, presiding over the highest–ranking Feathers, all of whom were obediently laughing at Bryn's distress.

Dawn led Bryn to the eating table she shared with her friends. Bryn stared vacantly at an empty plate. Jacinta, Alyce, and Willow sat worriedly, not eating. "What did they do to you?" Dawn asked, trying to get Bryn to look at her. Bryn shook her head, eyes on her lap.

"Ellerth is weakened by Keldes today," Dawn muttered, fear squeezing her heart.

Moving slowly, Bryn said good night to Dawn and drew her curtain. She set her candle on the small bedside table, stowed her shoes, and hung her robe in the wooden wardrobe.

Sitting on the bed in her nightgown, she drew her knees up, clasping them with her arms. Her head drooped, resting on her knees. Clea's words echoed in her ears. *In tomorrow's prophecy class, you'll be last. . . . If you tell anyone, I'll put death curses on your friends.*

Bryn didn't want to blow out the candle. It seemed as if the world itself would darken forever if she did. The shadow thrown by its small light loomed on the curtains, waving like Clea's feather.

Then the flame sputtered and went out.

Bryn trembled as she lay down, pulling the covers high. She remembered another night, a night when silvery light had filled her curtained nook, cast by a plume of thistledown.

And she remembered Kiran's words: *If you ever see that light again, you must follow it. No matter where it leads.*

Eleven

In the morning, Bryn skipped her chores with Kiran. She hardly touched her breakfast. She drank water, praying that the cool liquid would somehow have the power to cleanse her of Clea's curse. She scarcely heard Dawn's worried whispers and couldn't respond to the confused sympathy of her other friends.

Taking her seat in prophecy class as usual, she avoided Ilona's glance. She didn't look at any of the Feathers, especially not Clea. Not even when Ilona spoke of the exceptional importance of today's quest for a vision did she raise her head.

"The Master Priest suspects that someone outside the Temple is practicing unsanctioned prophecy," the First Priestess announced gravely. "It may be a gifted young man or woman, as yet undiscovered, in need of training here at the Temple. Or it may be someone who knowingly transgresses the laws of the Oracle. Your task is to seek a vision that will clarify who and where this renegade may be."

Bryn studied the whorls fanning out from a knot in the wood of her desk, her heart beating much too fast.

"We have no tea leaves to guide us," Ilona continued. "Do your best without them."

Bryn closed her eyes, afraid the First Priestess would notice her agitation over what Renchald was seeking. She fully remembered her dream of Selid, and Kiran's words about it: *It may be that Selid was writing a prophecy when you saw her. . . .*

Concentrating, Bryn waited for the play of light that would usher in a vision. Maybe she would be able to locate a young girl or boy who was rightfully a handmaid or acolyte, thus turning Renchald's thoughts from Selid.

Nothing happened. Blood drummed loudly in Bryn's ears. Her stomach clenched.

"Bryn? Are you ill?" Ilona stood beside her desk, smooth face expressionless.

Bryn shook her head. If only Ilona would leave, would forget about her. But the First Priestess slid a blank sheet of parchment closer to her hand, tapping it with her ivory stick.

Bryn glanced at the other students, at Ilona, at the embroidery on her sleeve. The first time she'd seen that embroidery, its threads had carried her away, had shown her the wind, had whispered to her the promise of prophecy. She gazed at it now, but it failed to come alive for her.

I could write the prophecy about Selid. They'd never know I see nothing now.

And why not? Wouldn't others see what Bryn had seen, know what she knew? If she said nothing, whom would she be protecting? If she spoke, she might save herself. *In tomorrow's prophecy class, you'll be last,* Clea had said. If those words didn't come true today, maybe the curse would be weakened; maybe Bryn would have a chance to get back what Clea had taken.

Don't tell him. She'll never read my words. The voice was so faint in Bryn's mind it sounded like a whisper from the dying.

"If you're not ill, write your prophecy," Ilona commanded.

But Selid's face appeared bravely in Bryn's memory. She bowed her head. "I have no prophecy," she said.

Kiran whistled Jack's call, his frosty breath swirling in the lowering sky. The dog hadn't been in his normal place the evening before when Kiran stepped outside to get some air after spending a stifling afternoon studying with Brock. Come to think of it, this was the longest he'd gone without seeing Jack since they'd crossed the Lyden Desert together when Jack was a half-grown pup with mismatched eyes that spooked most people, and Kiran was a twelve-year-old boy fresh from the Eastland slums. He would never have consented to leave Jack behind, and the Master Priest had agreed to bring him along.

Kiran pulled the hood of his cloak over his head and went looking for his dog. As he trudged the grounds, he listened for Jack's silent language. People thought animal speech was heard like human words. How foolish. Only humans contrived words and sentences and disturbed the truth with layers and shades. Only humans lied; animals didn't know how.

Ignoring thickening clouds, Kiran walked on. Late afternoon and it felt like evening. Soon it would be the longest night of the year.

As he neared the pond, the skin along Kiran's forearms prickled, the hairs standing up under his shirt. Jack was nearby, he felt sure, but something was wrong. The dog seemed distressed, as though he wanted to run but could not move, wanted to bite but was prevented, wanted to bark but had lost his voice.

Kiran followed the sense in his skin, thinking of how dogs followed their noses, homing in on one scent among many. He opened the door to a small shed not far from the pond, a place seldom used except for temporary storage of orchard fruit during the harvest season.

Jack lay on the dirt floor of the shed, his sides heaving. He didn't rise when light from the dim sky fell through the door, nor did he bark. He couldn't. His legs and his jaws were tied.

Kiran pulled a knife from his cloak, bending to the dog. He forced patience into his angry hands, cutting through the strong, slender sash that bound Jack's jaws, removing the cords that tied his feet. The poor animal's tongue lolled as he tried to stand; he whimpered when his legs, bloody from straining at the cords, collapsed.

Kiran balled up the cords, thrusting them into a pocket. He gathered Jack in his arms. The dog was about as heavy as two fifty-pound sacks of oats. Kiran carried him down to the pond. He set him close to the water's edge, then scooped freezing water for him in cupped hands. Jack slurped the precious moisture. When he was strong enough, he crawled forward, lapping the water himself.

After drinking, Jack began licking at the blood on his legs. Kiran brought out the wad of cord, examining it. Fine-woven silk, dyed the deep blue of ordinary student robes. Gently, Kiran held it to Jack's nose, sending a question. *Who?*

Jack bared his teeth. Kiran received an impression of two females. "Someone brought you a treat? Jack, I wish I could teach you not to take food bribes. Tied your legs while you ate. Then slipped a sash around your jaws?"

He waited for more about Jack's tormentors, but the dog was worried about something else. "Someone you wanted to protect . . . but failed to keep safe." *Who?* Kiran got a sense of Jack's strong devotion. "You wanted to protect . . . Bryn!" Jack's tail thumped the ground. *Was she hurt?* The dog seemed confused. He whined softly, putting his long black nose up to Kiran's cheek.

Kiran recalled Bryn's wan, hopeless face as Ilona tried to get her to write a prophecy. He had guessed she was concealing the vision of Selid. She'd been silent and distracted, staring blankly at nothing. And she'd missed chores that morning.

He frowned as he jammed the sashes back into his pocket.

* * *

Lord Bartol Errington arrived at the Temple of the Oracle several days before the winter solstice. He occupied the suite of rooms Queen Alessandra had once stayed in.

In the evening, Renchald, bearing wine, joined him for a private conference in a spacious room with a warm fire. Errington dismissed his servants, and the Master Priest directed his guard to remain outside the doors.

Errington, chosen by the cormorant, was one of the few bird-chosen who had never aspired to the priesthood of the Oracle. He had used his time in the Temple simply to gain an education before returning to worldly affairs.

The Master Priest took the stopper from the bottle. "Congratulations on the continued success of all your enterprises," Renchald said, pouring for his guest. "As always, the gods favor you." He set the bottle carefully down. "Tell me your news of our sovereign."

"Her Majesty continues to search for a cure for Zorienne, Your Honor." Errington raised his eyebrows.

Renchald paused. "The queen, as you know, is very determined."

"Despite your prophecy, sir. Why does she not accept the word of the Oracle?"

"In time, inevitably, she will." Renchald sipped moderately. "Meanwhile, Her Majesty continues to make herself beloved."

"Yes," Errington said dourly. "The people are

besotted with Alessandra and her weakling daughter. But if they knew the words the Oracle has spoken, they would change their minds."

"Alessandra has not chosen to make public my prophecy for her and Zorienne. The queen is no fool." Renchald frowned.

Errington bowed his head. "I humbly urge you to exert yourself again, Your Honor."

Renchald's frown deepened. "You forget. I exert myself daily to keep our actions from being seen by other prophets."

Errington set his goblet down. "Forgive me, Your Honor. Please accept my gratitude on Raynor's behalf."

Renchald nodded gravely, wondering if Errington adequately understood the risks they took. Perhaps it was just as well if he did not. The Master Priest had put thick etheric cloaks in place to conceal their doings from other prophets or prophetesses. There were only two people who might be capable of piercing those etheric cloaks: Selid and Clea. Both had demonstrated the ability to penetrate such disguise.

Clea was not a worry to the Temple. If she happened to learn of her father's efforts on her brother's behalf, she would be unlikely to complain. She might even know of them already.

And Selid?

Selid had survived the desert. Clea had been able to follow the faint traces of prophecy being practiced outside the Temple. She had found Selid alive and well, living in Bewel.

How dare Selid compound her previous crimes by continuing to prophesy? How dare she tempt the gods so brazenly?

She would soon pay for her arrogance. She would fulfill her consecration to the Lord of Death.

Twelve

The day before the Winter Solstice Festival at the Temple, Ilona paused outside the Master Priest's sanctum, arranging her outer face and her secret heart before entering. The guard ushered her in. Renchald rose to greet her, and they both bowed formally.

She seated herself across from him. "Please excuse me for disturbing you," she said. "There are two matters at hand about which your guidance is called for, Your Honor."

"Yes?"

"First: regarding the renegade prophet. Clea was the only one to provide a useful vision of Selid. Every other prophet could see only mists."

He nodded. "Yes. Clearly, Selid has created an etheric cloak. Our decision to cast her out was quite correct; she has proven herself contemptuous of the Temple's most sacred laws. Fear not—she may have temporarily concealed herself from other prophets, but she is only tempting the Lord of Death." He sighed. "Her understanding of Keldes was always weak."

"She lived through the desert," Ilona said softly. "She must have powerful protection."

"Monzapel is no match for Keldes," he answered.

"The Moon Goddess is often underestimated. Monzapel is both darkness and light, which endows her with great power."

Renchald gave a slight shake of his head. "Keldes will claim Selid."

"I'm sure you're right, Your Honor." Ilona put her hands together. "May we speak of the other matter I bring before you?"

His face was solemn. "Certainly."

"It concerns Bryn Stonecutter and Clea Errington."

He brought his index fingers together. "Ah."

"All through the autumn, the wind-chosen girl was more adept at prophecy than Clea Errington."

"And now?"

"During the week before classes closed for the winter holiday, Bryn fell from first in the class to last."

"You know how unreliable the wind-chosen are." His voice was cold.

"I believe Bryn may have been unlawfully cursed."

A short pause. Renchald rose from his chair. He looked out of the window at the blank, wintry night. The stillness gathered. He turned around again. "I have had a message from Sliviia. Lord Morlen is alive and powerful, becoming a thorn in the emperor's side." He advanced to stand in front of Ilona. "Bryn may have done well in prophecy for a time, but her predictions about larger matters cannot be relied upon. Moreover, we cannot afford to offend Lord Errington.

As you know, he has arrived for the festival. We met to-day and I gave him a favorable report of Clea."

Ilona returned his gaze. "Curses must be sanctioned by both you and me. If a curse has been cast unlawfully, we must see to it that justice prevails."

He was quiet for a moment. "After the festival, when her father has returned to the east, I will meet with Clea to impress upon her that she may not issue a curse unless it is sanctioned by the Temple. I shall discern whether or not a curse has been cast."

Ilona's bow before leaving displayed all her mastery of protocol: First Priestess taking leave of the Master Priest after receiving a promise from him.

At the Master Priest's command, Bolivar took with him only two other guards to Bewel to find Selid: Finian, a young warrior recently recruited to the Temple, and Garth, who had served for two decades. They didn't wear the Temple insignia, for the Master Priest had charged them to be discreet.

"Don't ask for Selid by name," he ordered. "She is doubtless using an alias. Inquire about a young female scribe."

Though cold, the morning was clear, and boded well for their journey.

"Eat something," Dawn urged Bryn. "You're skin and bones."

Bryn looked at the table. Eggs, potatoes, and bread. She wanted none of it. To please Dawn, she sipped tea. Its slightly bitter flavor suited her.

"The festival's tonight," Dawn said, clasping her hands excitedly. "Winter solstice! Solz's Day." Snow fell past the windowpanes behind her. She nudged Bryn. "Your birthday."

I'll be sixteen, Bryn thought dully.

"Won't it be thrilling to see the grand hall lit by more than five thousand candles?" Dawn went on.

"It's a chance to see gentry from all over Sorana," Alyce put in. "The guest wing is full. We'll see lords together with commoners in the Grand Hall."

What does it matter? Bryn thought. No stonecutters from Uste would be there to mingle with the likes of Lord Errington. Simon didn't have the means to make his way to the Temple. She thought longingly of her father and wished it were possible to exchange letters with him. But Simon could neither read nor write, and with Dai dead, the quarry village had lost its scribe. She had to be content with putting her father in her nightly prayers.

"I don't care about the lords," Dawn replied. "I only want to hear the Gilgamell Troupe."

The Gilgamell Troupe's fame had spread throughout Sorana. Four troubadours, they played both lyre and lute and beat upon tall drums, entertaining royalty in many lands. Dawn behaved as if she were in love with their master singer. "No one could hear Avrohom and not feel as if her heartstrings were being played upon," she had said many times.

A few weeks ago, Bryn had imagined herself among the crowd of handmaids and acolytes, enjoying the music, perhaps dancing with Kiran. But now, she didn't care to go. Clea would be there, leading the Feathers and charming the Wings, basking in the admiration of lords and commoners alike. Bryn didn't think she could bear it.

"The Master Priest spares no expense at the solstice," Alyce chirped, "or you wouldn't have the chance to see the troupe, Dawn."

"Well, this *is* the Temple of the Oracle," Dawn answered cheerily. "Winter solstice. Great meaning for the gods. Without the solstice, Solz would disappear from the earth. Tomorrow his light begins to grow again. And where would Ellerth be without Solz?" She turned to Bryn. "You'll have the time of your life."

Bryn shook her head, sorry to disappoint Dawn. "I waited too long to look for a gown in the castoffs closet. Besides, I don't feel well." She lifted her tea again, hiding behind the mug.

Her friends all began to remonstrate, but Bryn wouldn't hear of changing her mind.

Kiran padded down the hallway from the acolytes' washroom, shaking his dripping head. Brock hurried to catch up with him. "Going to the festival, Mox?" he called, using his nickname for Kiran, a shortened version of Lummox.

"I'll be there, Owl-face. For the music."

"The music?" Brock toweled his curly black hair as he walked. "I'll be there for the maids."

Kiran thought of Bryn, hoping to dance with her. She'd be light on her feet like a breeze in a field. He hoped the festival would lift her spirits. She'd been tired and gloomy lately. When he asked what was wrong, she wouldn't say. Sometimes, she didn't even join him for chores.

"What'll you wear?" Brock asked.

Kiran held up the bundle he carried. "Clothes."

Brock lifted an eyebrow. "That sheepshearer's outfit you serve barn duty in?"

"Sheepshearer?"

Brock stopped short. "It's the Solstice Festival. Everyone will be in their best finery."

"I have no finery." Kiran punched his bundle with one hand. "I've been to the festival four times, always dressed in clothes like these."

Brock measured him with shrewd black eyes. "What a hopeless lummox." He looked down at his own wiry frame. "If I'd taken after my father, I'd look like you, more bear than man. As it is, I've nothing that would fit you." He grabbed Kiran's arm, tugging him into the acolytes' hall. "Wait here."

A moment later, Brock returned with Jorgen, a senior acolyte. "He says he can get you clothes."

Kiran shrugged but went along, allowing Jorgen to supply him with a cream shirt, red vest, and black trousers. Then Jorgen and Brock urged him to get his hair cut.

"You look like a beast," Brock told him pleasantly. "Tonight is for humans."

Two hours later, having been pronounced human by Brock, Kiran walked through the doorway of the Temple's Grand Hall.

Tall tapers, hundreds of them, in crystal sconces and candelabra, shed light throughout. The high ceiling was hung with chandeliers holding fifty candles apiece. The crystal candleholders created an illusion that multiplied the flames, making the room sparkle like a giant fiery gem. Fireplaces blazed. Tables spread with white cloths stood end to end along one entire wall, laden with platters of food and jugs of wine.

During previous festivals, Kiran had found a place near the troubadours and thought of little else besides the music. He'd eaten and drunk, and sometimes danced. He'd paid no attention to what people were wearing. Now he noticed that everyone glittered in fine dress.

Kiran went farther into the hall, moving toward the platform where the troubadours would stand. It was easier to get across the crowded room than he'd expected, but the troupe hadn't arrived yet, so he and Brock edged toward the tables of food.

"Quite an entrance." Brock's brown hand reached for a napkin.

"Entrance?" Kiran asked, puzzled. He reached for a handful of walnuts, sparing a thought for the cook's helper who had shelled them into perfect halves.

Brock looked at him incredulously. "You didn't notice?"

"Notice what?" Kiran glanced over his shoulder.

"All those maids moving aside for you and whispering?"

Kiran frowned.

Brock spoke low. "The Wings aren't going to like hearing the Feathers coo over you, Mox."

Feathers cooing over him? Brock wasn't showing the half-smile that normally gave him away when he was joking. "Never mind the Wings," Kiran said. "They're all beak and no talons."

"Is that so?" Brock picked out a cheese pastry, careful not to get crumbs on his linen cuffs. He turned to gaze across the hall. "D'you see Willow? I want to be near her when the troupe begins to play."

"Willow?"

"Keep that growl of yours down. Yes."

Kiran grabbed a pastry. The two young men headed for a corner that didn't look too crowded and wasn't far from the stage. Kiran saw Dawn, dressed in a lavender gown too short for her long legs. Spotting Willow close to her, he caught her eye and waved her toward him, disappointed not to see Bryn among the group of friends. Alyce wore pale yellow; Jacinta's thick hair was twined with lace flowers; Willow floated in something soft and gauzy. But no Bryn.

"Oh, the Gilgamell Troupe is coming in!" Dawn cried.

Kiran hurriedly finished his food. He watched as the four troubadours made their way to the stage. Last year he had noticed only their instruments. Now he took in their appearance, starting with the smallest man, the red-haired fellow with an elfish face, known to the world as Avrohom, the troupe's strongest singer. He could fill the largest halls in every land he traveled with his famous voice. He wore a gold satin shirt and embroidered trousers. The troubadour who carried a lyre—a small, delicately made harp that he treated like a beloved child—was a slender man whose luxuriant black mustache contrasted with his bald head. He had a costume similar to the singer's, but his colors were black and green. The lute-player, round-faced and paunchy, wore orange and yellow, while the drummer stood out because he didn't wear a shirt; his purple vest showed muscular brown arms.

The four of them bowed to the room, and a hush came over the hall.

"Ladies and gentlemen!" The red-haired troubadour's voice carried over the uplifted faces.

"Avrohom," Dawn whispered, looking smitten.

"We are honored to be here in the Temple of the Oracle once again to celebrate the triumph of Solz—the winter solstice!"

Applause.

The lutist strummed a note, the harpist picked out a chord, the drummer set a swift tempo, and Avrohom lifted his voice.

> *"Keldes vanquished, Solz behold,*
> *His brightness brings us through the cold."*

People were shifting to clear a circle in the middle of the hall so dancing could begin.

Brock bowed to Willow with a rakish smile: foolish acolyte asking lovely handmaid to dance.

Willow bowed back: humble handmaid foolishly agreeing to dance. They headed toward the dance floor.

Kiran tapped his feet, wishing for Bryn. He watched Calden, a skylark-chosen youth with a thick blond mustache, bow to Jacinta, asking her to dance. Alyce too was borne away, by Marvin.

Kiran turned to Dawn. "You're not dancing?"

"Too tall," she said, her wistful eyes level with his own. Then her face tensed. She glared past him.

Kiran turned and saw Clea and Eloise approaching. Almost bumping into Dawn, he stepped back against the wall. The music swelled in his ears as a rush of drumbeats ended the song. He applauded fiercely, ignoring the people near him.

When the drums began again, he couldn't ignore Clea in front of him, saying, "Good evening, Kiran."

Clea. Standing opposite her, he remembered the way she'd treated him on her first day in protocol class. Each time he bowed apology to Alamar, who had not yet released him from the punishment, her sneer was sure to be seen, a sneer remindful of her brother, Raynor.

Kiran had been ten years old when he met Raynor, but he'd never forgotten:

A curbside in the streets of Rington, capital city of the Eastland. A blond boy in a temper, beating a terrified young horse for being terrified. Unable to endure the sight, Kiran had run out into the street, crying, "Stop! You must stop!" And laid a hand on the other boy's arm.

The boy had shaken himself free of Kiran's grasp, flinging him to the ground under the very hooves of the maddened animal. And continued the beating, laughing at Kiran's frantic efforts to scramble away.

A stray miracle landed on my head that day and took me out of harm's reach.

It was only later that Kiran learned it was Raynor Errington who had almost killed him for casual sport. He could have forgiven the fright he got himself, but not the cruelty toward an innocent horse. Time had not softened his ill opinion of the young Errington. He had neither seen nor heard anything of Raynor to change his mind. Rumors of the young lord's reckless whims were frequent.

Kiran knew that a sister could be different from her brother. He didn't condemn Clea for being Raynor's relation. However, he'd seen her taunting Bryn mercilessly, seeming to take pleasure in it, goading other Feathers to do the same.

And now she was smiling at him in the Temple's Grand Hall. Her gown was pink like the inside of a shell, a gold necklace fit for a princess adorned her throat, and the hand she laid on his chest sparkled with rings. "Why aren't you dancing?" she asked.

Kiran looked into her eyes, the color of cornflowers lit by the sun. He didn't like her expression of smug confidence. She seemed to think he had only been waiting for the chance to be allowed to worship her. He picked her hand off his chest as he would take a burr from Jack's coat. "I was about to dance." He turned to Dawn, standing rigid beside him in her too-short gown. He grasped her hand. "With Dawn."

Clea's shapely mouth looked pinched. She spun round so fast her elbow jabbed Eloise, who stood next to her. Eloise pouted. Clea flounced off, leaving Eloise to catch up with her.

Dawn beamed. "I warn you," she said into Kiran's ear, "I'm not sure of the steps."

"We'll get through this dance," Kiran told her.

The troubadour sang,

"I was born in a land both near and far—
Too near to leave, too far to find again.
I wander here, keeping my sorrow in my heart—
Wander here between the now and then."

Kiran and Dawn danced with more determination than skill, but they were getting through it.

"No one could guess all the places I've seen—
If you ask I won't tell where I've gone.
I wander here, keeping my sorrow in my heart—
And all you will hear is my song."

For the rest of the evening, Kiran found himself sought after as a dancing partner. Each time he finished a dance, another handmaid stood at his elbow, smiling expectantly. He did his best to lose himself in the music, but it wasn't as easy as it had been in other years.

That same evening, in the darkness outside her home in Bewel, Selid raised a lantern to check the saddlebags on her horse. She looked wistfully one last time at the house where she and Lance had begun their marriage.

143

She'd seen a vision of Renchald striding toward her, keltice ring raised like a weapon; Bolivar beside him, wielding a sharpened dagger.

She must get away from Bewel immediately.

Beside her, Lance cinched his saddle. Selid had tried hard to persuade herself to leave her husband behind. She didn't want to risk condemning him to the same peril that followed her. But when forced to decide, she couldn't abandon him. To do so would break his heart, and hers.

"Tonight?" he had said when she told him. "What about the solstice celebration?"

"With so many in the streets for the celebration, we won't be noticed. I know how you honor Solz, but it's Monzapel who will be guiding us."

Lance had given her one long look from his kind eyes. Then he'd nodded and begun packing his tools. Now, he locked the door as if they were going on a temporary journey, though Selid had assured him they would never return.

"Does it bother you terribly?" she asked, watching him.

Wrapping her in an embrace, he kissed her. Lance always smelled like freshly cut wood, a mixture of pine and cedar. "It will be an adventure," he said.

"Without me, you could live the rest of your life in peace." She stroked his rough cheek lovingly.

"You're wrong. Without you, I wouldn't feel that I lived at all." He kissed her again. "All's ready." He turned and mounted his horse.

Selid stared through the gloaming at the spruce

tree, looking for the cardinal. Whistling, she circled the yard, but the bird did not appear.

They rode through the gate. Lance dismounted to close it behind them. Monzapel opened a pathway of light as they set out into the cold.

And a streak of red cut through the dark to land on Selid's shoulder.

Thirteen

The day after the Solstice Festival, Bryn stumbled out to the field near the Temple's pond, the place where she'd last seen the thistledown. Sitting curled small, she looked out at the water. Its surface was as icy and fixed as the curse over her mind. Dead grasses and weeds surrounded her. A lone larch tree etched bare branches against gray sky.

A furry muzzle pressed against her. "Jack," she said. The dog whined softly, then laid his head in her lap.

Kiran appeared and sat down across from her. He looked different; his hair had been trimmed. He pointed to where, across the pasture, Obsidian galloped. "Look at him run," he said, and then startled Bryn by adding, "My father was a drunk who dragged me into the gutter with him, but he knew horses better than anyone, and he taught me what he knew. Obsidian is worth all the rest of the Temple horses put together."

Bryn didn't know what to say. It was the first time Kiran had told her anything of his life before coming

146

to the Temple. She felt suddenly awkward and shy, just as she had the day she met him.

He turned to her. His keen cinnamon-colored eyes studied her. "Jack noticed you and insisted we follow," he said. "He's missed you. Obsidian misses you too."

And you, Kiran—do you miss me? She stroked Jack's speckled fur, and felt the color rushing into her face.

Kiran leaned toward her. "You missed the festival. What's wrong?"

Bryn swallowed, thinking she might as well tell Kiran part of the truth—the part that everyone must know. "My visions have grown terribly murky." She didn't like saying it out loud; the spoken words seemed to give the curse finality. "The Oracle doesn't speak to me, and I don't believe she ever will again."

His eyes were steady. He couldn't be surprised, for he'd seen her fall to the foot of the prophecy class. "Why?"

She wanted to tell him, but Clea's words circled her mind: *I'll put death curses on your friends. Don't think I wouldn't.*

"The lighted thistledown came to me," Bryn said. "I didn't follow." Her eyes stung.

"Where did it want you to go?"

"Toward those sheds, I believe." She pointed to the outbuildings beside the pond.

Kiran looked from her face to Jack. A long minute passed as his hands slowly formed into fists. When he spoke, he said the last thing Bryn expected. "She cursed you."

"What?" Bryn flinched, startling Jack, who took his head from her lap and then sat on his haunches beside her, ears pricked.

"Clea. She cursed you. Didn't she?" Kiran's voice was as gruff as she had ever heard it. His face looked hot, his freckles darkening as if singed.

"But how did you—?" Bryn broke off. She looked about frantically. What if someone else had heard?

Kiran pulled a brittle stalk from a clump of dry weeds. "If I promise to keep the secret, will you stop looking like a ghost?"

Bryn gripped her hands together. *You're all right,* she told herself. *This is Kiran. He won't talk about it with others.* "Yes," she answered. "Yes, and you mustn't tell anyone."

His eyes fastened on her. "If a curse can be cast, it can also be lifted."

"But a vulture-chosen curse is forged by Keldes and backed by the other gods."

He shook his head. "If the gods want you cursed, I don't hold with the gods."

She looked fearfully at the sky.

"Afraid Keldes will strike me?" He inspected his hands. "Still whole." He pretended to examine his legs, patted his chest and head. "Aren't you wind-chosen?" he asked, voice gentle.

She looked at the ground. "I don't know anymore."

"Bryn, the gods gave you the wind and allowed me speech with animals." He touched Jack, and the dog's tail wagged devotedly. "I hold with that."

"But you haven't gone against . . . you haven't done

148

anything against . . ." At his puzzled look, she rushed on. "I didn't follow the thistledown and now I don't think it will ever help me again. I'm afraid the wind has unchosen me. I don't hear its whispers anymore, don't feel it lifting my hair or brushing against my face. It's all stillness now."

There. I've said it. Not only prophecy, but the wind too has gone from me.

Kiran scooted closer to her, reaching out his hands. He waited for her to take them. When she did, he rubbed her fingers, his skin full of heat despite the frosty air. "Bryn, I'm not sure of much. But I'm sure the gods would not withdraw from you forever after one mistake."

Shutting her eyes, she clung tightly to Kiran's hands, praying he was right.

"Bryn?" he said, as if he thought she might not be able to hear him.

"Yes." Letting go of his hands, she opened her eyes, hoping the wind would touch her. She searched for any movement, any sign of a breeze, but the only thing stirring was a branch of the young larch. A bird had landed on it with a flash of scarlet wings.

"Look," Bryn cried, pointing.

"The red cardinal. Selid's choosing bird." Kiran cocked his head. "Cardinals normally leave for the winter."

The bird flew toward them. They watched it make a circle over their heads before winging away.

"Is it Ellerth who watches over the cardinal?" Bryn asked.

"The cardinal belongs to Monzapel. Ellerth governs the wind, though." Kiran looked into her face. "And the swan, too." He rose, stretching his long legs. "As I said, Obsidian misses you." He extended a hand. "He's grumpy without you."

Bryn got to her feet. "Thank you for not reporting all the times I've skipped chores to the Sendrata."

"I'll say nothing so long as you'll help me now."

Bryn resolved to act as if all were well with her again. She knew her friends had been worrying, especially Dawn, who had been scrubbing latrines alone, letting Bryn sleep in. Dawn had been murmuring many prayers to Vernelda and Ellerth, asking that Bryn be looked after.

Before going to lunch, Bryn washed her face and hands and combed her hair. She entered the dining hall, and took her place. Dawn welcomed her anxiously. "Are you feeling better? Stars and luminaries, you've got to stop looking like death."

Bryn forced herself to push through her cloudy de-spair and smile a little. "I'm much better. No more ducking out of scrubbing. But you'll still have to wake me in the mornings."

Dawn put an arm around her, gave her a quick squeeze.

As soon as the grace had been spoken, Eloise's voice pierced Bryn's ears. "Each time I begin to feel safe from vermin, I see another rat."

"They creep right out of the *stone*," Clea replied.

Her laugh joined Narda's raucous cawing and Charis's humming twitter.

Dawn had a mug in her hand. She slammed it down so hard it shattered, the milk splattering. "Did you know," she said, raising her voice into the sudden quiet, "that woodpeckers spend all day looking for *grubs*? And crows love garbage better than anything else, while vultures are particularly fond of maggots!"

The entire dining hall seemed to have stiffened into shock, handmaids staring openmouthed and frozen, particularly Eloise, who was chosen by the woodpecker.

Then Alyce, who had just taken a drink of milk, began to splutter helplessly. Jacinta pounded her back, trying to be helpful while exploding into giggles herself. Willow too went off into gales of laughter.

As she stared at the three of them sitting across the table, Dawn's frown vanished. She let out a whoop.

Conversation resumed in a loud buzz. Bryn tried desperately to laugh along with her friends, but all that came out were dry sobs. She covered them up as best she could, hiding her face while the others held their sides. At least no one could hear her crying.

Desperately, she stifled her sobs. She looked up. Two senior handmaids were bearing down on their table, carrying whisk brooms, faces set in severe lines. They swept up the shards from Dawn's smashed mug and put a fresh one in its place, muttering about carelessness as they sopped up the spill.

For the rest of the meal, if any of the handmaids at Bryn's table whispered "grub" or "maggot," the others would laugh, half choking on their food. Even ominous glares from the Feathers didn't stop them.

Bolivar's frustration was growing. He'd roamed the streets of Bewel, questioning the inhabitants, trying to discover news of Selid. He and Finian and Garth had arrived in the late afternoon the previous day, the day of the Solstice Festival. Too many of the shops had closed in preparation for the festivities; far too many of Bewel's townspeople had begun their celebrations early by drinking strong wine. Bolivar wished he still wore the Temple insignia that made common people treat him with respect. The fools he talked to here were barely courteous. A young scribe? No indeed, they knew nothing of a young woman who might have come among them sometime late last spring.

Finian and Garth fared no better. Once Solz's celebration began in earnest, the hubbub in the streets was so tumultuous as to give all three of them splitting headaches. They had resorted to watching the comings and goings of the people, hoping to catch a glimpse of Selid by chance. Finian had been quite morose over missing the Gilgamell Troupe; Bolivar had to reprimand the young soldier sharply to keep him from accepting tankards of wine from passersby.

Now it was the afternoon of the following day. The town had been nearly deserted for most of the morning, the shops sealed tightly.

Dissatisfied and hungry, Bolivar finally found a baker's shop opening its doors. He asked for a dozen hot rolls. The baker's wife was exceedingly friendly, so he chanced repeating his question about the scribe. The woman answered delightedly, "Oh, you must be looking for Zera, who's married Lance the carpenter. She does a bit of scribing."

Her directions were only slightly confused. Bolivar found the carpenter's gate with no more than a few wrong turns. He lifted the latch, noting that it was well oiled. Stepping into the yard, he approached a snug cottage. Selid's carpenter, whoever he might be, was a fine craftsman.

He rapped at the door but received no answer. He broke the lock with a swift blow from his knife. Entering the house with his men at his back, he made a quick inspection.

"Gone," he announced. He kicked over a chair.

"Shall we wait, quiet-like, until they come back?" asked Finian.

Bolivar shook his head. The hearth was swept clean. "We come too late," he said.

Renchald was not pleased with Bolivar's report. He dismissed the soldier and sat alone in his sanctum, considering.

Oh, how bitterly he missed being able to see the future.

As Master Priest, he was heir to exceptional training, skill, and power: training in the most closely held secrets of the ancients; skill to hold effective ceremonies; power to perceive what was invisible to others.

None of it could keep him young.

His prophetic ability was failing at a disturbing pace. He was unable to foretell the simplest events anymore.

He had been told it would be so: the gift of prophecy, like Solz's journey through the day, waned with age, eventually sinking. Temple teachings declared that, as Master Priest, he would value wisdom more than the heady show of prophecy. But the wisdom Renchald possessed did not console him for what he had lost.

He knew he ought to be more grateful for the gyrfalcon's secret gift, a gift that would give him ascendancy for as long as he lived. But to use that gift upon others, they had to be in his presence.

Selid was far away, he knew not where.

Renchald sighed. Blind to the future though he was, he would not give up the search for his former pupil.

Clea had seen through Selid's etheric cloak, but not clearly; only the vaguest outlines of her life. It would require more than that to find the renegade prophetess again.

Renchald turned to face the gyrfalcon tapestry on the wall. "The best hope left to me," he said, speaking aloud to the spirit of his choosing bird, "is to train Clea to link with a male prophet for greater clarity of vision."

He stared into the fire burning on his hearth, reviewing in his mind the young male prophets. Whom should he choose to pair with Lord Errington's daughter? It would need to be someone with extraordinary abilities.

* * *

A few days later, after classes had resumed, Kiran headed back toward the stables from a trip to the storage shed where the oats were kept. A chilly wind flew in his face. He smiled as Jack bounded through the cold to meet him. Setting down the heavy sack, he rubbed Jack behind the ears.

Ahead, he saw Bryn sitting on the pasture fence, hand outstretched to Obsidian, who bent his magnificent head for her to stroke his nose.

"Do you see that, Jack?" Kiran said softly.

A bubble of stillness surrounded Bryn and the horse; the stallion's mane lay flat against his neck, and Bryn's hair didn't stir either. Dead grasses bent in the wind all along the rest of the pasture but stood quiet at the fence where she sat.

Kiran stood and stared for several minutes. He kept waiting for the breeze, which blew so strongly everywhere else, to touch Bryn.

It didn't.

He thought back to their talk by the pond after the solstice. What was it she'd said about the wind? *I don't hear its whispers anymore . . . It's all stillness now.*

All stillness.

Watching her, Kiran wondered if the curse on Bryn might also be making her somewhat invisible. Why else would the change in such a gifted prophetess fail to draw everyone's notice?

He approached the pasture fence as she climbed down. He wondered what it must be like to live as an echo of what she had once been; to move through her days, seeing wind in the trees and on the path but never feeling the smallest breeze.

"The wind doesn't touch you," he said.

She looked suddenly so bereft that he didn't fight the urge to put his arms around her. For a moment Bryn sighed against him, but then she pulled away.

Kiran captured one of her slender hands in both of his. "There must be some way to lift the curse," he said.

"Perhaps so." She sounded hopeless, her golden-brown eyes sad.

I'll find a way, Kiran vowed to himself, but he didn't speak aloud. And thinking of Clea, with her pretty airs and graces, her sneers and sideways smiles, he felt rage so hot it seemed the grass beneath his feet should rightfully catch fire.

Summoned to the Master Priest's sanctum late that afternoon, Kiran gazed through the window at the sunset flaming the skyline outside. Failing red light clung to the heavy drapes, dulling the cords that bound them; it spread onto the Master Priest's robes, washing the gold embroidery at his collar and cuffs with darkness.

This time Kiran was invited to sit.

"It's time you took your rightful place in the Temple," said the Master Priest.

"Rightful place?"

"You're a black swan prophet, Kiran. I would like to begin training you in the techniques of paired prophecy."

Kiran tensed. Paired prophecy was such a secret technique, he had heard only rumors of it.

The growing shadows seemed to transform Renchald's lean face into that of a gyrfalcon. "You're a gifted prophet, Kiran, though you hide it well. The Temple needs you. Your prophetic powers will begin to decline in less than ten years. By pairing with another whose powers are also at their height, you can bathe in the brilliance of the Oracle's light, walk at will through the future. You can travel effortlessly wherever the Oracle sees fit to take you. Your mind will fill with insight and become a thousand times more powerful."

Fill with insight. Kiran thought of Bryn. Might Renchald be able to teach him something that could help her? "What *is* paired prophecy?" he asked cautiously.

"A method for linking with the mind of a prophetess."

"How would I learn it?"

"Report to me for evening study. A class of one."

Could Kiran bear Renchald's company—alone? Could he endure learning from the Master Priest, while watched by a vulture statue and a tapestry of Keldes?

"Because the pairing techniques are so secret," Renchald continued, "you will be required to give your solemn word not to reveal what you learn and not to discuss that we are meeting." He laced his fingers together, his two hands like one large fist. "If you begin, you must agree to complete *all* the lessons I set for you."

Kiran's mind churned. *I swore to help Bryn. What if this is my chance?* He took a deep breath. He nodded reluctantly. "I agree. I give you my word."

The Master Priest leaned back in his chair, face inscrutable. "Because the black swan is your choosing bird, you'll have an extraordinary aptitude for learning to link with a prophetess."

Kiran glanced at the vulture statue, so smooth and darkly shining. He felt suddenly cold. "Which prophetess?"

"Clea Errington."

Kiran gripped the arms of his chair.

"As her prophecy partner," the Master Priest's relentless voice went on, "you will have firsthand knowledge of all her clearest visions. You will see them too."

Kiran remembered Bryn's dream of Selid. *If Clea had seen that vision, the Master Priest would have been told of it instantly.* Kiran ground his heel into the carpet. Clea bore watching, but the idea of linking with her mind revolted him. He crossed his arms. "Will she know *my* thoughts?"

"No. You have powerful inner barriers. Besides, she will not be trained to form links herself. She will have to rely on her pairing prophet for that."

"You promise this?"

"I promise."

SPRING

Fourteen

Dawn and Alyce swung between them a large basket filled with food they'd wheedled from the Temple kitchens for a Velday picnic to celebrate the warmer weather. Just ahead, rays of sun played with the pond waters; a few early butterflies skimmed the air. Marvin, Jacinta, and Calden sat on a blanket spread a short way from the sandy edge of the pond. Leaning against the larch tree, Kiran watched Brock, Willow, and Bryn skipping stones. Jack explored the weeds that grew on the far banks of the pond.

Marvin stood as the two young women approached with the basket. "Food!" he called to the others. He smiled at Alyce. "And beautiful maids," he added, taking the basket and setting it on the blanket.

Kiran lifted a pitcher sitting in the shade next to him. Pouring two glasses, he handed them to Alyce and Dawn.

"Mmm. The wine is almost good," Dawn said, grinning.

Brock chuckled. He'd been assigned to the Temple vineyards when he first arrived. Now he clapped one hand against his chest. "Yes, m'lady, you drink the nectar of fermented grapes that have been expertly tramped on by smelly-footed acolytes." He lifted his own glass high. "To nectar!"

The others joined his toast, laughing.

Dawn folded herself onto the blanket. "Is anyone else hungry, or am I the only one doomed to grow forever?" She motioned to Kiran. "You're my only hope of equality. Have some food?"

Kiran sat. "I wouldn't want you to eat alone."

Brock dug in the basket. "Look! Not only mashed cheese pastries, but also squashed jam tarts."

Dawn pushed him aside. "Don't you know what I mean by *hungry?*"

Brock threw up his hands. "You and Kiran. Don't forget, those of us who aren't natural-born giants need to eat too."

Rolling her eyes, Dawn replied, "There's nothing natural about being a giant, but there's something *un*natural about an owl-chosen boy who's never serious."

Brock rumpled his black curls, making them stand up all over his head. "You didn't accuse me of not being serious when I subtracted the math crown from your head, Oh Queen of Numbers."

Dawn snorted. Brock was so endearing she enjoyed their classroom rivalry. "Watch yourself, Prince of Theorems, or you'll find it taken away again."

She passed pastries around, and everyone began eating with gusto while Brock kept up an ongoing stream of banter.

As Kiran reached for his fourth cheese pastry, Brock punched his shoulder. "You're a glutton, Mox. Or did the swan give you the secret gift of oafishness?"

Kiran shrugged good-naturedly. "Not so secret," he said with his mouth full. He lifted his glass. "To oafishness."

They clinked glasses together, guffawing.

"Look," Bryn said, "we have company."

Eloise and Clea, Charis and Narda led several more of the Feathers toward their picnic spot. Brock's merry expression vanished, and Kiran scowled. The two of them got to their feet and stood defensively in front of their friends as the Feathers approached.

Clea and Eloise stopped a few feet away from Kiran and Brock, their friends behind them like maids of a court. "Hello, Kiran," Clea said, stepping forward. She put a hand on his chest, drawing a circle with her fingers. "We're going to have a picnic. Join us?"

"Just eaten," Kiran answered, his scowl deepening.

Clea smiled seductively. "Maybe you'd like to see what else we have besides food." She put her other hand on his arm, squeezing. "Good company."

Kiran lifted her hand off his chest, removed her other hand from his arm. "I expect my dog will be here soon," he said. "I doubt he'd enjoy your company." The freckly patches on his face darkened as he reached into his pocket. He brought out a wad of blue cord. Catching up Clea's hand, he thrust the wadded sash into it. "This belongs to you." He wiped his hands on his shirt.

Clea studied the bunched-up silk. "What are you saying?" She widened her eyes innocently.

"Don't pretend with me," Kiran said through clenched teeth. His fists bunched.

She gave a little shrug as if he were incomprehensible, then turned gracefully, her silk robe swirling. She linked her arm through Eloise's. They moved away, the other Feathers following.

Kiran stared after them as they disappeared behind a knoll.

Brock slapped Kiran lightly on the back and then dropped onto the blanket. "Have a jam tart, Mox."

The furious heat in Kiran's eyes died down. He rejoined his friends and took a tart. "To oafishness," he said.

Across the Lyden Desert, Selid waved to Lance as he headed out through the gate of their new home in Tunise. Lance, going by the name of Glenn, had joined the carpenters' guild; he had all the work he wanted. Buildings were springing up in expanding districts, and improvements being made in the older sections of the city.

Selid was known as Lorena now. She cautiously acted as a scribe again, but only in service to the poor, providing her skills to them in exchange for whatever they could give in return: handfuls of lentils, perhaps a potato or an egg, but most often simply earnest goodwill.

Selid went into her workroom. She stood in the middle of the floor, breathing the fragrance of cedar and pine. This place soothed her heart. It seemed built not only of wood, but also of Lance's love. He'd created a slanted writing desk for her. He'd even made a mosaic along the walls out of chips of oak, mahogany, and maple.

Selid gathered ink, quill, and parchment. She put a threadbare scarf over her head. She set out on foot for the impoverished district known as Scat Alley.

She reached the tea shop where she read or wrote letters for the uneducated poor. The owner of the shop called himself Sir Chance, "patron of the unlucky," and had named his establishment the Little Best. Sir Chance devoted his enormous girth to spreading cheer and his brawny arms to keeping order. He kept a great kettle of soup warm, doling out generous portions to anyone who could spare the small payment he asked. He replenished the soup continually by flinging unrecognizable scraps into the kettle, stirring, tasting, and then adding pinches of flavor from his spice kegs. He brewed strong tea in vats and served it in large steaming mugs along with buns the size of platters.

"Lorena!" he called heartily when Selid entered. "Hungry, m'dear?"

She never bothered to tell him no. He would urge food upon her whether she arrived empty or full. She submitted quietly to being plied with soup, tea, and bun.

"Ginette!" yelled Chance. "Scribe's here." He pointed a beefy finger at Selid.

A woman drew near Selid's table. Though her hair

was gray, her expression was that of a hopeful child. She fumbled in the folds of her ragged skirt and brought forth a dingy parchment. "From my son in the queen's capital city," she said, sliding it toward Selid.

"You'd like me to read it?"

"Please, ma'am." Her mouth quivered with eager anticipation.

Selid smoothed the creased parchment. She read aloud:

"My dear Mother,

I have found a scribe to write you so here is my news of Zornowel City. I arrived at your brother the draper's. We fill orders every day, all manner of curtains. You would love to feel the brocade and the silk. We have an order from the queen's own physician for bed curtains—"

Selid stopped. Her forehead ached, and she saw a telltale play of light begin washing the parchment she held. She dropped it as if it would burn her fingers.

No.

She had vowed, when she and Lance arrived in Tunise, never to prophesy again. It was too dangerous, not only to her, but to her beloved husband for being near her. She reasoned that if she didn't prophesy, the Master Priest would cease to hunt her; if she didn't prophesy, it would be simple to hide herself with only a thin etheric cloak, for she'd have nothing more to conceal than her own presence.

The cardinal still dwelt nearby, making its home in

a tall pine, and Selid still fed the lovely bird. But she refused every vision.

She had hoped to gain a measure of peace that way, but peace eluded her. During the day, shadows seemed to pursue her. When she looked over her shoulder, they vanished; when she looked ahead they returned to haunt her. Nightmares broke her sleep; nightmares of the Master Priest bringing his keltice ring close to her face and Bolivar lifting a gleaming dagger.

"What is it?" Ginette's eyes widened. "Is something the matter?"

Selid snapped back to awareness of her surroundings. She was in the Little Best, scribing for the poor. She rubbed her forehead, deliberately darkening her visionary eye. She picked up her mug. "No, your son is quite well." She took a long drink of tea before reading on. ". . . *We have an order from the queen's own physician for bed curtains and an order for Lord Laversham's front windows. My uncle sends his kind regards. Be of good cheer. Your devoted son, Gel.*" Selid looked up. "Would you like to send a reply?"

A few days later, Renchald waited in his sanctum for Kiran and Clea to arrive for their first prophecy pairing. Spring was well under way, and the two young people had been studying separately long enough. Both had demonstrated mastery of the techniques he had been teaching them. It was time to bring them together.

Clea arrived first. She bowed deeply as protocol dictated, holding the bow longer than normal.

Kiran was several minutes late. His bow as he entered was perfunctory at best. He dropped into the chair beside Clea. The Master Priest looked from one to the other. Clea, in her silk robe, with gold clasps fastening her yellow hair; Kiran, wearing what must be the shabbiest robe he could find, with his hair uncombed.

Renchald poured tea into prophecy cups on the table beside him. He handed each student a teacup. "You will begin with a prophecy of minor significance. The leaves are from Lord Lindenhal, who resides in the Northland. Newly married, he asks for a prophecy regarding children."

Clea sipped daintily. Kiran tossed his tea down, the delicate cup appearing overly fragile in his large fist.

"I will assist you through the pairing," Renchald told them. "Are you ready?"

Clea's eager "Yes" contrasted with Kiran's sullen nod.

After guiding Kiran and Clea back from the prophecy, Renchald allowed them a few minutes to compose their thoughts. Clea gazed at Kiran. Her eyes, for once, held no disguise, as if her choosing bird looked out of them; as if she'd caught the scent of a kill and knew it would lead her to all the meals she wanted. Kiran leaned back in his chair, breathing as if he needed more air.

The Master Priest dipped his pen. He turned to Clea, his hand poised above a fresh parchment on the table beside him. "Tell me your vision."

She dragged her gaze from Kiran. "Lord and Lady Lindenhal will have no children, Your Honor."

Renchald's quill hovered. "Ever?"

"She is barren, sir. Nothing can be done for her." Her voice was cool and sure.

Renchald raised his eyebrows to Kiran. The young man nodded tiredly.

"Did you see anything else?" the Master Priest asked Clea.

"Her white stallion will go lame," she answered. "He has a black star on his left flank."

Such details were invaluable in prophecy. The pairing seemed to have brought the added clarity that Renchald had hoped for.

Kiran roused himself. "The wording should be: *Put Lady Lindenhal's favorite white stallion, the one with a black star on his left flank, out to pasture and allow no one to ride him.*"

Clea gave her head a little toss.

Renchald wrote the prophecy. He would have preferred a more auspicious tiding for Lord Lindenhal, but he wouldn't tamper with the vision—the Oracle's reputation depended on prophecies that would be borne out.

He laid down his pen. "You are dismissed," he told Clea. "We meet again in one week at the same hour."

When the door closed behind her, Kiran sat more upright. "Clea wanted to give Lord Lindenhal the means to break his young wife's neck if he liked," he said. He kicked at the carpet. "I don't want to pair with her again."

Keldes, give me patience. "Your lessons are not yet complete." Renchald spoke calmly. "You will learn a great deal more through practice."

Kiran looked furiously angry. But the Master Priest knew he would not break his word.

Kiran left Renchald's sanctum, his heart aching, mind churning. He took a side passageway, fearing that Clea would be waiting for him somewhere along the main corridor. The passageway led into a tangle of unknown halls. He was glad to come upon a senior acolyte, who directed him to the nearest outer door.

Once outside, he gulped air desperately. He heard the dinner gong but ignored it, heading for the pond and woods, whistling softly for Jack. The evening breeze lifted his hair, stroked his cheek, caressed his neck. Jack bounded to his side. Kiran was moving so fast that if Jack hadn't been with him, he wouldn't have seen Bryn sitting on the flat rock by the pond, staring at the water. The dog greeted her enthusiastically.

Kiran noticed, as he always did now, that the breeze he'd been so grateful for didn't touch her. His frustration rose.

"Kiran?" Bryn said. "Are you all right?"

He sat beside her. Her brown braids lay limp against her worn robe, and her face looked tired. Kiran took a long breath. It was time he made some attempt to help her.

"Bryn," he said gently, "do you trust me?"

She bent to pet Jack, one of her braids falling over

her shoulder, partly hiding her face. "The only one I trust more than you is Jack." The dog grinned wickedly at Kiran, tail thumping.

How restful it was to be next to her instead of Clea. Bryn didn't run her eyes over him as if he were a rich delicacy, didn't speak with Clea's glittery tones.

He cleared his throat. "Do you trust me enough to let me link with your mind?"

She blinked at him, golden-brown eyes wary. "The way you do with Jack?"

"Something like that."

A flush crept up her face. "Would you know my mind the way you know Jack's?"

"I'd be looking for one thing only."

"What?"

"Clea's curse."

Bryn hugged her stomach. "How would you know where to find it?"

"I think it would be different from the rest of your inner landscape," he said, and then realized he had spoken one of Renchald's secret phrases aloud: "inner landscape."

According to the Master Priest, all people had landscapes within them that reflected their inner nature. Such private landscapes were part of the *abanya*, the vast etheric lands that existed, unseen by most, alongside the physical realm. People visited the abanya during sleep, but lived out their lives without consciously glimpsing its reality.

Part of Kiran's training for paired prophecy involved learning not only to perceive the abanya but

171

to walk within it consciously. To do so, he had developed a strong and focused *dream body*. Renchald taught that just as everyone had an inner landscape, everyone had a dream body, but most were not aware of its movements (beyond remembering fragments of nightly dreams) and had no control over where it traveled. Gifted prophets used the dream body to journey to other places and times, but very few were trained to move freely through the abanya at will.

Kiran had learned how. He knew he could enter Bryn's inner landscape, but it would be unethical to do so without her permission.

"The curse would be different from the rest of your mind, I mean," he said hurriedly. "It might try to appear as if it belonged there, but it would seem out of place somehow, like a desert plant growing beside this pond."

She looked down. "It's just that there are things in my mind I don't want you to see."

Kiran thought he understood. "Would it help if I gave you one of my own secrets to keep?"

She jumped up so quickly that Jack got in her way, and she tripped over him, nearly falling. "I don't want a secret from you to be like a bargain," she said. Her feathery eyebrows lowered. "Thank you. But no, I don't want you to link with my mind." She began walking fast toward the Temple.

Kiran didn't go after her. "Hmmm," he murmured to Jack when she was out of sight. The dog looked at him reproachfully. "Oh, *you* would have known what to say," Kiran said, answering the look. "Humans are complicated, Jack." The dog whined.

"Renchald would know what to do about the curse," Kiran said softly. "But I won't ask him. I think he knows what happened to Bryn. He's done nothing to help her. He's elevated Clea instead." Kiran looked at the sun's fading rays sinking their light into the pond. "And now, our Master Priest has Clea's curses at his command."

FALL

Fifteen

On the fall equinox that year, the acolytes of the Temple were granted a day of freedom. If they wished, they could go to the Harvest Festival held in Amarkand City. There would be no festival in the Temple.

Kiran swung a staff in a wide arc. It felt good to be outside the towering Temple wall, walking through stubbled fields with Brock and Jack. They were taking the shortcut cross-country and would meet the main road farther on.

Jack took off at a run, chasing a gray rabbit. Kiran's staff whistled as he swung it again.

"Easy, Mox," Brock said, taking a step to the side, trampling barley stubble.

Kiran grunted. "Have confidence, Owl-face. I may be thickheaded when it comes to math, but sticks I understand."

"It's not your thick head that daunts my confidence," Brock answered. "It's the thick arms that do its bidding. I wouldn't want to be on the wrong end of that stick."

"It's never *your* head I imagine hitting."

"I'm comforted." Brock high-stepped over more stubble. "Whose head, then?"

Kiran looked sideways at his friend. He frowned. "Clea's."

Brock chuckled. "Why does she trail you like a buzzard after blood, when you'd like to see her head on a stick?"

Kiran slashed at a dry barley stalk. "Like a buzzard after blood" was all too apt a description. Each time he paired with Clea, he could feel her seeking chinks in his inner barriers, trying to get more from him than he wanted to give.

And though he'd hoped to help Bryn, Bryn wouldn't let him help her.

Brock pointed ahead. "Trouble."

They were approaching a stand of trees, and Gridley Laversham was leading a band of Wings out of the woods: Lambert, Haig, Everett, Leonard, and Fulton. All were sons of lords. Each carried a sturdy-looking cudgel.

Looking around quickly for Jack, who was nowhere in sight, Kiran planted his staff. "I advise you to run," he told Brock. On a different day and in a different mood, he might have been willing to turn around and avoid a fight. But not today.

Brock folded his arms. "I stand with you, Mox."

Gridley and his followers stopped when they were a few feet away, forming a ragged line.

"Is there something you want?" Kiran said, his deep voice rough with anger.

The peacock-chosen young man smiled nastily. "Don't want much," he said, enunciating his words. "Something so simple even you should be able to understand it. Stay away from Clea. She's spoken for."

Kiran gripped his staff harder. "Why not ask her to stay away from me?"

Lambert snickered. Gridley scowled, his finely chiseled features scrunching together. "What would she see in an animal like you?"

"She has no taste," Kiran said.

The other Wings moved to surround him and Brock. *Jack. Where are you?*

Gridley's face flushed. He slipped a hand inside his silk shirt.

Kiran lifted his staff. He thumped it against Gridley's chest. "You wouldn't be reaching for a peacock feather, would you?"

All the students had been repeatedly told that it was rare for acolytes or handmaids to be able to use their secret gifts before they went through the formal initiation to the priesthood. But Kiran knew that just as he himself could speak to animals without being a priest, other acolytes, including Gridley, might have active gifts. It would be stupid to assume that the leader of the Wings could not use whatever gift the peacock had given him. If he couldn't, why would he reach for his feather? Kiran had no intention of allowing an unknown gift to be brought against him in a fight.

Gridley grabbed Kiran's staff with both hands, pushing back. Just then Lambert, cudgel held like a sword, rushed at Brock, who ducked aside but wasn't able to avoid a glancing blow off his shoulder.

Kiran yanked his staff away from Gridley's grasp and swung it, hitting Lambert's arm. The dull *thwack* sounded very loud. Lambert dropped his cudgel and jumped back, rubbing his arm and groaning.

Gridley roared. Haig rushed forward, cudgel raised in both hands. Leaping, Kiran drove his staff into Haig's stomach. Haig doubled over, retching. Gridley scrabbled to open the feather case he'd succeeded in pulling from under his shirt. Everett and Leonard stood in front of him, swinging their cudgels.

Kiran jabbed Everett in the chest with the end of his staff. Everett tumbled back. Kiran barely had time to switch his stance before his staff met Leonard's cudgel with bone-jarring force. "Behind you!" he heard Brock yell as a blow hit his back.

Kiran whirled, swinging blindly. His staff struck Fulton on the knee. Yelping, Fulton hopped backward and then fell. Brock was on the ground, his lip bleeding. He scrambled to his feet, motioning frantically for Kiran to turn around.

Kiran did so just in time to jump aside as Leonard charged him. Leonard crashed into Brock and both fell.

Kiran faced Gridley. The leader of the Wings was holding up a blue-green feather.

"Don't look!" Brock called out.

Too late. Kiran looked straight into the feather's shining eye, and suddenly, that eye was all he could see. He struggled to focus, blinking furiously, but each time he blinked, the peacock's eye multiplied until he was looking at a great fanning tail of blue-green. He held out his stick, groping blindly, and heard triumphant laughter as the other end of the stick was seized by his invisible opponent.

Panic surged through Kiran as he jerked his staff violently; just as he did so, whoever had hold of the other end let go. Kiran landed on the stubbly ground.

Brock's voice next to him spoke quietly. "Stay down. Keep your eyes closed."

Kiran took a deep breath, puckering his lips to whistle for Jack.

"If you call your dog, I'll smash your mouth," said Gridley's voice above him.

Jack, Kiran called silently. *Help us.* He aimed his thoughts at the surrounding woods.

Footsteps crunched close to his head. He strained to see, but his vision filled with swirling peacock feathers.

"Keep your eyes closed," Brock said again, whispering beside him.

Panting, Kiran shut his eyes. The glittering fantails disappeared even as he heard Brock groaning.

"One more word from you, Smith-boy, and you'll pray you were in your father's forge." Gridley's maddening voice so near made Kiran's urge to open his eyes nearly overpowering. "Get up!" Gridley was yelling now, but his shouts seemed to be directed away from Kiran and Brock. Must be calling his followers.

The end of a cudgel thunked Kiran's chest; he made a grab for it and missed, involuntarily open-ing his eyes. Immediately, the peacock fantails reappeared, blue-green and dizzying. He shut his eyes, throwing himself sideways. He heard the cudgel hit the ground where he'd been moments ago. Arms protecting his face, he rolled onto his side. *Jack.*

A booted foot crashed into his ribs. "Stop trying to get away," Gridley said. "You can't." A blow struck Kiran's side. He gasped in pain, kicking out in the direction of the voice but meeting only air. Blows began to come at him from every direction. "What do you want with me, Gridley?" he yelled.

Another kick bruised his back. "You don't belong in the Temple."

And then the sound of ferocious barking split the crisp air. Kiran imagined the Wings, startled and frightened as a large speckled dog burst upon them, running at full tilt. *Jack. Watch yourself. Take down the leader if it's safe. Scare his wits away, but don't hurt him.*

Sudden pandemonium. Fierce snarling, mingled with shouts. "Look out!" Kiran heard scuffling sounds and growls he knew couldn't be coming from Jack. If only he could see.

"Give me back my sight, Gridley," he shouted through the noise.

Snarls.

"Lie still!" one of the young men cried. "The bear won't attack if you lie still."

"Call them off!" Gridley yelled, panic-stricken.

Kiran opened his eyes upon clear sky. He sat up painfully and looked around. Nearby, Brock was getting to his feet. His mouth streamed blood. A few paces away, Jack had Gridley pinned. Growling deep in his throat, the dog was plainly enjoying himself, with his forepaws braced on Gridley's chest, slavering jaws dripping on Gridley's chin, mismatched eyes menacing.

Just beyond Jack, a huge brown bear wagged its massive head from side to side, watching the other five Wings, who cowered in the barley stubble, trembling and sweating. Kiran smelled the spiky scent of terror. He waited a few moments before communicating with the animals. *Thank you, my friends. These men have been defeated. You can safely let them live.*

The bear looked at Kiran. With a shambling gait, it set off for the woods again.

Brock extended a hand. Rising, Kiran groaned. His ribs were very sore. "Jack," he said aloud. *Jack, let him up.*

Jack backed down. He sat on his haunches, grinning widely enough to show all his teeth, while Kiran and Brock stood over Gridley. The rest of the Wings stayed on the ground, looking nervously from Kiran to Jack.

Brock dabbed at his bleeding mouth with the edge of his sleeve. "Your feather looks the worse for wear," he said to Gridley. "Put it away before it loses all its beauty."

Gridley slowly sat up. He stared at the feather he still clutched. Dirt dusted its flanges. "You're not going to take it?" he asked, chin quivering.

"You agree to let us alone?" Kiran demanded.

Gridley nodded yes.

"Let's forget it, then."

Gridley put his feather back in its case. Kiran helped him up. The leader of the Wings looked him in the eye for an instant, grudging respect on his face. Then he turned to his followers and began urging them to their feet.

Jack had followed Kiran's instructions to leave Gridley unhurt; despite having been tackled, Gridley, unlike the other Wings, had no injuries except his battered pride. Haig's face was badly swollen, and Kiran wondered if he might have been swatted by the bear—if so, the bear had been quite restrained, for there was no blood. Fulton, nursing his knee, leaned on Lambert's good arm.

Kiran sighed as the Wings limped out of sight. "Sorry you took a beating on my account, Owl-face. That lip looks bad."

"You didn't leave much for me to do," Brock answered, making a show of talking out of one side of his face.

"Not true. How did you know I should close my eyes? How did you keep your head?"

Sweat shone on Brock's deep-brown skin. His swollen lip was still bleeding, but his black eyes were calm. "Owl's gift," he answered absently.

Kiran looked closely at his friend. "It's the owl's gift to keep your head?"

Brock didn't answer.

Kiran narrowed his eyes. "Owl's gift?" His mind raced. "Somehow, you used your gift to help me. I know Gridley didn't confide in you how to defeat the peacock's weapon."

Brock stood quite still, uncharacteristically quiet. Kiran became aware of the slight noises around them: Jack snuffling, the rustling of orange-veined leaves on the trees beyond, the buzz of insects and cries of unseen birds.

"Brock. You know the secret gifts?"

Brock sighed. "And now you know mine."

Kiran gaped at his friend. "It's the owl's gift to know the other gifts? But you didn't take out your feather."

"Nor did you," Brock answered. "Yet you called Jack without a whistle. And did that bear turn up by coincidence?" His lopsided grin was so comical that Kiran felt a laugh trying to push its way out. When he swallowed, he choked. He began to cough, his bruised ribs aching. Jack barked in sympathy.

"You must admit," Brock said wryly, "that what we learned here could help us another day."

"What more did you learn, Oh sage Owl-face," Kiran said, "beyond what it's like to have a split lip?"

"Important things, Oh Bear-caller. You and I can both use our gifts without touching our feathers—something we've been taught only a Master Priest can do. Also: it is wise to befriend dogs and bears."

Jack yipped sharply and Kiran broke into ragged laughter. He shook his head at Brock. "So will you tell me the gyrfalcon's gift?"

Merriment drained from Brock's face. "The Master Priest's choosing bird?" He eased himself down on the ground. "I can't tell you," he said.

"Why not?"

"He isn't endangering you now. And if I revealed gifts willy-nilly, Winjessen would *not* be pleased." Winjessen, Lord of Thought, looked after the owl-chosen.

Kiran thought hard. He had to concede that it might be wrong to spread sacred secrets. What a fool Gridley had been to expose his gift out of pride.

Brock looked suddenly older, black eyes deep and wise as he stared up at Kiran. "Besides," he said, "I don't know another's gift unless that gift is used in my presence."

Kiran hunched his aching shoulders. "Now that I've done combat with another gift," he said, "I see how dangerous they can be." He looked uneasily at Brock. "Whatever the gyrfalcon's gift is, the Master Priest doesn't need his feather in order to use it."

"It's sure to be a fearful power," Brock said. "I've seen gyrfalcons attack their prey."

Kiran thought of all the hours he'd spent alone with the Master Priest. In his mind's eye, he saw the peacock's dizzying fantail again. He shuddered.

Unaware of Kiran and Brock's battle, Bryn sat with Dawn and Alyce on the east side of the Temple pond where the weeds grew high. The three young women had created a nook by tramping down weeds and then spreading their cloaks. Dense stalks of wild grass and weeds topped by seed pods taller than Bryn formed a makeshift enclosure.

Bryn breathed deeply through her nose. "I love

the scent of late summer," she said. "Like stored-up sunshine." She lifted her cider glass and took a sip.

Dawn stretched her lanky arms. "Always the poet, Bryn. To me, it smells like dead grass, and besides, it's the day of the equinox so we've entered autumn."

Bryn laughed. Dawn poked Alyce, who was lying back staring at the sky. "Isn't it a shame to be stuck inside the Temple wall while the acolytes can go to Amarkand on their own?" Dawn asked.

"If you wanted to go to the festival, why didn't you go into the city with Jacinta and Willow?" said Alyce.

"And be herded like sheep by the Temple guards?" Dawn snorted. "Much rather be here with all of you. I wish the Temple would celebrate the equinox. This day is sacred to Vernelda!" She took a gulp of cider. "And I have something to celebrate. I think I've finally stopped growing."

They congratulated her. "You're the Queen of Tall," Alyce said.

"How deep shall your subjects bow?" Bryn asked. She leaned forward to clink her glass against Dawn's. "You and I have a most holy reason to celebrate, don't we?"

"No more scrubbing latrines!" Dawn whooped. "Unless, of course, I open my mouth to the Sendrata again. Vernelda forbid."

"Or I stand up at the wrong time," Bryn answered, smiling.

"I still say the Temple should give the equinox a grand celebration," Dawn grumbled.

Alyce crushed a dry seed pod. "Because of the equinox, or because of the Gilgamell Troupe?" She scattered fine powder from her hand. "Only think, soon it'll be winter. No more warm days like this."

"You'll be cozy enough, standing next to the ovens," Dawn said. Alyce had been permanently assigned to the Temple bakery, as she had hoped. "You won't have to endure Ishaan's temper as you try to comprehend why Keldes at the midheaven means long life but Keldes on the horizon brings nothing but gloom."

Alyce snickered contentedly. "I don't care about the Lord of Death. Tell me when Marvin will ask me to marry him."

Dawn threw up her hands. "You're asking about Vernelda, Goddess of Love," she said glumly. "Inscrutable. She's supposed to be foremost in *my* chart, but she neither answers my prayers nor favors me."

"Maybe you need to fall in love before she'll favor you," Alyce said.

"I'm too tall for love to find me," Dawn answered. She twitched her black braid forward and played with the tassel of hair at its end.

Alyce tickled Dawn's nose with a fuzzy weed stalk. "Isn't there anyone you fancy?"

Before Dawn could reply, rustles were heard among the weeds. She rose like a lookout tower, hand shading her forehead. "Blast," she said, sinking back down. "Clea and Eloise. I shouldn't have stood up—now they'll know where we are."

"What are they doing here?" Alyce complained. "I thought they'd gone to Amarkand."

Bryn looked up to see Clea framed by weeds, her shining hair twined with ribbons, her richly embroidered robe belted with silk. "Sorry, Clea, but there's nothing dead and rotting here to tempt you into staying," Bryn said, surprising herself. She'd fallen into the habit of avoiding Clea and never speaking to her. *But what more could she do to me? She's already taken the wind. And why would she risk cursing my friends? I'm nothing now—nothing to the Temple and nothing to her.*

Clea dropped gracefully onto Bryn's cloak. Eloise remained standing, looking on with a sneer.

"Did you know," Clea said, pinning her blue gaze on Bryn, "that Kiran meets with me secretly?" She smiled the same smile she'd worn in the desert when she lifted a full water bottle to her lips while Bryn had nothing to quench her thirst.

"What nonsense!" Dawn said.

Clea ignored Dawn, kept looking at Bryn. "He holds the most famous feather among the acolytes," she said. "It's only fitting he should be mine. Your darling Kiran is quite a different man when he's alone with me." She smirked.

Your darling Kiran. Were her feelings obvious to everyone, or did Clea possess some uncanny ability to see into her heart? Turning red, Bryn hoped that Dawn or Alyce would say something. Nobody said a word.

Clea gave an elaborate sigh. "Well, this little place

you've made in the weeds has charm," she said. "It's a step up from a sinkhole, at least. But the conversation is rather dull."

Bryn rallied to say, "Because *you* did most of the talking."

Clea's blue eyes glinted coldly. Her robe whispered as she stood. She and Eloise stepped out of the weed enclosure, and soon their scornful voices faded away.

"May she fall in a sinkhole," Bryn muttered. "Carrion creature."

Willow and Dawn sniggered.

"Do you suppose it's true about Kiran and Clea?" Alyce asked, looking at Bryn.

Dawn shrugged. "Clea wants Kiran for herself, that much is plain." She stood, gathering her cloak and draping it over her arm. "I suppose I'll go finish the calculations Ishaan left for me." She picked up the empty cider pitcher.

"And my bread dough will be ready to punch down," Alyce said, getting up.

They headed toward the Temple, burrs clinging to their robes. As she walked beside her friends, Bryn kept hearing Clea's words: *Your darling Kiran is quite a different man when he's alone with me.*

WINTER

Sixteen

When the Solstice Festival was drawing near, Bryn asked Dawn's help in finding something to wear for the dance.

Dawn made a face. "You're coming to *me*? You're the proper size to look delightful in any rag, but what am I to do? I'll have to find *two* rags in the castoffs closet and sew them together to make something long enough to cover me." She rolled her eyes.

The castoffs closet was where gowns discarded by wealthy handmaids from past years were kept. Poorer handmaids were allowed to choose from among them.

A memory glimmered in Bryn's mind of the day of her first Ceremony of Birds. She recalled Jacinta's deft hands winding white ribbons over Dawn's bandage. The dove-chosen young woman always looked lovely and elegant. "We'll ask Jacinta to help us," Bryn said.

They found Jacinta behind her curtain. Dawn launched into their plea. "Vernelda favors you. Help us!"

Jacinta smiled, soft eyes glowing warmly. "How would you like to look?"

"I don't want people staring at me because of my height," Dawn grumbled.

Jacinta cocked her head. "People *will* stare at you, Dawn. Why shrink from it? Give them something to admire when they stare."

Dawn drooped. "No chance of that."

"But you're exotic," Jacinta said. "If you can give every spare minute to sewing, you'll look like a queen." She turned to Bryn. "What about you?"

Bryn bit her lip. She often felt invisible. "I don't want to look as drab as I usually do."

"That will be terribly easy," Jacinta assured her.

Several days before the winter solstice, a messenger from Emperor Dolen of Sliviia arrived at the Temple of the Oracle. Ilona was summoned to Renchald's sanctum to hear the message.

Renchald stood looking out at the dark winter evening. Candlelight reflected off the silver streak in his hair. He turned to her and bowed.

"Lord Morlen is dead," he said without preliminary. "Killed by a young woman with a knife."

Ilona's legs felt suddenly weak. She sat quickly. "Bryn foresaw his death." She calculated the timing in her mind. "A year and a half before it occurred."

He stared down at her. "Precisely. As I suggested to you long ago, Bryn is an extraordinary prophetess. Yet under your training, she has produced no prophecies of note for a year."

Ilona's throat constricted. "But—"

He held up a hand. "Tell me, what is her progress in class?"

She swallowed. "Her visions are foggy, lacking in detail."

"But are they truthful?"

"As predictions, her prophecies are useless. They can be understood only *after* the events she foretells take place." Ilona compressed her lips. Was he holding her responsible for the way Bryn's gift had failed? But hadn't he said that Clea had never cursed the stone-cutter's daughter?

Yes, Ilona was quite sure he had. It was after she'd told him she suspected Clea of casting a curse unlawfully. He had solemnly assured her that after meeting with Clea he had determined her innocence.

Could the Master Priest have lied?

"Something is interfering with Bryn's abilities," Renchald said. "I intend to test her prophetic strength by training her in paired prophecy. If she can regain her abilities, she will serve the Temple well. More prophecies such as that of Lord Morlen's death would greatly benefit the Oracle's reputation."

Ilona's thoughts spun as she listened. *Did the Master Priest lie to me, First Priestess of the Oracle?*

"I'll begin teaching Bryn after the solstice," he went on. "She can be paired with Kiran."

"Kiran?" Ilona choked out.

"As I've told you before, he's more able than he lets on. He may not do well in your class, but he's chosen by the black swan. He's fully trained; pairing Bryn with him may help her become an able prophetess again." The Master Priest bowed to Ilona. "When classes resume, send the stonecutter"s daughter to me."

Kiran and Brock entered the Temple's Grand Hall for the Solstice Festival. The candelabra shone as brightly as they had the year before, but Kiran's eyes didn't linger on the flames. His glance roved from the tables laden with food and wine to the troubadours' platform as he searched the crowd for Bryn's face.

He saw the Master Priest, authority draping him as if his high rank had been woven into the threads of his robes. Watching him nod gravely to wealthy lords, Kiran was reminded again that Renchald ruled the Temple as surely as Alessandra was Queen of Sorana.

Clea glittered in the midst of a group of Feathers and Wings. Kiran instantly drew his eyes away from her. He and Brock started through the throng toward the stage, away from the Master Priest, away from Clea and her admirers.

He spotted Bryn standing with her friends. She glowed in a gown the color of her eyes, soft golden-brown, open at the neck. Her hair was arranged so that tendrils curled about her face. When she saw him, she smiled, warm and bright as goldenrod in a summer field. Beside her towered Dawn in white, her gangli-ness transformed into grace, slender hands waving as she talked.

Kiran and Brock plowed through the crush of peo-ple to join the young women. Brock lifted Willow's hand, kissing the ends of her fingers, murmuring, "You're the Oracle of my heart."

Next to Willow, Alyce giggled. "What does your Oracle prophesy?"

Willow smiled. "Music and dancing."

Kiran edged in next to Bryn and Jacinta; the wall behind him felt comfortingly solid, steadying him as he watched the entrance of the Gilgamell Troupe.

The four troubadours ascended the stage and bowed to the hall. Avrohom, the red-haired singer, resplendent in a cream costume embroidered in black, stepped to the edge of the stage, waiting for silence. His roguish glance swept the hall. "Ladies and gentlemen! Again we have the good fortune to celebrate with you the return of Solz's power, the winter solstice." He lifted his hand and brought it down with a flourish. The lutist strummed, the harpist plucked his strings, and the drums began.

"Keldes vanquished, Solz behold,
His brightness brings us through the cold."

People had cleared the center of the floor. Brock and Willow were already joining other couples ready to dance.

Kiran turned to Bryn. "Will you dance with me?"

But she was staring hard at the troubadours and didn't reply. At Kiran's elbow, Dawn reminded him, "It's the first time she's heard Avrohom sing. Sometime tonight you must dance with me, Kiran, or I won't get to dance at all. I won't embarrass you this year; I've been practicing the steps."

"Of course." Kiran touched Bryn's shoulder. "Bryn? Dance with me?"

She gave a start. "Dance with you?" she answered breathlessly. "Yes, oh yes."

They made their way to the dance floor just as the first song ended. The troupe didn't wait for the roar of applause to finish before launching into the next tune, a lively melody that urged dancing the *zenga*, a sprightly set of steps Kiran had learned years before from Selid. The zenga involved couples standing across from one another, stamping up and down and back and forth, punctuating their steps with hand-clapping.

Kiran was surprised to find that Bryn kept missing the steps; several times she even trod on his toes. When she did, she blushed deeply. She clapped at the wrong moments. Kiran could see her trying to do better, a frown puckering her forehead, her lips moving to count the strokes of the drum. It didn't seem to matter. The harder she tried, the worse she danced. How unhappy she looked, alternately blushing and turning pale, sweat on her face, fumbling the steps. Kiran longed to comfort her, but didn't know how. It wasn't the sort of dance where he might have steered her.

When the song ended, he bowed deliberately: humble horse-trainer to lovely friend. Bryn stood stricken, chewing her lip.

The music began again, a medley of gentler

harmonies. This time, the dance would be the *trell*, a gliding dance during which partners kept close to each other. Kiran leaned toward Bryn. "Another dance?" Maybe he could help her through this one. His left hand would be on her back, his right hand joined with her left.

Her eyes met his, incredulous. "Please," he said. He placed his hand against her back, feeling her warmth; took her hand, which was icy cold.

Kiran gave himself over to the music; Bryn beside him, slipping and stumbling as if her shoes were stuffed with pebbles. When she stepped on his feet, he only held her closer, lifting her along, dancing for both of them.

> "*I was born in a land both near and far—*
> *Too near to leave, too far to find again,*
> *I wander here, keeping my sorrow in my heart—*
> *Wander here between the now and then.*"

When the music ended, Kiran drew her very near for a moment, to let her know he didn't mind that she had danced so badly.

He stepped back, reluctantly dropping her hand. Bryn's eyes looked almost feverish. She pointed toward the wall. "Dawn's there alone. Will you give her a turn?"

As they walked back to Dawn, Kiran hid his disappointment. What if he were trapped again as he had been the year before, dancing with one handmaid after another? Bryn was a terrible partner. *And yet, she's the only one I want.*

Dawn greeted them happily, tapping her foot, eager to dance. Bryn took her place leaning against the wall.

As Kiran and Dawn reached the dance floor, the troupe started another fast-paced tune. The zenga again. Kiran clapped and stomped, pounding the floor. Opposite him, Dawn drove up and down, dancing hard, believing this would be her only chance for the evening. By the time Kiran noticed that others were staring at him and Dawn, the dance was almost done. A flurry of drumbeats closed the song.

Avrohom pranced to the edge of the stage, calling over the crowd. "I honor you, beautiful lady in white!" He pointed to Dawn. "My lady, I must be your partner. Please?"

Dawn was looking behind her for a lady in white. "He means you," Kiran murmured. "Say yes. That is, if you would like to dance with him."

In the hush that grew after the troubadour's question, Dawn could be heard panting. "Don't fall," Kiran whispered, putting a hand on her elbow. "He's asked you to dance."

"Oh!" Color flooded her face. "Oh, yes," she called up to the troubadour.

"Thank you, lady." Avrohom gestured behind him at the other musicians. "My brethren can play a melody without me." And he leaped to the floor.

People made way for him. He bowed low in front of Dawn. When he straightened, the top of his fiery head barely reached her chin. He held his hand out to her, and she clasped it rapturously.

Kiran saw Clea nearby. He turned hastily, wanting to hold Bryn again.

"Good evening, Kiran." Clea blocked his way.

Kiran looked around for Gridley. Why couldn't the peacock-chosen young man stick to Clea?

Since their fight, Gridley and the rest of the Wings had stopped jeering at Kiran. Though they could hardly be called friendly, they were at least civil. But now, when Kiran wished he were around, Gridley was nowhere to be seen. "Excuse—"

"Dance with me." Clea stepped closer.

Glancing at Dawn, Kiran stopped himself from shoving Clea aside as he wanted to. He wished he'd never met her and fervently wished he hadn't been forced to know her as well as he did. He guessed she wasn't only inviting him to dance, but telling him that if he refused to be her partner, she'd do something dramatic. And whatever she chose to do, Kiran suspected Dawn would be the one to suffer.

Dawn had waited too long for her moment of happiness. Kiran couldn't bring himself to chance anything that might spoil it. He would simply have to endure one dance with Clea.

The music struck up again. Another medley. Kiran put his right hand out stiffly and allowed her to clasp it. He began the steps of the trell, merging onto the floor with the other couples, forcing himself to keep time.

"It's a pleasure to dance with a man who knows where to put his feet," Clea said. "What a pity you had such a clumsy partner earlier." She looked smug.

Kiran didn't answer.

"You have so many abilities, Kiran. Why do you keep them hidden?"

He wouldn't look at her face, focusing instead on the sleeve of her gown. Glistening garnets had been sewn into the cloth from which it was made.

"Answer me," she said, beginning to pout.

"There isn't an answer."

She tossed her head. "Just because we can't tell others about pairing together doesn't mean you have to keep such a distance." She leaned in close, dancing on tiptoe, her lips at his ear. "One day I'll be First Priestess, and you'll be the Master Priest."

Kiran stiffened his arms still more. "I will never be the Master Priest."

Would the medley ever end? He glanced at the troubadours' platform. The drummer played rippling beats; the lutist's fingers traveled up and down the neck of his instrument; the harpist plucked his strings, brushed them, strummed them, caressed them into a blend of heady notes. Kiran began to fear that this dance wouldn't end until Avrohom and Dawn dropped from exhaustion. They weren't showing any signs of tiring; they danced like birds flying in tandem, soaring ecstatically on and on.

"You can't avoid destiny." Clea's voice cut through the music.

Kiran's chest hurt from the effort of reinforcing his inner barriers against her. His arms ached. He wanted to stop abruptly and send Clea spinning. But if he did, the people near him would trip, perhaps fall.

Dawn's dance would be ruined, would be remembered only for how it ended. Badly.

And so he kept dancing.

At last the music finished. Kiran dropped his arms. He turned away from Clea rudely, not bothering to bow. He began pushing through the crowd, regretting that the dance had ended when he was at the far end of the hall from Bryn.

The troupe announced that it was time to eat and drink. Everyone started milling about. Kiran was glad of his height, which made it easy to shoulder his way past others. Ahead was the wall where Bryn drooped like a flower overcome by frost. Kiran tried to catch her eye, but she wouldn't look at him.

"One moment, Kiran." Renchald's sonorous voice had never been more unwelcome to Kiran. Controlling his irritation, he bowed to the Master Priest.

"I would like to introduce you," Renchald said, "to Lord Errington."

Errington's blue eyes were set beneath his brows as if the gods had measured the best distance from the bridge of his nose. It was easy to see where Clea and Raynor got their looks. His blond hair, graying at the temples, brushed his shoulders. He wore several thick gold chains; a large medallion set with gems was suspended on his chest.

Kiran felt a nearly overwhelming urge to smash Lord Errington's shapely nose. He'd spent the first twelve years of his life in this man's realm. He knew more than he wished to about Errington's greed. But tonight Kiran wanted to get across the room to Bryn, so hc bowed instead: student without rank to wealthy lord.

"Ah, Clea." Lord Errington stretched an arm to welcome his daughter, who had followed Kiran through the crowd. "Lovely dancing, my dear."

"I had an excellent partner," she answered coyly, smiling at Kiran.

Kiran knew he was expected to murmur something about how enchanting Clea's dancing had been, but he looked past her to the wall. He couldn't see Bryn, but then Brock and Willow, Jacinta and Calden, Alyce and Marvin crowded the area where she had been standing. His friends. He should be among them, not here with the people he liked least in the world.

Kiran bowed: student taking leave. He added the precise motion to say he needed to visit a privy, a gesture rarely used but always honored. He backed away and then swerved toward his friends.

Brock welcomed him, slapping his shoulder. "Sorry you got waylaid by the vulture princess, Mox."

Kiran looked about for Bryn. He didn't see her.

"Our Dawn is queen of the evening," Jacinta said proudly. She pointed to where Dawn stood with Avrohom. Though they made an incongruous pair, they seemed at ease, with eyes only for each other. As Kiran watched, Avrohom fed a bite of cake to Dawn, and then she gave him a sip of wine from her glass.

Kiran's chest was aching again. "Where's Bryn?"

"She was here a moment ago," Alyce answered.

"She'll come back," Jacinta assured him.

Bryn sat curled within an alcove of the corridor that led to the Grand Hall. The hard stones she leaned on were cheerless, but how could she go back to the dance? As she had watched Kiran and Clea dancing, her heart had throbbed louder than the drummer's beats. Clea's gem-encrusted slippers had twinkled; the sleeves of her gown swayed like curtains of blood-colored stars. How did she always manage to look as if she ought to have been chosen by a beautiful bird; by an egret perhaps, or even a swan?

Kiran hadn't let go of her until the dance was done. Afterward he had stopped to talk to the Master Priest and Lord Errington.

Bryn's cheeks burned when she thought of how she'd begun to hope Kiran might return her feelings for him. He'd been so terribly kind to her, supporting her through the trell while she clumped about, unable to put her feet where she meant them to go.

Cursed.

She hung her head. Was it any wonder that Kiran wanted to dance with Clea, a lovely, graceful girl who'd never dream of missing a step?

Because of her, I can't dance. Because of her, Kiran will never think of me as more than someone to share chores with.

Bryn knew Clea pursued Kiran at every opportunity, lavishing smiles on him, speaking in a special tone when he was near. *He meets with me secretly,* she'd said. Could it be true?

How chilly it was in the stony recess. Bryn shivered. She shouldn't be sniveling alone in this alcove like a silly child. *It's the solstice. Solz triumphant. My seventeenth birthday.*

Still, she couldn't bear the thought of returning to the dance. She'd never be able to hide her misery if Kiran and Clea were partners again. It would be better to slip away.

Taking one last look at the door to the Grand Hall, Bryn turned from the music and fled to the quiet of her pillow.

Seventeen

Kiran thought that the morning after the Solstice Festival always seemed colder than any other. Colder and bleaker. Few would be stirring in the early hours, for most preferred to sleep off the revelry that had lasted through the night.

Carrying a bone wrapped in sacking for Jack, Kiran nodded to a bleary-eyed guard and went outside. Shafts of cold pierced his lungs. He headed through the snow toward the stables, where Jack had a bed of straw. Early as it was, smaller feet had already left prints ahead of him. Recognizing Bryn's footprints, Kiran hurried forward. She hadn't returned to the dance the night before; Jacinta had looked for her; Alyce too. Dawn had been so lost in the glow of dancing with Avrohom, she hadn't noticed Bryn's early departure from the hall. Bryn's other friends had decided she must have taken ill.

Not wanting to chance Clea again, Kiran had slipped out himself as soon as it was plain Bryn wouldn't be back.

Now, he slipped inside the stables. Jack jumped

excitedly around him as he uncovered the bone. "Here's breakfast."

The dog settled himself with the bone between his paws as Kiran lit a torch. The light showed Bryn hunched on a straw bale close to Obsidian's stall, hidden in the folds of her cloak, its hood covering her head.

"Morning," Kiran said. "Are you feeling better?" He put the torch in a sconce nearby.

She caught him off guard by saying, "I don't exist to Lord Errington, except perhaps as an annoyance to his daughter."

Kiran wondered why Bryn would care whether she existed for Lord Errington or not. "Maybe that's a mark of character," he answered.

"But *you* exist for him." Her hood fell away as she lifted her head. Tangles of hair hung around her face. "When I came here, they said, 'This is the Temple of the Oracle, the most sacred ground in Sorana. Here, we learn to serve the gods.' She put a hand to her forehead, rubbing as if she could ease her thoughts. "Nirene insists all the handmaids are equal, though she knows it's a lie," she went on. "Ilona says the bird-chosen love and understand one another, and she pretends not to see all the meanness done by the Feathers." She took a shaky breath. "The ones who *do* love and understand—those like Jacinta and Willow— are given no favor. But everyone, from the Master Priest to *you*, defers to Clea. And what are her virtues? She's pretty, she's wealthy, she's related to royalty— and she casts curses."

"Bryn," he said, "I don't defer to Clea."

Her eyes were so shadowed he couldn't see them clearly. "Why else would you dance with her?"

"But I—"

She jumped from the bale. "I thought you were my friend," she said. "My dearest friend. But if Clea puts death curses on my friends as she threatened, she won't be cursing you, will she?" And she ran to the door and out into the cold.

Kiran sat blinking for several moments. "I *am* your friend!" he yelled, too late for her to hear.

Obsidian neighed in answer. Jack stopped gnawing his bone and looked up, black ears sagging.

"You might have done something to get her to stay," Kiran said to Jack. "*I* can't put my paws on her anytime I want the way you can."

Jack sniffed.

"I do *not* need a lesson in where to put my paws," Kiran said. "Humans are different. You wouldn't understand. *I* don't understand." He shook his head in frustration. "*She* doesn't understand."

Jack yipped and returned to his bone.

A week after leaving the solstice dance early, Bryn sat morosely in the handmaids' dining hall. Classes would begin again in a few days, and her entire holiday had been hollow. She felt a perfect fool for the way she'd behaved at the dance—going off to bed without saying goodnight to anyone; missing hours of music. Worse, she'd blurted out her feelings to Kiran the next morning.

Though they'd continued doing chores together, Bryn felt awkward with Kiran now. When he looked at her, his eyes, usually so warm, were cool and distant.

"I wish I could ride Obsidian to Uste," she said to Dawn. "See my father."

Dawn rested her elbow on the polished wood of the table, chin on her hand, looking dreamily at nothing.

"She's still getting over dancing with Avrohom," Alyce said.

Bryn nudged Dawn, making her jump. Dawn's dreamy look disappeared. Tears sprang to her eyes. She picked up her napkin, covering her face.

"What's wrong?" Bryn asked, alarmed.

Dawn mopped her face with the napkin. She blew her nose. "I'm so happy," she said. "But I'll miss all of you so much."

"Miss us?" Alyce stopped spreading butter.

Dawn dabbed at her eyes. "I'm leaving the Temple," she said. "To be married."

"Married!" Bryn and Willow shrieked. Several of the Feathers turned to stare. "To whom?" Bryn asked.

"Avrohom," Dawn answered. "I wouldn't marry anyone else, would I?"

"Avrohom?" Bryn cried. It had been only a short week since the red-haired troubadour had leaped from the stage to dance with Dawn. Since then, Dawn had been mysteriously absent many times, but Bryn hadn't thought to question her. "You're going to marry the troubadour?"

"Tonight," Dawn said, nodding. "The Master Priest

has agreed, but I've never seen him so angry." She made a face. "He was hoping I'd become a star-caster for the Temple. Now he's probably afraid I'll tell Avrohom too many Temple secrets and they'll be sung to the world."

"The troubadour," Jacinta said. "You're marrying the troubadour *tonight*?"

"Tonight." Dawn's eyes streamed. "I wish you could all be there for my wedding, but Renchald won't allow anyone. Only the smallest of ceremonies," he said. She rolled her eyes. "The Sendrata of Handmaids will stand up with me."

Bryn wanted to cry when she thought of meal-times without Dawn, of waking in the morning without Dawn's cheerful whispers, of mathematics without Dawn's explanations. But she smiled at her friend. "Congratulations."

Dawn grinned through tears. "I'll travel with the troupe. We're leaving tomorrow morning." She clasped her hands. "I'll see the world."

"You'll cast star charts for kings and queens," Willow said.

Dawn crumpled her napkin. "Remember when you said Vernelda would favor me if I fell in love, Alyce? And so she has."

She began to talk in raptures of Avrohom, how his music had always spoken to her heart but she'd never considered he'd feel anything for her. "Jacinta, the dress you designed got him to notice me. Once he did, love found us. Did you know he writes the songs the troupe performs? He told me he'll be able to write

211

true love songs now instead of the bittersweet ballads he used to sing. Isn't that romantic?"

Nirene looked at the four determined young women who had insisted on a meeting.

"We're Dawn's friends," Bryn was saying. The stone-cutter's daughter wasn't recognizable as the girl Renchald had plucked from the dirt of Uste. Her hair was neatly braided, her robe smooth, her face clean.

"We can't let her go away without a celebration, however small," Jacinta declared.

"Let us use one of the rooms where guests are entertained?" Alyce asked.

Nirene frowned. "And whom will you be inviting?"

"Only a small group, Sendrata," Bryn answered. "Ourselves. The guest of honor, naturally."

"Her groom," Jacinta put in.

"Brock and Kiran," Willow added.

"Calden and Marvin," Alyce finished. "And you, of course, Sendrata, to be chaperone."

Nirene looked at their expectant faces in silence for a moment. "Oh, very well," she said. "But I won't be bothered with preparations or cleaning up."

"Of course not," Bryn answered. "We know how to clean."

Nirene showed them into one of the less imposing rooms kept for entertaining and watched sourly as they laid out a tablecloth, covering it with festive foods: delicate puff pastries, small frosted cakes, beribboned bowls of shelled nuts. Where had they got so many dainties? Nirene looked suspiciously

212

at Alyce, who was setting forth plates with an innocent air.

Dawn arrived wearing her old student robes, looking flustered, her black hair hanging loose. The acolytes came through the door in a disorganized bunch a few minutes later, their voices loud in congratulation.

Brock had brought a vial of sand. "From beside the pond," he explained, presenting it to Dawn with a flourish. "If you get lonesome for your friends you can open it, take a big sniff, and remember you're getting along quite well without us."

Dawn clutched the sand, not knowing whether to laugh or cry. She settled on laughter.

Alyce gave a collection of recipes. "Though I know you may not get a chance to try them now that you'll be rich." Jacinta brought a box of hair ribbons, while Bryn surprised everyone by producing a Star Atlas.

"Bryn," Dawn squealed, "did you become a thief for me? This book isn't even battered."

Bryn beamed. "Let me show you what I said to Ishaan to get it." She went into an elaborate bow.

"Humble friend of student about to be married requesting book from esteemed instructor," Brock shouted.

Everyone clapped. "Kiran helped with the bow so the book is from him, too," Bryn said, somewhat stiffly, without looking in Kiran's direction. "And Ishaan pronounced you 'fully adequate,' Dawn."

"Fully adequate, no less." Dawn fingered the book delightedly. "Thank you, Bryn." She hugged the stonecutter's daughter. "Thank you, Kiran." She shook hands with the tall freckled acolyte.

When Avrohom arrived, he awed the company by singing a newly written love song to Dawn: "*Through the soft night air, Monzapel's light . . .*"

Nirene refused to be drawn into such sentimental nonsense, but she had to admit the melody was haunting.

The friends talked and laughed. Brock glued himself to Dawn's side for awhile, talking with her about theorems.

Evening was approaching when the four young women grouped themselves beside Dawn. Bryn put an arm around her. "She may be yours for eternity, Avrohom, but she belongs to us now until the wedding tonight."

"We're going to help you dress," Jacinta announced, smiling at Dawn.

"Thank you for offering to clean, Kiran," said Alyce.

"Don't thank only me," Kiran answered. "Brock will be here too."

"I will?" Brock said, acting shocked.

In the first prophecy class of the new year, Bryn slumped in her chair. Deciphering her vision was like trying to read a page of smeared ink. She saw no point in setting it forth. *For that matter, why do I study any of the subjects taught at the Temple? I'll never be a priestess.* During math class, numbers would jump about in her mind like pebbles knocked wide by a quarry hammer. She found history fascinating but suspected a great deal was being omitted. Geography was interesting too, but since most of the handmaids didn't leave the Temple grounds, the rivers, mountains, and oceans on maps seemed farther away than the moon and stars. *Farther away than Dawn.*

Bryn had watched her friend ride out of the Temple gates, tall and straight beside her husband Avrohom, famous troubadour. Dawn's hair had been gathered into ribbons tied in bridal knots, her gloved hand waving goodbye.

Bryn fiddled with the ragged end of her quill pen. Her blank parchment reproached her as the First Priestess collected the prophecies. When the gong sounded, Ilona said, "Bryn, remain after class."

Clea paused beside her. "Are you feeling well, Bryn? You look like death."

"Better than smelling like something that died long ago." Bryn made her way to the front of the room, where the First Priestess stood beside the marble table that held the prophecy teapots and cups.

"You're to come with me to meet with the Master Priest," Ilona said calmly.

Bryn bit her lip. Her poor showing in prophecy must have come to the Master Priest's attention. She'd been expecting the Temple to forbid her to continue studying with the bird-chosen. She had no feather, and the wind had deserted her.

For a moment she thought Ilona would say more, but the First Priestess turned and led the way out with her usual quiet dignity.

When they arrived in Renchald's sanctum, Bryn knew, this time, what bow to make: humble student to Master Priest of the Oracle. She'd grown since the day she'd occupied the same seat in front of Renchald. She feared him much more now than she had then. She hardly dared look at him. When she did, she noticed that there was more silver in his hair, and that the lines in his austere face had deepened.

"A year and a half ago, you predicted the death of Lord Morlen at the hands of a young woman wielding a knife," he began. "Your report seemed unlikely at the time, but we have received word from Sliviia that Lord Morlen has died in the manner you described."

Bryn remembered the rushing winds of prophecy, the visions seen while dreaming in the Oracle's alabaster chamber. Such things seemed removed from her now; as if someone else, not she, had found the golden couch in the shining room. She had since learned that the deep chamber was reserved for priests and priestesses who had undergone special purification. "The vision was true, then?" she asked faintly. *If Lord Morlen has died, then the dream of Selid must also have been a true vision.*

"Yes. You are a gifted prophetess."

She met his cool, opaque stare. "Perhaps I was when I arrived. I no longer see clearly."

"You're troubled," he said. "Something is interfering with your prophecies. I can teach you a method for improving the clarity of your visions."

"*Troubled*" *by a curse*, she thought. *How much does he know?*

What if he could teach her something that would dispel Clea's curse? What if she could learn to hear the voice of prophecy again; what if her visions, borne upon the wind, could return clear and full once more?

If not, I can be no less than I am now.

"What would I need to do?" She looked directly at the Master Priest, willing her eyes to show nothing, like his.

"You would train with me personally. You need not bring your quill. Everything must be remembered, not written. And you must not discuss this training with any other person." The keltice ring glittered on his hand, reminding her of the day they had first crossed paths. *She will be with others of her kind. She will serve the Oracle,* he had said.

The vulture statue loomed upon its pedestal. Would she go mad, watched by those black marble eyes and the Master Priest? But if she didn't learn from him, she might as well journey back to Uste. Either that or stay on in the comfortless Temple, becoming a senior handmaid, abandoned by the wind and bereft of visions.

The gyrfalcon tapestry glared at Bryn as she nodded.

SPRING

Eighteen

Spring had come, scenting the breeze with leafy buds and new flowers. The city of Tunisc was thriving. Throngs of people worked to repair the roads from the ravages of snow, rain, and frequent travelers.

The talk of the town was the Gilgamell Troupe. They were to perform an open-air concert on the commons. There was hardly a person in the city who planned to stay home.

Lance persuaded Selid to go with him. Though eager for the music, she was hesitant about showing herself among so many.

"What if the Master Priest has spies posted?" she said.

"Wear your ugliest kerchief and no one will know you," Lance answered, grinning, his brown eyes alight with anticipation of hearing the famous troubadours. The Temple didn't hold the same fear for him as it did for her. Hadn't Monzapel protected and guided her thus far?

When they arrived on the green, mingling with the happy crowd, Selid felt queasy. She told herself to relax, but couldn't seem to do it. Hundreds of strangers jostled and shoved for position, pressing close, too close. Lance didn't seem to be bothered. He staked out a place for Selid and himself, then forgot about everything but the Gilgamell Troupe.

From the moment the troubadours appeared, Selid knew she shouldn't have come. She saw a glow around them, an ethereal glow that had nothing to do with the sunshine. She tried to ignore it, but the more she did the more it gathered force until it pressed against her forehead, a fisted hand of light.

She couldn't darken her visionary eye. Light beat and pulsed, blending with the music, swarming in her head. She fought for calm, fought for air.

She murmured to Lance that she wasn't feeling well and went stumbling through a forest of rough shoulders and sharp elbows toward the edge of the crowd, not looking back to see if Lance followed or not, overcome by the driving need to get away. He did follow, of course. He caught up with her and helped her, clearing a passage to the perimeter of the crowd. There Selid sank to the ground, holding her head and panting.

Lance sat beside her, an arm around her, murmuring quietly. "There, it's all right. It's all right."

"Selid? It's surely you?"

The voice close to her ear startled Selid badly. She looked up into a familiar face bent over her.

Dawn. It was the tall handmaid she had known in the Temple of the Oracle. It seemed ominous that she should appear at such a moment, when Selid was struggling to shut out the Oracle's light. What was she doing here? She wasn't dressed as a handmaid. More like a princess, in flowing white. Sapphires sparkled at her wrists and throat. Maybe she was an apparition.

Dawn helped Lance get Selid on her feet and lead her farther from the crush of people. "Selid, I knew it was you the moment I saw you. Something about the way you hold yourself. I'm so glad. I was afraid . . ." Dawn stopped.

Selid forced herself to gather her wits. Dawn's face was becoming strangely lit, as those of the troubadours had been. The light threatened to thrust Selid into a future she did not want to see. Refusing the Oracle had never been more difficult!

"You look lovely, Dawn. This is Lance, my husband. I'm sorry to be unwell, but I really must go home." Each word was an effort.

"Is it far?" Dawn asked. "I can take you to the inn where we're staying. It's close by."

"No, thank you, no. I just want to go home." Selid groped for Dawn's hand, not sure, when she found it, if she was pleased or sorry to find that it was real. "Please promise you won't report seeing me."

Dawn squeezed her fingers softly. "I'm not part of the Temple anymore. Even if I were, I'd never tell the Master Priest where you are. I've worried about you ever since you disappeared."

Selid could feel the truth in Dawn's words. "Thank you."

"But you must visit me when you're better." Dawn told them where the Gilgamell Troupe would be staying. "I'm with them," she said, smiling. "I've married Avrohom. The troupe has to be terribly careful to hide where they're housed, or they'd get no peace. Adoration has its price, you know. But I trust you, Selid. Come and find me."

Selid blinked, not sure she had understood what Dawn said. More light poured from the tall young woman's face, so bright it blurred her features.

"Thank you," Lance said. "We'll find you, or, if you're careful, you can come to us." He gave Dawn quick directions and then they parted.

As they walked home, Selid's head pounded and sparks of sharp light jabbed her eyes so fiercely she was unable to see where she was going. Lance kept his arm around her waist.

Selid went to bed. There, encroaching visions beset her. She poured sweat, using everything she knew to prevent herself from being taken over by prophecy. When she finally slipped into sleep, she dreamed again of the Master Priest. He thrust the keltice ring close to her eyes; sharp and burning, it cut through her sight, her mind, her soul. She tried to look away but couldn't. All the worst moments of her life rushed upon her at once; she couldn't fight off the memories. Then Bolivar appeared, menacing her with a long, killing blade.

Selid tried to cry out, to call for Lance, but her throat closed uselessly.

When the new day arrived, she concealed her exhaustion, telling Lance she was well, she didn't know what had come over her, he needn't worry about her. And had she really heard Dawn say she was married to Avrohom, the famous singer?

Lance assured her it was true. He kissed her and left for the job he had with the carpenters' guild, finishing cabinets and banisters in Lord Evensol's new mansion.

Selid decided not to go to the Little Best, although Sir Chance expected her. He and his patrons would have to do without her; she wasn't fit for company. Restlessly, she fed the chickens and cared for her horse. The cardinal swooped close as soon as she stepped out of the house, nor would it leave her as she completed her chores. Finally, she darted into her workroom, shutting out the persistent bird.

There she paced the morning away, fighting the Oracle's light until her strength was gone.

She wrapped her shawl close. Sunlight played over the ripples of the wooden mosaic as she sank, defeated, onto the couch Lance had put there for her comfort. She closed her eyes.

This time, when the prophecy came, she let it take her.

Borne upon beams of dazzling light, Selid found herself standing in an alcove built into a massive stone pillar, one of dozens of pillars supporting a domed hall. If an eagle had flown to the ceiling within this dome, the bird would have appeared as a speck high above. Along the marble floor stood crowds of lords and ladies.

Twenty feet away sat Queen Alessandra on a throne. She wore her crown, though it seemed heavy for her slender neck and stooped shoulders. Her eyes, deep-circled and sad, shone with dignity and command. Near her stood soldiers in green doublets, swords at their belts.

Upon a smaller throne, a painfully thin young woman watched the proceedings. An opal tiara sparkled in her black hair; her purple gown was decked with opals, but it was her face that caught Selid's attention. Her skin was translucent, delicate blue veins visible just beneath the surface. Intelligent eyes, far too large in their pale sockets, were glassy with tears that did not fall.

The voice of the Oracle knelled in Selid's mind: *Princess Zorienne, near death, poisoned by the hand of Mednonifer, queen's physician. Not by food or drink, but by the air she breathes while sleeping.*

Then Selid glimpsed her former mentor, the Master Priest, writing a prophecy addressed to Queen Alessandra.

False prophecy, the Oracle said.

A few days later, Kiran tramped the familiar path next to the pasture at night, Jack by his side. He stopped at the fence where he'd often seen Bryn sitting untouched by the wind. Starlight cast a silver gleam over the ground, lighting the old fence-posts dimly.

Kiran leaned against a post. "How wrong I've been," he said. "Mistake after mistake."

Jack perked up his ears.

Kiran lifted his face to the quiet sky. "I should never have paired with Clea." Earlier that day, Renchald had asked, once again, for news of Selid. This time Kiran and Clea had seen her. Writing a prophecy.

Kiran had severed the pairing immediately, but not soon enough.

The ink in the Master Priest's quill, as he inscribed what Clea remembered, ran like blood.

"I haven't helped Bryn," Kiran told Jack. "I've helped the ones I despise instead."

And now the Master Priest wanted to begin pairing him with Bryn.

"I won't," Kiran said to the sky. "Renchald can leave me in the desert or throw me back in the gutter." He looked into Jack's mismatched eyes. "And I swear by Ellerth that I won't pair with Clea anymore."

The next day, Velday, Bryn watched wind dance over the pond, creating ripples across the water. A breeze swished through the fresh grass until it reached the little knoll where she sat alone. There, the air became blank and still. She told herself she should be used to the stillness. But she wasn't.

She heard Jack's bark and saw Kiran coming toward her around the pond with Jack at his side. Her emotions scudded and eddied and stormed as he got nearer, walking with his long stride.

The constraint between them, begun after the solstice dance, had continued. Though they still did chores together, Kiran acted as if what he wanted most was to be left alone. Sometimes he'd pause in his work, looking at nothing. Once Bryn had ventured to ask what was bothering him, but he'd only shrugged his shoulders heavily.

What if it's me? she thought.

Yesterday the Master Priest had told her she was ready for paired prophecy and that Kiran would be her partner: *With his help, you'll see clearer, broader visions.* He had not asked for her agreement, and something in his tone frightened her when he said, "Those who are gifted in prophecy *owe* the Temple their service."

Bryn felt a nervousness bordering on panic when she imagined linking with Kiran's mind in prophecy. And yet, it was also something she wanted. She longed to be near him, truly near, not just doing chores side by side with neither of them disclosing anything.

Jack ran up, knocking Bryn backward with playful paws. Kiran, however, didn't stop, though he waved to her before heading off along the path to the woods.

"I should go catch up with him," Bryn whispered to herself. "Tell him I'm sorry. Get it done with."

She started after him, but soon her steps slowed. Wasn't it plain he wished to be by himself? If he'd wanted her company he would have stopped to talk with her.

Bryn veered off the path into the trees. Among them, she felt comforted. She pushed through tangled undergrowth to a broad boulder that jutted from the ground. Climbing it, she settled herself into a hollow in the rock to think. How she missed the sound of breezes soughing in the branches and stirring against the leafy buds. Clea had taken that sound away.

Images of Kiran paraded through her mind: *If a curse can be cast, it can be lifted. . . . The gods would not withdraw from you forever after one mistake. . . . Do you trust me enough to let me link with your mind?*

And now she *would* link with him, formally, and in the presence of the Master Priest.

228

She remembered what Kiran had said about looking for Clea's curse: . . . *It would be different from the rest of your inner landscape.* . . . *The curse might try to appear as if it belonged there, but it would be out of place.*

"Inner landscape" was a phrase the Master Priest used while teaching the concepts needed for paired prophecy; concepts such as the "abanya" and "dream body." Bryn wondered how long he'd been training Kiran.

"I should use what Renchald has taught me to search for the curse myself," she said softly. "Now, before Kiran and I must pair together."

Yes, that was what she would do. She shut her eyes, remembering how the Master Priest had helped to direct her into her dream body: *Recollect a place you've been where you felt peaceful.* Bryn would remember the fields of Uste and the bright thistledown she had seen the day she left for the Temple.

On that peaceful thought, Bryn moved into her dream body. She felt the now-familiar sense of light becoming more solid, the peculiar tingle as she switched her awareness out of normal existence and into etheric life.

She entered her inner landscape.

When she'd visited this place under Renchald's direction, he never allowed time for exploration. But now, alone and undisturbed, she would see all she could.

The feet of Bryn's dream body felt light and delicate on the ground of this place, a ground similar to earthly terrain and yet different. The sky here wasn't the same as normal sky. Instead of blue, it was a deep golden color. Flowered fields glowed with jewel-like hues. Rainbow fish swam in a brook. A grove of trees shimmered in the golden light.

Bryn had been taught that everything in this landscape reflected a part of her own spirit. She remembered to look for anything that didn't seem to belong. Now and again she bent to examine a rock or a bramble, but everything seemed to be as it should.

She came to a well in the center of a meadow. She scrutinized the stones that lined it, stones that looked as if they'd been hewn from the quarry of her childhood, rough-cut but fitting well together. A windlass held a bucket over the water.

Certainty burst upon Bryn. *I use this well to bring up prophecies.*

Both the bucket and the chain attaching it looked new, with a steely sheen that nothing else in the landscape possessed. The bucket threw shadows into the waters of the well and along the ground.

A stalk brushed Bryn's hand. She kneeled to see the plant it grew from. It was dark beside the well, darker than it should be, and chilly. She peered closely at the cluster of plants.

Thistles.

They looked very sickly. Close to the roots, small patches of green hid inside clumps of limp brown stems. The plants had once thrived, for their stalks rose as high as the edge of the well, but now they smelled of decay. The damp ground had been overwatered.

Using the bucket.

Bryn put her arms around the thistle plants as if she could revive them. Here beside her inner spring, the thistles that could guide her were meant to grow. Instead of growing, they were dying.

Every time I drew upon the waters of prophecy, the bucket tainted the water and killed a little more of what could have saved me.

Curse.

Bryn stood. She gazed at the bucket, at the cold gleam of its metal and the hard links of its chain. She had no doubt she was seeing Clea's curse upon her.

How was she to get rid of it?

"Solz and Ellerth help me," she prayed.

Then a sharp sound from outside pierced the quiet.

Bryn left her inner landscape in a rush, and opened her eyes. She heard careless footsteps in the woods. Squinting through branches, she glimpsed Clea, walking purposefully along the path a little way off.

The blood drained from Bryn's head. How had Clea known? What would she do now?

If she adds another curse, I'll surely die.

But Clea didn't seem to see her huddled on the boulder, shivering in despair. Instead, she called hello to someone else who was coming along the path in the opposite direction.

It was Kiran, on his way back from wherever he had walked.

Neither of them saw her, and Bryn didn't want to be found. Jack wasn't with Kiran, and she hoped the dog had found something interesting to pursue else-where. If he caught her scent he was sure to come bounding to greet her, and she couldn't speak to him in her mind the way Kiran did.

Weak and trembling, Bryn crept to the boulder's edge and jumped behind it to the ground. A bed of leaves caught her, but the sound as she landed seemed louder than a gong.

Clea and Kiran paid no attention. Bryn hunched behind the boulder, listening to them.

"Kiran," Clea said. "I knew you'd be outdoors on such a fine day."

Bryn waited for Kiran to answer, but he didn't.

"Why so silent?" Clea spoke sweetly. "Why not greet your pairing partner?"

Pairing partner! Bryn nearly gasped aloud. Had the Master Priest been training Clea also? *Naturally. She's first in the prophecy class.*

But paired with Kiran? He would never endure such a thing. Or would he?

She heard him clear his throat. "I'm not your partner," he said grimly.

She laughed seductively. "There's no one about, Kiran. No need to deny that you're my partner."

"I won't be. Not anymore."

"What are you saying? The Master Priest would have no reason to exchange you. Brock is the only other prophet he might train, and I'd never consent to pair with *him*."

Silence.

"Hasn't Renchald told you how well we're getting on?" she asked.

"*We* are not getting on well," Kiran answered, gruff and cold.

"Of course we are. You should be thankful to be improving your prophetic skills." Her voice sharpened. "Don't you want to see more visions?"

"Not with you."

"With whom, then?"

"We have different aims, Clea," he said, side-stepping her question. "Our pairing was a mistake."

"Don't be a fool. Together, we will become the most noted voice of the Oracle."

"Being noted is not what I live for."

"What *do* you live for? The animals? Or is it your dirty little peasant friends?"

Kiran gave a whistle that would tell Jack to find him. When he spoke, his voice was tight with anger. "As I said, we have different aims."

"I could change your aims, make you serve the Oracle as you should. The gods have gifted me, gifted you, too, and then brought us together. Our visions belong to the Temple, not to you."

"From now on, your visions have nothing to do with me." Bryn could hear him walking away, and she heard Jack's bark, much too close.

"I could change you," Clea said, voice rising. "I could change you with a wave of my feather."

Please, Ellerth, don't let Jack come snuffling around the side of this boulder. Don't let Clea find me here. Bryn waited, every muscle tensed, listening for Jack.

When his bark came again, it was farther away.

Faint with relief, Bryn rested her back against the rock while Clea's retreating footsteps faded.

When Clea claimed they met together secretly, she wasn't lying.

And now? Clea was angry enough to do something against Kiran.

Oh, Kiran, please be careful. Don't let her curse you.

Bryn's thoughts returned to the bucket hanging at her inner well, the steely poisonous metal of Clea's curse, the thistle plants nearly dead.

She was more determined than ever to lift that curse, stop the spread of poison, and give the thistle plants a chance to revive.

She quieted herself by breathing slowly and deeply. When she was calm enough, she sent her dream body into the abanya and entered her inner landscape once again.

She rushed to the well. Kneeling beside the thistle plants, she called upon the whole pantheon of gods. *Solz and Ellerth, Winjessen and Monzapel, Ayel and Vernelda.* She paused before adding, *And Keldes. Lend me your wisdom.*

Then she waited.

Warmth and heat began covering the plants, burning away blight. Healthy life replaced brown rot. New stems reached upward.

Now for the bucket.

Bryn leaned on the edge of the well. She reached for the bucket. The metal handle was so cold! She unfastened the bucket from the chain that attached it to the windlass. She set the bucket on the ground.

Pulling the chain, she unwound it. The end was fastened with a large hook that bit into the wood of the windlass. Bryn wrestled with the hook until it came free. She threw it and the lengths of chain into the bucket.

Shivering, she considered what to do next.

Somehow, Clea must have transported the curse through the abanya to hang it on Bryn's windlass. Bryn thought she could carry the bucket beyond her own barriers, but she didn't want to leave it anywhere in the abanya. What if someone else stumbled upon it in a dream? What if it made things go terribly wrong throughout the inner lands?

I'll have to take it with me when I leave the abanya if I can.

Screwing up her courage, Bryn lifted the heavy bucket. It weighed on her frightfully and felt as if it could freeze through her soul.

She mustn't stop now. She headed for the borders of her inner landscape. It wasn't far to the edge of her barriers, but the bucket grew heavier and colder with every step. Weary and freezing, she dragged the bucket out of her landscape.

She made herself hold on to it as she sent her dream body back to the boulder in the woods.

As she left the abanya, an overwhelming brightness touched her head. An invisible hand took the bucket.

Nineteen

The following day Kiran woke filled with foreboding. He went through the motions of washing and dressing and eating, paying so little attention to what he did that Brock began laughing at him during breakfast.

"If you butter that piece of bread much longer, Mox, you'll wear down the knife."

Kiran looked at his hands holding a knife and a slice of flattened bread, well buttered.

Brock's merry eyes peered at him. "The post brought me a letter," he said, lowering his voice. "From Dawn."

Kiran snapped awake. Glancing around, he was relieved that he and Brock were alone at a table. Nevertheless, he spoke in code. "Did she explain those equations you were wondering about?"

Brock drew out a scroll. He unrolled it; it was covered with numbers and mathematical symbols. He winked. "Dawn's quite happy with the simple one-plus-one equation."

Dawn's marriage is going well, Kiran thought.

"I'll need to study it further, but it appears she's found the answer to the S problem," Brock said.

Dawn has found Selid? Kiran raised his eyebrows.

The gong rang. Brock whisked the scroll into a pocket of his robe.

"Meet out by the pond, after lunch?" Kiran asked quietly. Students would have an hour or two then.

Brock nodded.

Bumping into Bryn in the corridor, Kiran hoped she heard him whisper that he'd be at the pond; hoped that if she *did* hear, she'd be willing to meet him.

Later, standing by the flat rock near the water, where he and his friends had shared picnics and talked and laughed, Kiran was overpowered with eerie certainty: *This is the last time.*

He turned to Brock. "I've tried to keep you out of danger," he said.

Brock's black eyes lit up. "Do you mean you could have offered me more danger before now?"

"I'm serious." Kiran whistled for Jack. When the dog arrived, Kiran silently asked him to see if other people were around. Jack trotted off. He soon returned with Bryn. Kiran was very much struck by how unusually healthy and bright she looked, her skin rosy, her eyes animated and clear.

She and Brock perched on the flat rock and looked at Kiran questioningly.

Speaking in a low voice, he told them about training with the Master Priest, about Clea and their pairing and how he couldn't bring himself to do it anymore.

Neither of his friends interrupted, though they looked grave as they listened to him pour out the story of his secret life. Kiran hoped it was understood, now, that he did not "defer" to Clea and never had. "And now the Master Priest wants to pair me with you, Bryn," he finished; "to use us both to hunt for Selid—and for anything else he may wish to know. I can't be part of that, either."

"How will you tell Renchald?" she asked. "What if he sends you to the desert?"

"I won't tell him. I've decided to leave the Temple."

"Leave?" The word was a whispered cry on her lips.

"I must. The Master Priest plans to command my visions endlessly. If he learns I refuse to pair, he'll give it forth that I've broken my word to him. He'll consecrate me to Keldes or have me cursed into compliance."

Brock leaned forward. "After what you've said, I won't deny you should get yourself gone. But how?"

"Jack and I will leave just after sundown. I'm often out at that hour. The guards know it. We'll go through the woods to the far wall; there's a place where the roots have weakened the stone. You know where it is, Bryn." He raised his eyebrows to her, and she nodded. "Jack can dig a way out."

"Tonight?" Bryn said hoarsely.

"Tonight. And Bryn, we have a letter from Dawn." He looked at Brock. "Have you deciphered what it says?"

Brock pulled the parchment covered with numbers from one pocket and an abacus from the other. "One moment." He spun the beads of the abacus as his eyes darted over the equations Dawn had written.

"Selid is living on the outskirts of the city of Tunise, near the juncture where the north-south highway meets the east-west road," he said after a few minutes. "She's married a carpenter." He paused, tapping the page of numbers. "The troupe was performing, and Selid went to hear the music. Dawn happened to spot her."

Kiran pondered the news. "Even if I hadn't decided to go already, I'd want to leave now, to warn Selid. Someone needs to tell her Renchald is pursuing her."

Brock rattled his abacus. "If you plan to go to Tunise, you'll need a horse to get through the Lyden Desert."

Kiran shrugged. "Least of my worries. I *am* swan-chosen." He managed a smile. "I'll speak to the first likely horse I meet outside the wall." He fastened his gaze on Bryn. *Now for it.* "Bryn, I hope you'll go with me. If you stay here the Master Priest will surely train another prophet to pair with you and force visions from you."

Color rushed into her cheeks. "Go with you?"

"You could slip away by taking a guest cloak and using the door near the gardens, then meet Jack and me at the weak spot in the wall."

Bryn bit her lip. Jack went to her side and nudged her.

"Jack wants you to come with us," Kiran told her. "Will you?"

They were all quiet for a few moments.

"Well, my lady," Brock asked her, "must I say good-bye to you, too?"

Bryn stood up. Kiran couldn't read her expression. Joy? Sadness? "Yes," she answered. "Yes, say goodbye, Brock."

"You'll come with me?" Kiran said eagerly.

She nodded, giving him a look as she used to do, a look of trust and unbreakable friendship. "I'll meet you by the wall, after sundown." She bent to pet Jack, who was grinning broadly, showing all his teeth.

"We'll be waiting," Kiran said.

Within his curtained compartment in the acolytes' hall, Kiran threw off his student robe and exchanged it for shirt and pants. This time he would never put the robe back on. He checked his knife and wished he had thought to smuggle some food.

A tingle made the hair on the back of his neck stand up. He whirled round, feeling that someone else was there.

"Brock?"

No answer, and Kiran suddenly knew who it was that had entered his curtain. Not a bodily presence, but a tendril of awareness from his former pairing partner, Clea. Angry darkness rose in his mind as he reinforced his inner barriers. How long had she been prowling the abanya, waiting for him to let down his guard? What if she knew his mind and betrayed his plans to the Master Priest? Renchald had once promised him that Clea would be unable to know his thoughts. But if that were so, why had Kiran sensed her presence?

He couldn't risk waiting. He must leave at once.

Taking his cloak from its hook, he headed for the nearest outer door. The sense of Clea persisted. He looked right and left, behind him and in front, but didn't see her. How glad he would be to get away from her! *Once I leave, I'll never return.*

Never return, never return, he repeated to himself with each step. His boots trod softly in the corridor; shadows flickered across the polished granite floor ahead where guards were stationed at the door.

Kiran's eyes narrowed. Normally one or two guards protected this door, not five gathered in a knot, watching him approach. His steps slowed. Again he looked behind him, but no one was there. *Turn around,* his mind shouted, but it was too late.

All five guards closed in on him, grabbing his arms. "We're ordered to take you to the Master Priest," one of them said. It was Finian, whom Kiran considered a friend.

Kiran threw himself backward with such force that the surprised soldiers lost their grip. Lurching, he turned and bolted back the way he'd come. He raced toward a branching corridor. Turning the corner, he ran pell-mell into another group of guards, who surrounded him.

He didn't wait for them to seize him. He kicked the nearest man's knee and swung his fist at another's head. His boots cracked against bone and his fists met flesh. The groans and curses he heard only urged him to fight more furiously.

For long minutes he fought them off, but then several of them dived for his legs, yanking his feet out from under him. He fell heavily, rolled to the side only to meet the flat of a sword against his head; it half stunned him. His arms were grabbed, his wrists twisted. A booted toe kicked his ribs.

Still he struggled blindly.

After the evening meal, Bryn looked fondly around the curtained nook that had been her home for almost two years. How she wanted to say farewell to her friends, but that would be too risky. She murmured a quick prayer for Alyce, Jacinta, and Willow, wishing them happiness; her whispered voice caught in her throat.

Was she really about to leave the Temple and her dream of becoming a priestess of the Oracle? Had Kiran really asked her to go away with him?

Yes, and she was going.

But what did his desire to take her with him truly mean? It might simply be that he wouldn't leave a friend defenseless in the clutches of the Master Priest. It might be that he wanted a companion to travel with, though Bryn doubted that. Jack would be enough company for Kiran.

Does he care for me?

She opened her wardrobe. Inside hung her spare student robe and the gown she had worn for the

Solstice Festival; she brushed its lustrous cloth with her fingertips and then flung off her worn robe. She slipped on the gown, and put her spare robe over it. The robe bunched a little at the shoulders but she hoped it wouldn't be noticeable.

Starting down the corridor, she saw no one. Delighted, she continued on, her steps light. Perhaps the absence of guards foretold that she and Kiran would escape quietly.

As she reached the turn in the corridor that would take her to the guest wing, a shining plume of thistledown appeared in front of her.

Bryn's first feeling was joy—joy that beat in her ears like the drums of the Gilgamell Troupe. Oh, glorious happiness!

But then the thistledown moved, floating ahead of her, and she realized it was leading her away from the guest wing.

She hesitated. Every nerve quivered to join Kiran. He wanted her to go with him. He'd be waiting for her, wondering what was keeping her if she didn't arrive.

But hadn't she vowed to herself over and over that if she ever saw the thistledown again, she would follow it? *No matter where it led.* Hadn't she said that nothing was more important to her, or ever would be?

Now it was here, guiding her in a direction she didn't want to go. Bryn looked down the hall that would lead to the guest wing and Kiran. No guards to be seen. How easy it would be to slip out of the door to the gardens. If she waited, the chance to leave with Kiran might vanish forever.

Light streamed from the thistledown as it bobbed along the hallway far ahead. If she ran, she could catch up with it. "I'm sorry, Kiran," Bryn whispered, throat aching. "I can't ignore it again." She tore after the thistledown as it disappeared round a corner.

It sped along much faster than it had the night she'd first followed it through the Temple. Bryn had to run to keep up and lost her sense of direction as it flew through unfamiliar passageways. And as she dashed through the halls, a breeze touched the back of her neck.

Kiran didn't recognize the room he found himself in. There were no windows to give a sense of the time of day, and he didn't know how long he'd been unconscious. Candlelight from two chandeliers showed three chairs at one end of the room. The Master Priest sat in the middle chair; on either side of him were Ilona and Clea.

Clea's blue robe had been replaced with a black one traced with silver embroidery. Signs of the god Keldes wound about the sleeves, and her feather case hung free in front. The Master Priest and First Priestess also wore black, but their robes were threaded with gold.

Kiran's ankles were bound, as were his wrists behind his back. His ribs hurt with every breath; his face felt bruised and swollen. Pain throbbed in his head. Around him guards stood rigid.

"Awake, Kiran?" Renchald asked.

Kiran glared in silence.

"You have betrayed the gods," the Master Priest went on.

"You speak for the gods, Renchald?"

"You have plotted to withhold visions and to deprive the Temple of your skills in paired prophecy. Do you wish to atone?"

"If, by *atone*, you mean do as you say, I won't," Kiran answered.

Renchald drew himself up. "As you refuse to atone, the First Priestess and I have sanctioned a compliance curse upon you."

"Compliance curse?" Kiran looked at Ilona. "You would do this?" he asked her, and thought he saw a glimmer of emotion on her face.

"Do not trifle with the gods!" Renchald thundered so loudly that the wall sent back an echo. *The gods . . . the gods . . . the gods.*

Kiran thought of Bryn waiting for him. Or would she, too, be caught as she tried to leave? "You don't serve the gods," Kiran answered hoarsely.

"Silence him," said the Master Priest, nodding to the soldiers.

Renchald prepared to breach Kiran's inner barriers. It was what the rebellious acolyte feared most, he knew. Doing so would weaken Kiran and make him more vulnerable to being cursed. *He deserves no less for turning against the Temple.*

Kiran kneeled in obvious pain, the gag that bound his jaws cutting into bruised skin. Luckily, he'd depleted his reserves by fighting—but he might still be a formidable foe in a battle for the inner worlds where Renchald planned to meet him. The Master Priest found it hard to believe how much damage an unarmed, untrained student had been able to inflict on the skilled warriors of the Temple guard.

I must be quick, giving Kiran no time to respond.

Summoning his inner power, the Master Priest struck with all the might of his etheric weapons, smashing Kiran's barriers.

His dream body stood within Kiran's landscape, and for a few moments he was transfixed by its majesty—a place where tall mountains met sweeping plains; where animals roamed beside singing cataracts of water; where brightness permeated the air.

Then Kiran's agonized spirit stood before him crying out, *You have betrayed me.*

Renchald didn't answer. He set a wedge in the broken barrier to hold it open, concealed the wedge with a bank of fog. As he did so, he realized that the violence of his attack had destroyed more of the barrier than he'd intended, endangering Kiran's health. Well, it couldn't be helped now. He would mend the barrier later, after the curse was in place.

He sent his dream body back to the Temple room. He nodded to Clea.

"Cast the curse."

She opened the case that held her feather.

Twenty

Kiran felt the last of his strength draining away. Soon he would be unable even to kneel upright, would fall to the floor like a beaten child. He felt more naked than if he had been stripped. Eyes closed, he groped desperately within his landscape, seeking the damage he felt but could not find.

He heard a crash. His eyes flew open. Twisting his head, he was amazed to see Bryn in the doorway, her braids coming loose, her face damp with sweat. She gasped for air as if she'd been running hard.

The Master Priest rose to his feet while Clea and Ilona sat frozen in place. Renchald waved a hand. "Guards!"

Several soldiers lunged toward Bryn. She glared at them, and her robe began flapping like a flag in a storm. A sudden wind went shrieking through the room, buffeting the guards so ferociously that they put their hands in front of their faces and stepped back.

The wind has returned to Bryn. Through his pain, Kiran felt a pulse of triumphant joy. He watched a gust pull a guard's dagger from its sheath. The dagger shot through the air, its haft landing in Bryn's hand. She darted forward. Kiran felt the blade slip beneath his gag, releasing his jaw. She freed his hands next, while the wind continued beating against the guards, who took more unwilling steps backward until they stood pinned to the walls. Tapestries above their heads snapped free of their moorings to flutter madly about the room.

Bryn cut the bonds around Kiran's ankles. She pulled at him frantically, helped him to his feet. They stood together in a small space of calm as wind howled through the rest of the room. Gusts whipped around Clea, snatching the vulture feather from her hand, overturning her chair and those of the Master Priest and First Priestess, spilling the occupants.

Clea screeched a vulture's cry as she tried to reach her feather, but it began to spin, wheeling across the room to the hearth, where it plunged into the fire. The acrid smell as it burned was laced with the odor of carrion.

Ilona lay quietly, not fighting. The Master Priest thrashed on the floor, veins in his forehead standing out as he exerted himself to hold up the keltice ring. The wind wouldn't let him.

Kiran staggered with Bryn into the hallway. He forced himself to run, following the wind as it screamed through the corridors, where students and guards alike fell back, flattened against the walls.

The gale burst open the outer door, flinging aside two men who guarded it. Kiran stumbled as he went through. He could see the stable, its weather vane spinning like a top.

Bryn urged him forward. "Obsidian," she cried. "We need to get to Obsidian."

They ran until Kiran had to stop for breath. He clutched his chest. Looking behind, he saw guards pouring from the Temple. Some put arrows to their bows, but as the arrows left the bowstrings, they were caught by the wind and tossed into the sky. The soldiers looked like creatures of nightmare as they struggled against the gale, faces contorted, shoulders hunched, fists pummeling the air.

Obsidian, Kiran called. *Come to me, Obsidian.*

A tremendous crash sounded. The stable door burst open. Obsidian galloped toward them, a flash of black, swift as the wind that licked at his heels, his mighty flanks pumping, hooves pounding the earth.

The horse slowed when he reached them but didn't stop. Kiran flung himself onto Obsidian's back and Bryn scrambled up in front of him. They bent their heads to the stallion's neck. *Out through the front gates,* Kiran urged him.

Obsidian charged past the useless band of guards. The men wrestled with their weapons, trying to draw daggers or force swords from their scabbards while the gale battered them, whistling round their ears.

Jack. Kiran couldn't bear the thought of leaving his dog. Without Kiran, what would happen to him? Would the Master Priest order him killed to avenge the Temple's dignity? *Jack, my friend, come now, we are going away.*

Obsidian rushed between the Temple and the ancient trees that stood beside it, hooves drumming the wide way toward the iron gates. Guards stationed at the entrance ranged themselves in a line across the gates. As the stallion galloped toward them, they drew their bows.

A tempest raced ahead of Obsidian. It blew arrows awry and knocked guards to the ground. Men flailed powerlessly as the gates snapped open. Obsidian leaped over the guards, through the gates.

From the side, a streak of black and white fur skimmed the ground. *Jack.* The dog dashed into the road. Kiran smiled through the bruising pain that increased with each breath he took.

North. Run north without stopping.

Bryn would remember that ride always. When the Temple was miles behind them, she threw off her student robe; the robe would mark her to anyone they passed who happened to notice. Obsidian was also likely to draw attention just because he was so magnificent, but there was nothing to be done about that.

Kiran wrapped his arms around her, pressing her to his chest. She could feel the beating of his heart as they stormed down the road on Obsidian's back, and she'd never forget the warmth of his arms. She didn't know which was dearer to her—the wind at her back, or Kiran.

He whispered into her ear, saying it was all he could do to stay on the horse; that she would have to guide Obsidian. It was a long way to Tunise. The sun would sink, and they'd need to keep going through the dark. Tomorrow they'd be crossing the Lyden without water.

Two nights later, Selid kissed Lance before going out to her workroom. Some of her grief showed in her face and he noticed it.

"What's troubling you?" he asked tenderly. "You've been skittish ever since the concert on the green."

"Tomorrow," she promised him. "I'll tell you then. Now, I have work to complete." She turned from him quickly, unable to bear the trust and kindness in his face. What would he do when she was dead?

Resigned to the Oracle's power, she sat alone in her workroom, bathed in candlelight, putting the finishing touches to her final prophecy.

The prophecy was for the Queen of Sorana. Selid's quill glided over her smoothest parchment. *For this, Monzapel, you preserved my life.*

The candles guttered suddenly, all at once. Selid looked up. There, wavering in the air beside her, transparent as flame, an apparition stared. A girl. The face was familiar. Selid had first seen those golden-brown eyes in the desert, looking at her in horrified innocence.

Now, here she was watching, having a vision of her own.

"You lived?" she whispered to Selid.

Nodding, Selid heard the cardinal's call outside. Knowledge swept over her: the etheric cloak she had surrounded herself with had somehow parted, giving this young prophetess a glimpse of what she meant to do.

Prophecy of a prophecy.

If the girl was within the Temple of the Oracle, her vision would reach the ears of the Master Priest.

By receiving the Oracle's light again, Selid knew she was making it easier for the Lord of Death to find her. But if the queen never read her prophecy, Keldes would win more than Selid's life.

"Don't tell him," she cried to the watching apparition. "She'll never read my words."

The visitant took a step forward, and then vanished.

Hours later, Selid read over the finished prophecy. While she read, she listened with half an ear for hoof-beats that would turn off the north-south highway onto the narrow road where she and Lance lived.

The prophecy was everything it should be. *Renchald himself would swear he had written it.*

Then she heard the horse she'd been listening for, clopping wearily, coming closer. She bowed her head. Her heart hammered. *My vision was all too true, then.* Selid blinked back the tears that wanted to fall. She must not allow her sorrow over her own fate to ruin the queen's prophecy; no tears must smudge the words she'd worked so hard to write.

And though they arrive at midnight like harbingers of death, the friends who approach now are not the cause of my sadness.

Selid poured two glasses of water and went out to the gate. She waited for a knock. When it fell, she spoke. "Give your name." But she knew who it was.

"Kiran," said a low, hoarse voice from the other side of the boards.

She lifted the bar and opened the gate. How well she remembered the tall freckled acolyte. Others in the Temple hadn't known what to make of him, but Selid had thought him special. She had seen him calm a frenzied horse with nothing but a quiet word and had suspected he was hiding unusual intelligence behind his rough bearing.

He staggered through the gate. Livid bruises marked his face. Selid handed him one of her glasses of water. "Drink slowly," she urged.

A dog slunk in behind him, limping slightly. Selid bent to look in the dog's eyes. Mismatched. "Hello, Jack," she said. She pointed to a bowl of water close to the gate. Jack shot her a grateful look before he began lapping.

Kiran's hands shook badly as he took a drink. He gestured behind him. "Bryn," he said. "And we brought a horse."

Selid turned. The young woman who had appeared in her workroom only hours earlier leaned on the gatepost. Seeing her again, this time in the flesh, Selid couldn't keep the tears from springing to her eyes. "It's you," she whispered, holding out the other glass of water.

Bryn lifted the glass to her lips. And behind her nosed the most splendid black horse ever born.

Kiran and Bryn both refused food, insisting that Selid feed and water Obsidian first. Kiran collapsed onto a couch near the hearth. He fell asleep instantly. Bryn was having trouble speaking; she could talk only of the horse. It wasn't until Selid promised to care for the stallion that Bryn agreed to being shown to the couch in the workroom.

Lifting the candle high, Selid watched her visitor's exhausted eyes travel over the wooden mosaic and the writing desk. "I didn't tell," said Bryn. "No one but Kiran."

Selid heaved a long sigh. "I hoped it would be so," she answered softly. "Thank you." She faced Bryn. "And thank you for saving me from death in the desert."

Bryn crumpled onto the couch. Her murmured gratitude was lost in the blanket, covered in sleep.

Selid latched the workroom door behind her. Time to attend to the horse. As she fed and watered him and brushed his dusty hide, the red cardinal alighted on her shoulder. Moonlight shone like a silver blessing over the stall. How peaceful the world seemed: in that moment Selid found it difficult to comprehend that cruelty or treachery or any of the horrors the Oracle had made plain could be real.

And yet, these visitors bore out the beginning of the prophecies she had been given. The rest would follow. She knew it, but wished such truth had never come to her.

Please, Monzapel, I beg you, keep Lance safe.

When she went inside, Selid sat on the edge of the bed, rocking herself. Lance stirred. He sat up. He moved next to her, and put a warm arm around her shoulders.

"Tomorrow has come?" he asked.

"So it has." Selid poured out her story: what she had seen, and what she feared. When she finished, she said, "That is why, my darling, you must leave me now, why you must forget me."

Lance shook his head. "You believe I would leave you? Forget you because you're afraid?" His brown eyes, which always reminded her of the wood he worked with, looked into hers unflinchingly.

"It's more than fear, Lance. I *know* Keldes will come for me."

"He came for you before, and yet you lived."

"Monzapel spared me."

"She'll spare you again." The gentle carpenter looked fierce. "Don't ask me to leave you. I won't defend my life with cowardice. Our lives are joined. If Keldes hunts you, so be it. I stand ready to flee again, today, if need be."

"We can't leave until the Gilgamell Troupe answers my message."

"Then we'll wait for them. Afterward, *together*, we'll be on our way."

The next day, in the Temple, Renchald and Clea entered into paired prophecy together, breaking an

255

ironclad tradition that prohibited Master Priests from pairing with students.

To find the insolent traitors who had stolen the most valuable horse in the Temple, Renchald would try anything. If Kiran and Bryn were allowed to roam free in Sorana, they could cause untold damage to the Temple. He had to prevent it. Without knowing where they had gone, how was he to stop them?

Pairing with Clea was the only choice. Their quest for visions was enormously successful. His exalted skills combined with her prophetic talents not only revealed the whereabouts of the wayward students, but also showed Selid's plans.

At last, thought the Master Priest, *I've found a prophetess worthy of me. Clea shall become a priestess without further delay.*

When he thought of Selid and the message she had penned to the queen, he twisted the keltice ring on his finger. *The past two years of Selid's life have not kept step with the rightful march of eternity.* Now, it was high time Renchald acted for Keldes, to whom the renegade prophetess belonged.

As for Bryn, she would discover that a curse sanctioned by a Master Priest was truly unbreakable.

Late that night, Ilona rapped on the door of the Master Priest's sanctum. He answered at once. "Come in, and thank you for responding quickly. I apologize for the hour." He shut the door after her.

They bowed. He confessed to her that he had paired with Clea.

Almost dumbfounded, Ilona listened. "But the laws of the Temple forbid you to lend your power to a student," she said. "Particularly a vulture-chosen student."

His face remained calm. "Let me remind you, Ilona: a wind-chosen prophetess and a black swan prophet have defied my authority and betrayed the Temple. They have stolen a horse I've promised to Lord Errington—and injured more than a score of guards."

"And how," she asked, "will pairing with a student remedy those events?"

"Clea and I have found where they have gone," he answered. "Moreover, we received a clear vision of Selid, a vision of utmost importance."

"Selid?"

"Shall I tell you what threatens the Temple? Selid has penned a false prophecy for the Queen of Sorana. She plans to pass off her forgery as written by the Master Priest."

Ilona stared uncomprehendingly. "False prophecy? But how—?"

"Her chosen messengers to deliver this forgery to the queen are none other than the Gilgamell Troupe."

Her tongue refused to work.

He nodded. "The situation is dire. I regret that in my quest to preserve the Temple, I broke one of our laws. When these menaces are vanquished, I will perform every penance."

She looked at him doubtfully.

"I've scarcely slept for three days," Renchald told her. "Among other important tasks, I held a private ceremony so that Clea could be visited by her choosing bird. She has another feather." His robes shone crimson in the candlelight. "Tomorrow morning at first light, you and I and Clea leave for Tunise."

Ilona called back her whirling thoughts. "Tunise?"

"We have determined that Kiran, Bryn, *and Selid* are in Tunise. The Gilgamell Troupe will soon be on their way to the queen, bearing the false prophecy. You, Ilona, will continue on from Tunise to Zornowel with Clea to deliver a *true* prophecy that will take the place of Selid's forgery."

"You're sending me to the queen?" Her voice sounded thin. "But—why not you?"

"I expect Lord Errington here. I cannot be absent from the Temple when he arrives."

He strode to the door. Opening it, he motioned her out. Moving in a daze, she went past him, not looking at his face.

Twenty-one

Bryn stood in the carpenter's spare stall, rubbing Obsidian with a teasel brush. The stallion stomped restlessly. "I know you don't like being confined," she said soothingly. "But if I showed you in daylight, the Master Priest would be sure to hear of it. In a few hours, when it's dark, I'll take you for a run."

They'd been staying with Selid and Lance for two days. Kiran was still too weak and sore to do much beyond lie on the couch. Gruesome bruises colored his face beneath the freckles. It hurt him badly to breathe. He refused to hear of being seen by a healer. He shook his head stubbornly at Selid when she mentioned it. "Too much risk to you," he said. "I'll mend."

He wouldn't tell them what had happened to cause his injuries. "I fought too many guards at once" was all he would say. The expression in his eyes haunted Bryn—he seemed to be wounded in a way she couldn't see, a hurt that went deeper than bruises. Whatever it was, he kept it to himself.

A breeze kissed Bryn's nose, lifted her hair,

fluttered the sleeves of her gown, brushed through Obsidian's mane. The wind was always with her now, sometimes light as a downy seed, sometimes a gusty roar.

Obsidian gave a loud whinny just as Jack scampered past the stall, barking importantly.

Bryn followed Jack as he ran to the wooden gate and began jumping against it, whining excitedly. She reached the gate just as Selid drew the bar.

Dawn burst through. She threw her arms around Bryn. "Stars and luminaries, it's good to see you." Dawn turned to Selid. "We would have been here sooner, but had to ready ourselves for the trip to Zornowel, not to mention finagling so as to leave the inn without drawing notice."

Behind her, four men in nondescript cloaks held the halters of horses. Bryn saw Avrohom's elfin grin peeking around Dawn's shoulder. He winked. "Incognito or we'd never escape those who adore our music."

Selid motioned the men and horses through the gate into the carpenter's yard. Bryn could hear Obsidian protesting his separation from the five mares that had come with the Troupe. She hoped he wouldn't smash through the stall as he had done at the Temple stables.

Dawn barraged Bryn with questions. "What happened after I left? Brock got my message? Are you all right?"

Bryn held tightly to Dawn but answered none of her questions. Selid took everyone inside, where Kiran tottered up from the couch. He waved off Dawn's exclamations of pity when she saw his face. He shook hands with the troubadours, then sank back onto the pillows.

Avrohom's fiery hair and vivid blue eyes lit the room as he introduced the other members of the troupe. The lyre player, Negasi, smiled broadly beneath his enormous mustache, his bald head shining. Jeffrey, whose fingers could work such magic upon his lute, resembled a ripe apple with his red cheeks and round stomach. The drummer, Zeb, seemed to take up room for two men as he threw off his cloak, revealing muscled brown arms.

When all the troubadours had said hello, Avrohom turned to Selid. "We're here because your message spoke of utmost urgency."

"Thank you for coming," Selid answered. "I'll make tea before we discuss why." She was already moving toward the kettle on the hob. Bryn helped set out mugs.

When everyone was served, Selid held up a scroll tied with red ribbon. "A message for Queen Alessandra," she said. "It must get to her safely. None better to deliver it than the Gilgamell Troupe."

Frowning, Avrohom shook back his hair. "We are troubadours. Why not send your scroll by messenger?"

"The queen herself, not her servants, must read this. It is a prophecy."

"Prophecy?" Dawn looked askance at Selid. "But—"

"Unknown to Her Majesty, Princess Zorienne is being poisoned by Mednonifer, queen's physician,"

Selid announced. She spoke quietly, but something in her voice reminded Bryn of the way she'd shrieked at the Master Priest as she kneeled in the desert sand. *Ellerth will bury you, Renchald. I have seen it.*

"How is that possible?" cried Dawn.

"I received the vision only recently," Selid told them. "I fear the Oracle has wished me to see it for some time. I only hope I'm not too late. Peril surrounds Zorienne. Unless the poison is stopped, she cannot live much longer."

They stared.

A long-ago memory took hold of Bryn, of the first time she had heard the Oracle's voice: *Beware his sleeping death.* And she had been pointing at Princess Zorienne!

Dawn stepped forward. "But why must *you* give this prophecy? If the princess is being poisoned, why wouldn't the Master Priest send a warning?"

Selid waved the scroll. "So he will."

Bewildered, they waited for her to explain.

"I know how Renchald pens a prophecy. I watched him often enough." Selid held out the scroll. "This is written and worded as though it comes from him."

Kiran rose up from where he lay. "No," he said. "If he ever learned of it, he would summon Keldes from the underworld to find you and see you dead."

Selid shook her head at him. "This prophecy is more important than fear of the Master Priest. Without it, Raynor Errington will rule Sorana."

Bryn's thoughts spun sickeningly. She thought of Lord Errington standing beside the Master Priest at the Solstice Festival. Her stomach twisted. "It's Lord Errington behind the poisoning, isn't it?" *Beware his sleeping death.*

Selid nodded.

"And no warning has been sent by the Temple," Bryn said.

Selid nodded again, more emphatically.

Kiran swayed on his feet. "Why is Renchald to have the credit for such a vital prophecy?"

Selid gestured at the homey furnishings around the room. "Because if Alessandra knew it came from a simple scribe, she might never read it. It must appear to come straight from the Oracle."

Dawn waved her hands nervously. "Isn't it a crime to pretend it comes from the Oracle when it comes from you?"

Selid's lips tightened. "For centuries, those who received the light of the Oracle were revered whether they chose to be part of the Temple or not. Renchald has appointed himself guardian of the Oracle's word—" Her voice cracked. "He isn't. The Oracle's light followed me, even after the Master Priest took my feather and consecrated me to the Lord of Death." She clasped the scroll, lifting her chin. "When I was dying of thirst, Bryn gave me her water. Now I give Sorana my ink."

As she extended the scroll toward Avrohom, a breeze flapped against it and Bryn heard a bell-like voice echo in her head: *I give Sorana my blood.*

No, Bryn tried to say. Her lips felt numb, her throat closed. Not a sound came out.

"Please, Sir Troubadour," Selid said, "take this to the queen. And when you have done so, write a song about it."

Avrohom's eyes, usually so merry, were grave as he accepted the scroll. He bowed. "Her Majesty shall read your words," he said.

Frightened, Bryn looked at Selid. Kiran had warned her that the Master Priest was hunting her. She'd only nodded and said she knew. But what if Renchald found her? *Blood, my blood, is given.*

"There's more," Selid said. "You must be there when this message is delivered, Bryn. It's you who can bring the winds of change to Sorana."

Dawn spoke into the quiet, looking very serious. "Winjessen is about to align with both Ellerth and Monzapel," she said, "and Vernelda will oppose Keldes. Momentous events are poised to happen."

Kiran dropped back to his couch and watched Selid and Bryn, his uneasiness growing. They knew something they weren't saying; he was sure of it.

His head felt hazy and sick, as it had ever since Renchald had stormed his barriers, leaving him weaker than a newborn colt abandoned by its mother; wobbly on his legs, searching for what he could not find. He didn't seem to be healing. His ribs hurt as much now as they had right after the guards kicked him. Though he'd visited his inner landscape repeatedly, he could only stumble about in a fog, unable to find what was robbing him of strength.

The voices around him seemed distant, as if

spoken by people on the other side of a wall. With an effort, he concentrated. "We'll leave early. You can ride pillion with Jeffrey, Bryn," Avrohom was saying.

Kiran roused himself. How much of the conversation had he missed? "Obsidian can carry both Bryn and me," he cut in. "Selid and Lance must come with us too. They're in danger from the Master Priest."

Silence greeted his words. Zeb began drumming his fingers on the mantelpiece; Negasi and Jeffrey looked away. "Kiran," Avrohom said, "I'm no healer, but I can see you're not fit to stand up, let alone ride. And if that stallion is everything he's said to be, the Temple guards will be searching for him as hard as they search for you."

Kiran looked at Bryn. The golden flecks in her eyes were like sparks of sunlight. It seemed to him she shined brighter, now that the wind had returned to her. Who, upon seeing her, could doubt she was the most extraordinary woman in the world?

He forced himself to his feet. "We *must* go with you." He took three steps before he tumbled.

As promised, Bryn took Obsidian for a run after everyone else was asleep. Riding the stallion quieted her nerves only a little. After she'd returned him to his stall, she crept in to where Kiran slept by Selid's hearth. Jack was curled at the foot of his couch. He opened one eye at Bryn and then sank back into slumber as she kneeled beside Kiran's head.

"Kiran," she whispered to his sleeping face. "Kiran, I need to thank you."

He stirred. The bruised skin under his freckles looked sickly in the moonlight. "Because of you," she said softly, "I was able to lift the curse. I found what didn't belong in my landscape. You were right about that, as you've been right about so many things." She bowed her head over her hands. "I'm sorry I ever doubted your friendship."

She was startled when a rough finger brushed her cheek. She raised her head and saw Kiran's shadowed eyes squinting at her. "It's all right," he whispered hoarsely. He propped himself on an elbow, but then immediately slid down to rest on his pillow again, flinching in pain.

"What did they do to you?" she asked miserably, fear rising in her heart. He looked worse than he had the day before. How could she leave him? What if he died while she was away? "Did Clea curse you?"

"No. Master Priest breached my barriers. My landscape is covered in fog. When I enter it, I can't see anything else, nor can I think clearly. My dream body keeps weakening."

Bryn took his hand. "You can't get any weaker."

"I've done all I know to do."

She leaned in closer. "Maybe I could help. If you can trust me."

He didn't pull away, but a small frown appeared between his brows. "Trust you?"

"We could pair with each other to heal you."

"No. Too dangerous for you."

"Please, Kiran. It would mean everything to me."

"Can't risk you."

"Together we would have more strength, wouldn't we?" She squeezed his hand, willing him to listen. "Please."

His eyes met hers searchingly. "But you've never paired before, have you?"

"No. But the Master Priest said I was ready." She spoke firmly, though she felt unsure. "Please, Kiran. What harm could come to me?"

He moved his hand in hers to lace their fingers together.

"Agreed?" she pressed.

"You must promise to get away if you begin to feel weak."

"Of course," she lied.

He stopped resisting. He closed his eyes.

"Will you do it, then?"

"We can try," he murmured.

"Now," she urged. "Tomorrow will be too late."

He gave a slight nod. "Ready, then."

Bryn prepared herself. Kiran's link, when it reached her, was faint, but it was enough to take hold of. She felt an uneasy thrill as she fused with it.

Their dream bodies stood together on the ground of open pairing, a timeless place in the abanya, lit by clear light. From here, they might go to either of their landscapes, or to a different time; they might travel anywhere in the world.

Kiran's dream body looked even more ill than his physical one, his aura ragged. He nodded to her wearily and led the way into his landscape.

Heavy fog enveloped them instantly. Bryn couldn't

see him anymore. She strode determinedly into the mist, hand outstretched, hoping to find the border of his barriers. When she met a wall she groped her way along it, trailing a hand to feel for any fissure.

Her head spun. Her legs as she walked grew heavier and heavier, as if shot through with lead. Death seemed to seep from the ground and crawl through the air. Her legs wanted to give out, but she pushed on through the dreary fog.

There. She could feel a jagged break in the wall.

Here, she called, hoping Kiran could find her.

The break was sealed with something; Bryn felt along the edges of what seemed to be a wedge of stone. Touching it, she felt a deadly sense of futility. She stood with her hands on the wedge, summoning her will to fight.

Beneath her hands, a wind sprang up, a sudden forceful burst of bright air shaped like a quarry hammer. Warm and strong, it pounded the wedge, hammering against the darkness.

The wedge neither chipped nor cracked. It contained a will of its own, formed into density that refused to give in. As Bryn beat against it, her sense of futility deepened. A frightful tiredness weakened her.

No, she said, renewing her grip on the bright hammer. *I won't be turned aside. I will stay here and swing this hammer forever if need be.*

She swung against the impervious wedge. She didn't know how long she stood there in the dark fog, fighting the block of stone Renchald had set in Kiran's landscape. She only knew that she would keep going until she couldn't lift the hammer anymore. Weariness filled every part of her dream body, but she wouldn't quit.

At last she struck a blow that suddenly disintegrated the wedge all at once. The rock exploded into a cloud of dark dust that quickly vanished.

Utterly exhausted, Bryn rested her hands on either side of the gaping breach and called for Kiran. *Are you there? The wedge is gone. Can you rebuild the barrier?*

Thinning shreds of mist began drifting away, revealing more of the towering barrier wall. Then Kiran was beside her, the hands of his dream body replacing hers on the breach, his arms spanning the gap. *Yes, I can mend it*, he told her. *Thank you, my love.*

Bryn woke with a start. She was sitting with her legs tucked under her, her head cradled in her arms, which were leaning against Kiran's couch. A thin beam of grayish light streamed through the window. It must be near dawn.

The last thing she recalled was being within Kiran's landscape. He had told her he could mend his barriers. And called her *my love.*

Or had he? Bryn unfolded her legs, wincing. Even her bones felt tired.

Kiran's sleeping face looked very peaceful, and his color was better. She mustn't wake him from such a healing sleep.

Twenty-two

Selid couldn't sleep. For her, the bedroom was filled with bright silver light all the night through, light that enveloped and eased her mind.

At daybreak, she and Lance saw Bryn and Dawn and the troupe on their way. Bryn made them promise to follow as soon as they were able. Selid tried to reassure the young prophetess, but Bryn was deeply anxious.

The carpenter and his wife waved to the travelers, and then went inside to check on Kiran. He was sound asleep, Jack sitting watchfully at his feet.

"Don't worry," Lance whispered to Jack. "We won't wake him."

They tiptoed into their bedroom. "He's mending," Lance said. "His color is better. I'll begin the packing, get the horses ready. We can ride out as soon as Kiran wakes." He stroked Selid's hair. "We've another long journey ahead."

A very long journey, from which there is no return. Selid heard the Oracle's words, but somehow her fear had gone. She understood that it didn't matter where or when they went. Keldes would find her.

But Monzapel, too, would be with her. With her, and with Lance, forever.

She smiled at him. "I want to stay beside you today."

Kiran woke feeling refreshed. He sat up cautiously. When he drew breath, his ribs were only slightly sore.

Sensing the change in him, Jack jumped up and began licking his face.

The sun was low. He must have slept through the day. A fragrant smell drifted from the kitchen, where he could hear Selid and Lance moving about.

Kiran slipped outside, happy to be able to walk without help. He entered the washhouse, where he gratefully bathed. He was eager to see Obsidian but decided to eat first; he was famished.

He went inside. Selid set soup and bread on the table, inviting him to eat. His stomach rumbled. "Bryn kissed your forehead before she left," Selid said, sitting across from him. She looked different somehow. The day before, when she'd spoken so passionately about prophecy, she'd been lit like a candle, but a candle too small for the great flame burning within her. Now, she glowed as though the Moon Goddess had a hand on her head, tranquil and serene.

Kiran spooned delicious soup into his mouth. "Did they leave early?" he asked.

"At dawn."

Lance put a hand on Selid's shoulder. "We're ready to travel," he said. "We'll leave as soon as you've eaten."

Kiran took another bite. "Traveling at night will

help hide us." He heard a sound at the window, an urgent thumping. He slid back his chair. Peering through the curtain and fading rays of sunset, he saw a bird dashing itself against the pane. "The cardinal!" A sudden sense of peril overwhelmed him. He turned to Selid and Lance. "You waited. For me," he cried.

They didn't answer. Urgency made Kiran short of breath. Regret choked him as he thought of the time he had taken bathing. "We should go. Now." He turned to the door.

Jack was ahead of him, growling a warning. Kiran opened the door. The dog streaked out.

They all heard enraged neighing from Obsidian.

The shadowy yard was crawling with armored men. *Run, Jack. Don't let them capture you.*

"The animal is unimportant, let him go," said a familiar voice. The Master Priest stepped out of a squadron of Temple guards, the last rays of the setting sun smearing his face with blood-colored light.

Kiran didn't try to fight or run this time. There were too many of them, and besides, if he didn't resist, perhaps they'd let Selid alone. "It's all right," he said. "I'll go with you."

"That you will," said Renchald, coming up to the door and pushing him backward into the room.

Obsidian, Kiran called silently. *Run, Obsidian. Run away.* He heard the stallion's frantic snorting.

Renchald looked at him sharply. "I warn you, Kiran, the horse is well tethered. If you urge him to run, he will be injured. If he injures himself or comes near you, the guards are ordered to kill him."

Kiran called again. *Let them lead you.* The frenzied sounds of the horse trying to get his liberty faded. Renchald gave Kiran a grim nod and brushed past, flanked by Bolivar, guards swarming after them.

Selid and Lance stood before their hearth. They faced the Master Priest. "So," Renchald said. "Keldes claims you at last, Selid."

Lance put an arm around her protectively. "Please, sir. We do no harm."

"Ah," Renchald answered. "That is where you are mistaken."

Selid's gentle eyes looked through the Master Priest. "Ellerth will bury you, Renchald. I have seen it."

The Master Priest lifted the hand that held his ring. Selid stared back at him serenely.

"My regrets have flown, Renchald," she said. "They belong to this world no more." She turned to Lance. "Goodbye, my love. Walk in Solz's light."

Both Lance and Kiran flung themselves at the Master Priest, but guards grabbed them. Though they fought with all their might, they couldn't break free.

Renchald nodded to Bolivar, who stood near Selid. In one motion, the soldier drew his sharpened dagger and took hold of the back of her head. For an instant the blade seemed to catch time itself and hold it still, a silver edge of eternity waiting for all to bear witness. Then Bolivar struck with swift and hideous grace, cutting Selid's throat. He let her down, gently enough, on the hearthstones.

"No," Lance whispered as her blood poured. He struggled against the soldiers holding him.

Selid smiled at him, and him alone, as the life left her eyes.

The carpenter twisted his head toward the Master Priest. "You have killed the bravest, dearest soul of all."

Renchald nodded again to Bolivar. Lance saw the dagger coming for his own throat, but he didn't flinch under the blade. Reaching for Selid, a strange gladness filled his face. He made no sound as death came for him.

Kiran went rigid. He saw through a watery mist. The soldiers guarding him pushed him to his back on the floor and pinned him there.

A face leaned over him, cornflower-blue eyes and a spiteful smile. A long black feather fringed with gray waved in front of him. The scent of carrion filled his nose. Clea's lips formed words he couldn't hear through buzzing ears. He tried to escape, but his strength failed him. His lungs labored but seemed to bring no air.

At last she slid the feather into its case. Kiran could breathe again, and sound returned to him. He heard her say, "You will obey the Master Priest of the Oracle."

Blackness rolled over him, bringing welcome oblivion.

Standing in the doorway of the carpenter's house, Ilona grasped the doorjamb for support. The effort of concealing her shock and revulsion made her feel intensely faint. She trembled, exerting herself to keep upright. She had not been prepared to see Selid and

274

her husband murdered, Renchald's dark threats about the Lord of Death notwithstanding.

Gods of earth and sky, what have I become part of?

Every curse that Ilona had witnessed in the past had been conducted with utmost solemnity, with due regret that such a course had become necessary.

Not this time. Clea had been all too gratified to use her power to curse Kiran. She had positively gloated.

What if he was right to refuse to pair with a mind such as hers? Ilona felt a strong pang of guilt at having agreed to sanction a compliance curse against the swan-chosen acolyte. She looked at Lord Errington's daughter, whom she was now charged to take to the queen.

Ellerth forgive me.

When Kiran regained consciousness, he heard the sound of wheels moving and felt the motion of a carriage. He listened closely but couldn't tell who might be riding with him. He kept his eyes shut, feigning sleep, guessing he was guarded. If he didn't show he was awake, maybe he could take time, precious time, to think.

In his mind's eye Selid and Lance rose up before him. He saw them die again.

They could have been safe if they had gone without me. His despair mounted when he remembered Clea's curse: *You will obey the Master Priest. . . .*

What would he do when Renchald ordered him to tell what he knew? Would he become a traitor to his friends and to all he believed? *I know too much: how*

Brock and Dawn write in code; about the Gilgamell Troupe and Selid's message.

He vowed to fight the curse, but even the thought of resisting left him intensely nauseated. Worse, his mind felt fragmented, his thoughts like tired birds fluttering aimlessly.

Forcing himself to concentrate, Kiran imagined that Bryn was beside him. The thought of her comforted him. She, too, had known this sickness and hopelessness.

And overcome it. She had proved that a curse could be lifted.

He racked his brain to remember what she'd said. *I found what didn't belong in my landscape.* His idea that the curse would attempt to blend itself into the inner landscape must have been correct.

If only he had asked her to say more. Now she was gone, on her way to the queen. He would simply have to do what he could by himself.

Weariness urged him to go back to sleep, to wait until he was better rested before trying to undo the curse. But then he imagined the Master Priest commanding him to betray his friends and felt a frightening impulse within himself to obey.

No, he must keep awake.

Kiran squirmed on the carriage seat to ease his body, moving carefully, pretending continued sleep. To give himself heart, he summoned the memory of pairing with Bryn.

It took longer than usual to get to his inner landscape, but his dream body finally arrived there.

The sky shone golden. In the distance, scarlet mountains rose. Streams glittered as they poured down the mountainsides, weaving into bright waterfalls that leaped to join a silver river. The river sped across lush plains to a well-made stone dam. Below the dam, the water slowed, creating pools.

Kiran's gaze swept the landscape, looking for what didn't truly belong. Something was out of place—something that made him terribly uneasy—but what? He scanned the territory again. *Mountains. Waterfalls. River. Plains. Dam. Pools.*

Kiran approached one of the pools. He squatted beside it. A film of slime was coating the water. The slime thickened noticeably even as he watched. He looked at adjacent pools, and saw scum gathering over them also.

Of course. The curse had taken the form of a dam. Kiran himself would never have stopped the free flow of water within his landscape.

He rushed along the banks to the dam. Massive blocks walled off the river's current. What could he possibly do to remove such a structure? Who could help him?

The answer floated on the air. *Swan.*

Kiran remembered that Clea's curse had taken the wind from Bryn, sealed her in stillness that shut out her gift. Maybe he would be unable to touch the spirit of the swan. Then again, Clea had sought to *deprive* Bryn of prophecy, whereas Kiran's curse was for the purpose of making him obedient to the Master Priest's desire for *more* prophecies. He would be of no value to the Temple unless he continued to be a black swan prophet.

He must call the swan. Nothing else could help him now.

Kiran called. He stood beside the dam within his landscape, waiting, calling with all his heart. He kept his eyes fixed on the blank sky, pleading, *If I have done any good thing in my life, please help me now.*

After a timeless interval that seemed to last for hours, a great bird came into view, soaring out of the plains. Black wings glistened against the golden sky as it flew closer, its beak ruby red. Kiran watched as it came nearer and nearer.

It perched on a branch directly across from him. It shook its feathers and looked at him with eyes deeper than all the waters of the world.

Thank you for heeding my call.

Light rolled off the swan's wings toward him, light so thick he could gather it in his hands like silken rope.

And Kiran knew what to do. He arranged the coils of light into a web, a net big enough to throw over the dam.

He cast it. Alive with intelligence, the net slid under the blocks of Clea's curse, shining ever more brightly as it wrapped round the whole structure.

When the entire dam lay within the net, Kiran and the swan drew the edges of the net together, the swan using its beak, and Kiran his hands.

Now.

They tugged with their combined strength. The dam broke into pieces held by the net. The pent-up water burst free, flowing into the riverbed, overrunning the pools, catching them up in its pure current.

Energy and strength streamed through Kiran. He gripped the net. *What now?* he asked the swan.

The bird led the way out of Kiran's landscape. Dragging the net, Kiran followed the swan past his inner barriers. He understood that he must not leave the curse lying in the abanya. He decided to try bringing it with him into the outer world.

Thank you, he told the swan. *Thank you.*

Black feathers glinted as the bird soared out of sight.

Kiran sent his dream body back to the carriage that traveled toward the Temple of the Oracle. And as he passed out of the abanya, the net he carried and the stones within it vanished.

Twenty-three

Renchald regretted the need to push for a quick return to the Temple to meet Lord Errington. It would have been more suitable to travel at a measured pace. However, he took solace in knowing that he and Bolivar had done what they set out to do. And Clea had subdued Kiran before heading on to Zornowel with the First Priestess.

The Master Priest remained wakeful during the night journey through the Lyden, but he was able to sleep in his carriage for much of the next day. He woke in late afternoon. The terrain outside told him the Temple would appear within an hour. He took advantage of the solitude to reflect on the events of the past two years.

The actions of only a few insubordinate students had made his job excessively difficult. Now, calm would be restored—with Selid in the hereafter, Kiran under a compliance curse, and Bryn soon to be barred from the wind forever.

Renchald sighed. Sad that the cardinal-chosen handmaid had followed her own misguided views instead of serving the Temple. *But the gods ordained it so.* As for her husband, it was a shame that he'd become mixed up with her. Renchald did not approve of extraneous killing. However, one man's life was unimportant compared to preserving the reputation of the Oracle. Had the carpenter been left alive, he could easily have caused unrest. The Temple could not afford to be misperceived.

At the Temple, the Master Priest disembarked from his carriage. He noticed, with appreciation, the colors of sunset. Solz's daily gift of beauty was a reminder of the grandeur of all the gods.

He dismissed Bolivar for some much-needed rest. The captain of the Temple guard had stayed awake and vigilant during the long ride.

Alamar came scurrying to the carriage house to welcome the Master Priest. "Lord Errington arrived in your absence, sir,"

"Ah." Renchald caught sight of Obsidian being led toward the pasture by six tired soldiers, each of whom held a tether.

"He was perturbed to find his daughter absent, Your Honor," Alamar said.

"Send him to me at once." The Master Priest would rather have taken refreshment but thought it best to mollify Lord Errington first.

Renchald saw Kiran crawl from the carriage that had held him. The tall acolyte had shed his arrogant stance and was being courteous with his guard, a young warrior named Finian. Renchald caught

Finian's eye and beckoned. As Kiran docilely allowed the guard to take his elbow, the Master Priest chided himself for enjoying the sight of Kiran so subdued. His conscience smote him a little when he remembered how badly Kiran's barriers had been damaged. It was a wonder the young man could walk upright. Now that a compliance curse was in place, Renchald promised himself he would mend the barriers soon. Yes, that very evening, as soon as he had pacified Lord Errington.

"Thank you, Finian," Renchald said to the guard. "Go, and take your rest."

Finian saluted and stalked away just as Brock Smith, the owl-chosen acolyte, appeared from around the corner of the carriage house. Renchald frowned, but the young man bowed very properly: humble acolyte to Master Priest.

Brock's presence reminded him of the questions he meant to ask Kiran about his friends. Had Brock known he contemplated leaving the Temple? And how had Bryn and Kiran known of Selid's whereabouts?

"My business with Lord Errington will soon be concluded, Kiran," Renchald said. "Await me on the bench near the west entrance. I have questions for you." Kiran bowed politely, and began to move away with Brock. "And Kiran"—the acolytes turned back—"you are forbidden to hold silent speech with animals. Nor will you speak of anything that occurred while you were away, except to me."

Again, Kiran bowed respectfully. He walked off,

Brock murmuring to him something about the mathematics of time.

Alamar approached with Lord Errington. The lord bowed deeply; Renchald returned the bow, welcoming him.

"You've sent my daughter on a journey, Your Honor?" Errington asked. Alamar hurriedly excused himself.

"Clea is well protected, traveling with a squadron of Temple guards to visit the queen," Renchald answered, "on a mission of importance. But more of this later." He looked meaningfully at Errington. "Would you care to have another look at the magnificent horse you'll be acquiring?"

Errington bowed. Renchald led the way. He pointed out Obsidian, who paced at the far end of the field, his outline lit by orange rays of sunset. The Master Priest gathered his thoughts. He had carefully considered what ought to be said to Lord Errington. The pasture would afford them privacy to speak.

"I'll allow no one to ride him but me," Errington said, looking at the horse.

"You've sold Obsidian?" Renchald was startled to see Kiran and Brock appear beside him as if out of nowhere.

"This is no concern of yours, Kiran."

"Obsidian cannot go to this"—Kiran gestured at Errington—"this bloated Lord of Greed." Fists clenched, he took a step forward.

Errington's face purpled. "How *dare* you?" He faced Kiran, doubling his own fists.

Renchald stepped between them. "Stand down, Kiran, I command you."

Kiran gave a bitter laugh. "Stand down yourself, Renchald. You have ruled this Temple too long." And Kiran shoved him in the chest, making him stumble backward.

The Master Priest gaped in disbelief. How could Kiran be defiant with him? "Brock," he said, "fetch Bolivar."

Brock folded his arms and made no move to obey. Errington rushed at the smaller young man. Brock sidestepped. Kiran tripped Errington by hooking his shin with a foot. Errington landed sprawling, Kiran's boot on the back of his neck.

"Don't move," Kiran said. Errington went limp.

Renchald forced himself to think. *Kiran has overcome the curse somehow.* He whirled around, waving to a guard posted at the west entrance. Was the man addled? Did he suppose Kiran was having a friendly wrestling match—or was he simply blinded by the setting sun? Renchald pointed to Errington's prone figure. "Find Bolivar!" he roared. Shading his eyes with his hand, the guard nodded. More soldiers could not be far, but Kiran had timed his rebellion well. Was it by chance?

Fear clawed at Renchald as he realized that hardly twice in ten years had he been in a more unprotected position. Nearly all members of the Temple would be at the evening meal. "Be reasonable, Kiran," he said, lifting the keltice ring. "You can't fight the Temple guard alone."

But Kiran wasn't looking at him or the ring. "I left reason behind on Selid's hearth," he answered. "And I don't intend to fight alone." He closed his eyes.

Renchald threw a tendril of awareness toward Kiran. His fear increased when he found that the unpredictable rebel's barriers were intact. Who had mended them—and how?

There wasn't an instant to spare. Renchald drew on his inner power to smash the barriers again.

They held fast.

Renchald heard a trumpeting cry. A huge bird beat through the sky, black feathers gleaming, red beak shining.

But I never taught Kiran how to summon his choosing bird.

Renchald called to his gyrfalcon. A bird of prey could defeat any swan, no matter what size it might be.

The gyrfalcon appeared so swiftly it was only a dappled blur against the red sky as it dived for the black swan, razor-sharp talons outstretched, screech tearing the air. The swan swooped sideways; the plummeting falcon grazed its wing. Black quills fluttered to the ground, but the swan soared free and doubled back, speeding toward Renchald.

The gyrfalcon lifted high in the sky. *Attack!* Renchald thought, face raised to his choosing bird.

The two birds collided in midair. Both Renchald and Kiran fell to the ground. Renchald rolled to a crouch and then stood up. Kiran lay still. Brock kneeled beside him, while Lord Errington got ponderously to his feet, swearing angrily.

Bolivar and a dozen guards were coming at a run. Renchald motioned to them to hurry. Just beyond, his gyrfalcon hunched on the ground, blinking. The black swan sat unmoving.

"You see, Kiran, how fruitless it is to struggle? The gods watch over the Temple."

Kiran's eyes flew open, and Renchald, flashing the keltice ring, was ready. Kiran's gaze caught the ring.

Kiran fell under the force of the gyrfalcon's gift.

His mother, long dead, appeared before him, vibrantly alive. She mounted her horse. The saddle was poorly fastened; it would slip, and her foot would catch in the stirrup. She would be dragged to her death.

'No!" Kiran cried. "Don't ride today!"

She didn't hear him, didn't seem to see him. Someone beside him laughed tauntingly. Kiran turned and saw Raynor Errington as a boy, lifting his riding crop over a frightened horse.

"Stop!" Kiran yelled, and then felt himself hurled beneath the stamping hooves. He put up both hands imploringly. "No," he cried.

The elder Lord Errington, Raynor's father, took his son's place. He aimed a kick at Kiran's defenseless ribs. Kiran writhed, groaning, and a squadron of guards set upon him, the guards who had waylaid him in the Temple corridor. "We're ordered to take you to the Master Priest."

But the Master Priest was there already, nodding to Bolivar, ordering him to cut Selid's throat.

"No!" Kiran cried out. He saw his mother riding, the saddle slipping, her foot trapped in the stirrup; saw Selid's blood pouring onto her hearthstone.

"Kiran," someone was yelling, "it isn't real!"

Who was it?

Lord Errington kicked again, his heavy boot hard as a stallion's hoof. Raynor screamed with laughter. A horse's terrified neigh merged with Kiran's mother's shrieks.

"The gyrfalcon's gift, Kiran!" someone called, the voice barely audible above the noise of panic and death. "It's the ring."

Who was calling? What ring?

"Help her!" Kiran shouted to his father, Eston, who appeared just out of reach. Eston's eyes overflowed with grief as he lifted a bottle of whisky to his lips.

The disembodied voice came again, lanced with pain. "Renchald is making you bring forth the past, Kiran; the worst moments of your life all at once."

Brock's voice.

Renchald watched Kiran grapple helplessly with his own phantoms. Errington kicked Brock repeatedly, but Brock kept yelling.

Renchald froze. How did Brock know the Master Priest's most inviolable secret? *No one* living, except him, knew what he could do with the gyrfalcon's gift and the keltice ring.

"The ring, Kiran! What you see isn't real." Brock grunted as Lord Errington bludgeoned his shoulder. "What happened before . . . not happening now!"

And, unbelievably, Kiran seemed to hear. He stopped twisting and moaning. He shut his eyes, rolling away from Errington's boots.

Keldes, Lord of Death, you must claim Kiran! Renchald thought.

The Master Priest heard a sudden thunder of hooves. He turned to see more than a dozen horses, Obsidian at their head, jump the pasture fence.

Kiran. He's speaking to the horses.

Renchald called to the god of his choosing bird. *Keldes, I have served you well. Help me now.*

The horses galloped straight at the guards, who were closing in. The men yelled commands to stop, but the horses ignored them. Obsidian struck a man down with his hooves. A white mare plowed into another guard. Two matched brown horses knocked Bolivar headlong, pinning him to the ground with their forelegs. Confounded, the rest of the guards began to scatter.

Renchald threw himself at Kiran. Brock sprang up to block him, then lost his balance and fell. Kiran scrambled to his feet. Renchald lunged again, but Kiran jumped away.

The swan's wild cry resounded. The falcon's screech echoed eerily. The birds had taken to the air once more.

Something very hard hit Renchald's shoulder. He spun halfway round and then fell. Rolling painfully onto his back, he looked up. For an eternal moment everything was supremely clear: Kiran looking down at him, Obsidian rearing up, his striking hooves higher than Kiran's head. And in front of the great black horse, the Master Priest saw a vision of Selid: *Ellerth will bury you, Renchald. I have seen it.*

The hooves came down. The gyrfalcon tumbled earthward, shrieking as it fell.

Breathing hard, Kiran stood over Renchald. The Master Priest's chest was crushed, his blood seeping into the earth. The ground was darkening rapidly, the sun's last rim sinking below the horizon. Obsidian paced beside the body, shaking his black mane and twitching his tail.

"Keldes forbid what my eyes tell me." It was Lord Errington. "What have you done?"

Kiran was having trouble taking in the magnitude of what had just happened. He knew he'd battled the Master Priest and won. But death? It seemed unthinkable. He was startled by how quickly Brock leaped at Errington, crying, "Get back!"

Errington scowled. "Don't presume—"

"Or perhaps you'd care to argue?" Brock waved a hand at Obsidian.

Errington backed up a few steps, then turned and hurried away, past Bolivar, who still lay pinned beneath the forefeet of two horses.

Brock bent to Renchald's body and lifted the dead hand. He took the keltice ring. "For safekeeping from the likes of Errington," he said, slipping it inside his robe.

Other members of the Temple were beginning to pour from the west entrance, like shadows running through the gathering dusk. Seeing them forced Kiran to think, to act. "Brock," he said, "we've got to leave now, before every priest and priestess here gathers their gifts against us." He pointed to the white mare who had charged the guard. "She's willing to have you as a rider."

Brock pulled himself onto the mare.

Ribs aching, Kiran climbed on Obsidian. He sent out a call to all the animals in the grounds.

Honking and hissing ensued, as a flock of geese soared over the stables from the pond and flew at the people who streamed from the Temple. Maddened horses sped down the causeway toward the gates. A great lowing and bleating issued from cattle and sheep breaking down fences.

Obsidian and the white mare galloped to the gates, the black swan sailing above their heads. The guards at the entrance, fully occupied fending off animals and birds, couldn't stop them.

Thus Kiran and Brock took their leave of the Temple of the Oracle.

And as they turned onto the main road north, Kiran heard a bark. *Jack. I knew you'd find me.*

Twenty-four

Bryn concentrated on her steps as she entered the queen's palace with Dawn and the Gilgamell Troupe. The troubadours had provided her with an ivory satin gown, its full skirt almost overpowered by flounces. She was having trouble walking smoothly.

Avrohom's costume was so bedecked with ostrich plumes that he created the illusion of a man moving from the realms of the gods into the world of mortals. Concealed in the jacket he wore was Selid's prophecy. He led their group with a confident stride through the domed hall that dwarfed them all. When Bryn dared look up, she caught her breath at the height of the great ceiling, a vast expanse of arching stone.

They had arrived in Zornowel after making very good time on the north-south highway, but a day had been lost notifying the queen of their arrival and receiving her invitation to attend her at the palace during court hours. Now, as the heralded troupe advanced, their steps rang upon polished marble. Lords and ladies stood to the sides and looked out from galleries above. "Ooh"s and "ah"s greeted the troubadours, who kissed their hands to the crowd.

They reached the carpeted area in front of the dais holding the queen's throne. The troubadours and Dawn bent into deep bows. Trying not to trample her skirts, Bryn followed their example.

Queen Alessandra welcomed them from a throne of gold set with emeralds in a pattern of flaring rays above her head. She sat regally upright, wearing the seven-pointed crown. Her eyes were shiny and black as onyx. Wrinkles, traced by years lived in service to her people, wove across her face.

Beside her upon a throne of silver was Princess Zorienne, wearing an opal tiara. The bones of her skull pressed against her frail skin as if already belonging to Keldes. Blankets were piled around her.

"The arrival of the Gilgamell Troupe is always a cause for celebration," said the queen. "Doubly so when you arrive early. But whom have you brought with you?"

"Meet my wife, Dawn," Avrohom answered, gesturing adoringly to the tall figure beside him, "and her traveling companion, Bryn."

"Marriage, Avrohom?" the queen said. "You have sadly disappointed ten thousand maidens who dreamed of becoming your wife. How are we to send condolences to so many?"

A buzz of appreciative laughter circled the hall.

Avrohom bowed. Stepping forward, he drew out Selid's prophecy. "I hope, Your Majesty," he said, his famous voice pitched for all to hear, "to spare you and the people of Sorana a much deeper grief." He extended the scroll. "I bring you a prophecy entrusted to me by the Oracle."

The queen lifted her eyebrows. "You surprise me, my dear troubadour." She signaled a gray-haired soldier. "Please take the scroll for me, Gideon."

Avrohom drew back. "This is meant for Your Majesty alone," he said.

Alessandra lifted a hand. Ten more soldiers in green doublets, with swords at their belts, came forward.

"You and your troupe are well regarded for your music, Avrohom," said the queen. "But troubadours have never been used to carry messages for the Oracle. Did no one tell you that important prophecies, after being penned by the Master Priest, are guarded thereafter? Those who carry such messages are carefully chosen from among the most seasoned warriors the Temple can provide, and never travel without a squadron to add to their protection."

At that crucial moment, before Avrohom uttered a word in reply, when all waited for him to speak again, heralds in the doorway called out: "The First Priestess of the Temple of the Oracle!"

Along with everyone else, Bryn turned to look.

Ilona marched down the walkway toward the throne, unmistakable in her gold-embroidered robes. Beside her was a familiar yellow-haired woman, dressed in the red robes of a priestess. Temple guards filed behind them.

Bryn found it hard to breathe. *What is Clea doing here? And why is she dressed as a priestess?*

293

"Your Majesty—" Avrohom began.

The queen held up a hand. She waited until Ilona and Clea bowed before her.

"We come with an urgent prophecy from the Master Priest," Ilona said, thrusting forth a scroll.

The queen took it. "Your arrival is very timely, First Priestess," she said. She snapped her fingers. Men-at-arms grabbed the troubadours. Dawn and Bryn were also seized and forced back from the queen.

Gideon wrested Selid's prophecy from Avrohom's grasp.

The queen stared hard at her captives. "Perhaps, First Priestess, you can tell me why a prophecy has been brought to me by a band of troubadours."

Clea spoke, her lovely face expressing concern. "False prophecy, Your Majesty."

"The Gilgamell Troupe was duped into believing they would do Your Majesty a service," said Ilona.

Clea pointed at Bryn. "That woman is a traitor to the Oracle. It was she who planted lies in the hearts of these good musicians."

The hall itself seemed to flutter as everyone craned their necks to see.

"It's not true," Bryn cried. "The Temple of the Oracle has been lying to Your Majesty! Your daughter, Princess Zorienne, is—" Her throat swelled, choking her. She tried to see the queen, but found Clea's blue eyes instead. Clea waved a dull black feather, tinged with gray.

But her feather's gone.

Bryn's hands and feet froze in place, her legs giving way so that the soldier who guarded her had to hold her up. Her ears buzzed. Pain seared her spine. *This can't be happening.* Her strength was draining, running like water through the quarry sluices. She tried to call back the force of her life, but it was like calling to a sinking tide.

Death. She's cursing me with death this time.

Ellerth, please, please. Don't let it end this way. We can't have come so far only to give this day to Keldes.

Summoning every drop of life remaining, Bryn wrenched her captured gaze from Clea. She looked mutely at the First Priestess. Their eyes met. Ilona's gaze seemed possessed of an unearthly power that Bryn had never seen there before.

The First Priestess sprang suddenly into action. She leaped at Clea. She shoved her violently. Clea tumbled. As she fell, Ilona snatched the vulture's feather.

Temple guards stood transfixed. The queen's soldiers drew their weapons, ranging themselves between their sovereign and the strife. Jumping to her feet, Clea kicked out viciously. Her boot connected with Ilona's solar plexus. Ilona doubled over, the dark feather slipping from her hand.

The feather slid along the floor. Temple guards rushed to catch the First Priestess before she fell. Queen and soldiers watched, temporarily stunned to see members of the Temple battling one another in front of the throne of Sorana.

Bryn was regaining her power to move. Her own

feet could hold her. Her vision lightened and she could hear again. A breeze ruffled her hair.

Clea plucked the vulture's quill from the floor. She whirled upon Bryn.

But the breeze rose swiftly to a furious roar. A blast tore the feather from Clea's grasp. She lunged after it. It eluded her. As if held by a human hand, it moved in intricate whorls just out of her reach. It flipped in the air and raced at Clea as if shot from a bow. The shaft thrust itself into her forehead, where it quivered like an arrow. She screamed, sinking to her knees. The odor of carrion surrounded her.

The wind was not finished. It blew across the queen's soldiers, breaking their grip on their prisoners. Dawn stood like a flagpole, her gown a wild banner. Avrohom's ostrich plumes burst from their stitches and soared into the dome.

Soldiers made a grab for the troubadours. The howling tempest flattened them. Among them, only Gideon remained standing; he squinted against the gale, helpless to prevent the wind from snatching Selid's prophecy. A purposeful gust dropped it into the queen's lap.

The wind stopped.

Avrohom thought quickly. "Hear me!" His famous voice blared into the sudden silence. "Anyone who touches a weapon will feel the might of the storm once more!"

Bryn doubted it would happen as he said. A faint stirring of the air close to her skin was all that remained of the storm, but she was thankful Avrohom had spoken, and relieved that none of the soldiers raised their blades; instead they toiled to their feet and stood, dazed and swaying, weapons sheathed.

"Your Majesty," Avrohom said in ringing tones, "I ask you again, this time as a troubadour and faithful subject, to read the prophecy delivered to you by Ellerth's power."

Alessandra swallowed, staring at the scroll in her lap. She picked it up. "After such a delivery, what queen would refuse?"

She unbound the ribbons. She unrolled the parchment, revealing Selid's beautiful script.

As she read the prophecy, the only sound in the dome was the breathing of the crowd.

The queen's eyes misted. She turned to look at her daughter with love and hope. "Gideon," she said. "Take soldiers, and bring Mednonifer to me."

Gideon saluted. He and a company of soldiers marched out.

The First Priestess ordered the Temple guards to form a tight circle around Clea and secure her hands. They did as she asked.

Ilona beckoned to Bryn. "Come forward, wind-chosen prophetess."

Watched by queen and princess, Bryn did so. "Explain to Clea," Ilona said, "and to all gathered here: what is the meaning of the feather in her forehead?"

Bristling guards made way for Bryn to approach nearer. She looked down at the woman who had tried to curse her with death. "You are cursed with your own feather, Clea, and the curse is this: for the rest of your life you'll be powerless to cast curses."

Clea didn't answer. Pale and sweating, she glared while people stared in ghastly fascination.

"Not so pleasant when it's you who's cursed," Bryn said softly.

Ilona fixed Clea with a powerful glance. "You are no longer a priestess," she said. She turned to Bryn. "You shall determine her fate, wind-chosen prophetess. What shall be done with her?"

Bryn reached out, and took the dark feather from Clea's forehead. It slid easily into her fingers, leaving behind a small round mark. A little whirl-wind grew in Bryn's hand. It tossed the feather into the dome, where a current of air floated it toward the door. At the entrance, a strong breeze rose and carried it outside. For a moment it hung suspended, a fleck of darkness against the blue sky, and then it blew away.

"I put Clea into your care, First Priestess," Bryn said.

Ilona wondered if she should tell Bryn exactly what had happened. Should she reveal that before Clea could complete her curse, the wind's power had been augmented by the golden eagle's gift?

When Clea began cursing you, Bryn, I knew at once she must be stopped. A death curse was never sanctioned by me.

Ilona's gift—that of being able to magnify the gifts

of others, enhance and make them stronger—had caught hold of the wind's dying force and brought it back just in time.

Keldes was very eager for you, wind-chosen prophetess. He backed Clea with dreadful power.

Bryn leaned against Dawn; she looked tired but content.

If I tell her, my talent will no longer be secret. Ilona thought Bryn could probably be trusted, but then again, true secrets were meant to be kept. She would consider the matter carefully.

Gideon returned, escorting a tall, narrow-shouldered man with a long black beard and overgrown eyebrows: Mednonifer, queen's physician. Hustled along by soldiers, he endeavored to maintain his dignity by walking so quickly that it wouldn't appear he was being hurried. The resultant hasty shuffle only made him look ridiculous.

Pushed in front of Alessandra, Mednonifer gave a graceless bow. "My queen." He bowed to Princess Zorienne. "Princess, I fear you are weary."

Queen Alessandra studied the physician. "Weary?" she said.

He nodded his expert assessment. "Her unfortunate malady, Your Majesty." He lifted an eyebrow in carefully posed concern. "Is this why I have been called to your presence, madam?"

"Yes, it is. But I doubt you would recommend the remedy that shall cure her."

Puzzlement. "The remedy?"

Queen Alessandra lifted Selid's scroll. "I have

received a prophecy from the Oracle," she said, watching him closely.

"Ah. You wish me to hear it?"

"You, and all those present." Her wide gesture swept the hall. She turned to the Gilgamell Troupe. "Avrohom, I do not have a troubadour's voice, therefore I appeal to you to read aloud this prophecy."

Avrohom bowed. He took the scroll. Facing the gathering, he lifted his powerful voice:

"*To Her Honorable Majesty, Alessandra, Queen of Sorana: This prophecy proceeds from the Oracle's light. Princess Zorienne's illness is due to poison administered by Mednonifer, queen's physician. Not by food or drink, but by the air she breathes while sleeping.*"

Avrohom paused, allowing a collective gasp.

Mednonifer's face went ashen. "Lies," he cried. "I have tended her health!" He broke into a trembling run.

The queen did not have to signal her soldiers—a battle nearly broke out as each tried to be the one to bind him.

"*The poison,*" Avrohom continued, "*has been applied to the princess's bed curtains. Send for a healer from the Healer's Keep in Bellandra for Zorienne.*"

Avrohom paused again. Princess Zorienne had risen from her throne. She stood, a frail woman with eyes more luminous than the opals on her gown.

"*Look to the east, Your Majesty,*" Avrohom continued, "*for those who would supplant Zorienne's reign.*

"*Brought from my pen before the gods,*

"*Renchald, Master Priest of the Temple of the Oracle.*"

"No!" Mednonifer shrieked. "The Master Priest—"
Gideon clapped a hand over his mouth.

"Take him away," said Queen Alessandra, "lest I lose my conscience and order him spitted on the throne room floor."

As the former physician was led out, a bright scarlet bird flew in, straight to Zorienne. Circling her head once, it winged away again, leaving behind a single red feather that floated gently to the floor.

When the pandemonium died down, the queen declared that Mednonifer should have a chance to prove his innocence. He would be confined within Zorienne's bed curtains until a healer arrived from Bellandra.

Ilona bowed to the queen. "Your Majesty, these events I've been privileged to witness have made plain that the second prophecy you hold—the one I gave into your hand—may be false. Would you be so kind as to give me leave to study it?"

Queen Alessandra, radiant as Solz himself, needed a moment to recollect. She retrieved the sealed scroll. She handed it to Ilona, who concealed her passionate relief to have it back. Though she didn't know the contents, she suspected that if they were revealed and held up against the truth, the Oracle's authority would be damaged.

She would read it later, in private. She, the First Priestess, would break the seal of the Temple and find out what Renchald had written.

Reverently, she bent to pick up the red feather. *I will honor you always, dear cardinal-chosen prophetess.*

The Gilgamell Troupe filled the palace dome with music to celebrate the news that Zorienne might live to rule Sorana.

Thrilled though she was that Selid's prophecy had been delivered, Bryn couldn't shake an equally strong feeling of sadness. The sight of the red cardinal's feather landing on the floor had touched off a terrible dread. The First Priestess's face when she picked it up, and the way she had held it like a flower in homage to the dead, made Bryn want to burst into tears.

She longed to be gone.

Twenty-five

Days later, on the road north to Zornowel, Brock told Kiran, "We should stop to rest soon, Mox."

"The sun is still high," Kiran objected.

Just then, Jack yapped wildly and took off running. "Come on," Kiran yelled to Brock. *Run, Obsidian.* The stallion leaped forward, dashing after Jack. The white mare's hooves thudded behind.

Rounding a bend, they pulled up short just in time to avoid crashing into a party of riders led by the First Priestess. With her rode a squadron of Temple guards; the sun bounced off the gold and red insignia on their breastplates. Jack darted past them all.

In their midst was Clea, drooping in her saddle. Kiran looked at her warily. A puncture wound marked her forehead, and she wore a plain dress. Her blue eyes smoldered. Her mouth drew a bitter line. She said nothing.

Ilona bowed from horseback, her dark eyes full of questions.

Jack reappeared, weaving through the horses of the guard with Bryn beside him. Kiran jumped from

Obsidian's back. Bryn reached for him in welcome, and he took both her hands in his. Her eyes lit like pools of golden fire.

Ilona chose an inn for all of them to stay in. Avrohom insisted on gathering the group of friends into his room. "You also, First Priestess. True stories are best heard in song, but before they become songs, they need to be told."

Thus, Bryn learned from Kiran how Selid had died, and how Kiran had been cursed. The First Priestess hadn't told her about those events. Hearing of Selid's fate, Bryn bowed her head. Tears gathered in her heart. The cardinal-chosen prophetess had indeed given her blood for Sorana.

A soft breeze floated around Bryn; a gentle voice spoke in her mind: *Do not grieve. I walk with Monzapel now, and Lance is with me.*

Brock was the one who described how the Master Priest had joined Keldes. Listening to his story, Bryn felt furious elation tinged with sadness. Renchald had written false prophecies to the queen, plotted with Errington to prevent Zorienne's reign, pushed Kiran to pair with Clea, ordered Selid killed and Kiran cursed. For those crimes—especially for the horror of taking Selid's life—his death under the hooves of a valiant horse seemed fitting.

But it was he who had lifted her from her bleak life in Uste. Because of him, she had been educated in the Temple. She'd known the splendor of the Oracle's light. She had met Dawn and Jack and Obsidian, Alyce, Jacinta, Willow, and Brock, who would be her friends for life.

And she had met Kiran. He sat across from her, firelight illuminating his cinnamon-brown eyes.

Now Renchald was dead. She wondered who among the priests would take his place. She glanced at the First Priestess to see how she took the news, but Ilona's face showed little.

Avrohom told the tale of what had taken place at the palace, Kiran watching him intently as he spoke. When he finished with a report that Princess Zorienne had already experienced improvement after one night spent in a new bedchamber, Kiran's eyes glistened.

Everyone was quiet for a few moments. Then Ilona spoke to Bryn. "Will you return to the Temple and serve the Oracle, wind-chosen prophetess?"

Bryn recalled the dazzling light of the alabaster chamber filling her with visions; recalled that once she'd wanted to be a priestess more than anything.

"Before you answer," the First Priestess continued, "you should know that I gave Clea the choice to continue studying in the Temple if she wished. She has chosen to return to the Eastland. Though I pointed out the likelihood of civil war between our queen and her father now that his perfidy has been revealed, Clea was adamant. Therefore I have sent a message to the Temple so that Bolivar and several of his soldiers will meet us in Tunise and escort her eastward."

Bryn's heart lifted. The Temple without Clea

would be a much warmer place. *Without Clea and the Master Priest.*

In her mind, she heard Renchald's voice again: *There she will be with others of her kind. She will serve the Oracle.* Might those words come true at last? "Would I be welcome?" she asked the First Priestess.

"You would be welcomed by the First Priestess," Ilona answered.

"I would like to serve the Oracle, yes," Bryn answered. "And carry on Selid's legacy."

Ilona nodded her stately head. "And you, Kiran?"

Kiran lifted an eyebrow. "Bolivar might need convincing before he allows Brock and me within a mile of the Temple walls."

Brock snorted. "Convincing is a *kind* word, First Priestess. Bolivar may have to be assigned to the Eastland permanently after you make him escort Clea back to her papa."

"I will intercede with Bolivar," Ilona promised. "The Temple has need of wise owl-chosen and swan-chosen prophets."

"Where will you find a *wise* swan-chosen prophet?" Brock asked, and then ducked a punch from Kiran.

"But wait!" Dawn cried. "Where does that leave us? Bryn, you must agree to travel with the troupe every spring."

"So you must," agreed Avrohom, grinning mischievously. "We'll help persuade the new Master Priest— whoever he may be—that you are needed for inspiration to write ballads of courage and adventure."

Brock slapped his forehead. "Master Priest," he

muttered. He pulled something from his pocket. "Sorry, First Priestess, I meant to give this to you sooner, for the next Master Priest." He opened his hand. Glittering in his palm was the keltice ring.

Ilona drew back. "Only the Master Priest may hold the keltice ring."

Brock hung his head. "I probably violated at least two dozen sacred laws when I took it, but I only wanted to keep it from Lord Errington."

Ilona stared into the laughing black eyes of the smith's son. "I cannot take it from you. No one but the Master Priest may hold it."

Brock lifted an eyebrow. "You trust me not to lose it before another Master Priest is selected?"

Ilona shook her head. "If I were to hold the keltice ring, it would destroy my powers."

Brock frowned in confusion. Ilona rose from her chair and bowed to him: First Priestess greeting Master Priest of the Temple of the Oracle.

Kiran thumped Brock on the back. "She means you, Owl-face."

At Brock's dumbfounded expression, Avrohom flung back his head and gave a delighted ululating cry. Soon everyone in the room joined the merriment. Even Jack, curled next to Kiran, lifted his head and howled his imitation of human laughter.

Zeb began beating his drums with great jubilance. Jeffrey grabbed his lute, Negasi his lyre. And Avrohom sang.

"No one could guess all the places I've seen,
and no one believe where I've gone.
I wander in joy through the places you dream
And give you the heart of my song."

When the other guests in the inn heard the music of the Gilgamell Troupe, they broke in on the gathering of friends, begging the famous musicians to play for them, too. The troupe good-naturedly agreed to move to the main room of the inn. Word spread like fire until half the town joined them.

Kiran and Bryn danced together, dances of pure joy. No curse interfered with the grace of her steps; she dipped and rose like a golden breeze, her feet keeping perfect time with the drum. This night, there were no interruptions from unwanted partners. For song after song, they glided around the room until she laughingly declared she had to rest.

She went to sit with Dawn, and Kiran stepped outside with Jack. He gazed at the stars, dazzling flowers of light in the quiet field of eternity.

Jack's nose prodded his leg. The dog sat with his tongue out, grinning. "All right," Kiran said. "You're allowed to be smug." *Jack, it's time I found you a lady love.*

Jack snuffled, shaking out his fur.

"You don't think I could do as good a job for you as you've done for me?" Kiran said.

The dog sniffed disdainfully. Kiran kneeled beside him. "Thank you, my friend. You chose well."

*   *   *

Bryn sat next to Dawn in a corner of the crowded inn, watching a few determined dancers make their way around the floor. In another corner, four Temple guards, looking stiff and out of place in the gathering, guarded Clea.

"The Temple won't be the same without Clea, will it?" Dawn said, rolling her eyes.

Bryn shrugged. "It's her choice to go home. She'd rather be in the Eastland when civil war arrives than stay with us. Ilona said she could continue to study at the Temple if she wished."

"Without the power to cast curses? That would be like asking a vulture to live without carrion," Dawn replied. "Not in her nature."

"As a favor to myself," Bryn said with a wink, "I'm going to forget her."

"That reminds me—when you see Eloise, blast the sneer off her face, will you, Bryn? As a favor to *me*."

Bryn laughed. "May she meet with a cyclone."

"I'm glad Clea can't curse anyone again, but she can still make mischief—she's rich enough."

Bryn leaned forward to poke her friend's shoulder. "So are you. But what else have you got? Friendship, music, and adventure."

"True." Dawn's azure eyes sparkled. "Speaking of adventure, where shall we travel next spring?"

Bryn smiled. "There's a certain beloved sinkhole some call Uste that I'd like to visit. Beyond that, I want to go wherever the music is playing." She stood. "I'm going to find Kiran."

"I saw him go out with Jack." Dawn pointed to the door.

Outside, Kiran stood with Jack. Bryn gave a little skip toward them. Jack bounded to meet her, barking joyfully, leaping up to lick her face.

"You shouldn't let him paw you that way," Kiran said, smiling.

The moon's crescent shone beside silvery stars. With one accord, they turned toward the inn's stable, where Obsidian would be. "When Avrohom makes a tune of your journey to the queen," Kiran said, "your courage will be sung throughout the world."

Bryn shook her head, smiling. "Without friends I'd be a coward."

"I don't believe you." He stopped outside the stable door, and turned to face her. His arms went round her, pulling her close.

He leaned down. As she kissed Kiran, Bryn's heart danced like a breeze through green fields.

And above them, a plume of thistledown caught the light of the stars.

Glossary

abanya (uh-bon-ya) The abanya can be thought of as the territory of the mind. Most people—if they think of it at all—consider it to be a symbolic realm only. The abanya is where dreams occur. Unseen by most, it exists constantly, interpenetrating normal physical reality.

dream body The part of a person that travels through the abanya.

inner barriers The border of an individual's inner landscape; the barriers may be fortified and strong or relatively weak. Broken barriers bring about ill health.

inner landscape The part of the abanya that reflects an individual person's inner nature.

* * *

Ayel (ai-yel) A member of the pantheon of gods of Sorana. Ruler of battle and warriorship. Associated with a planet that appears red in the sky.

Ellerth A member of the pantheon of gods of Sorana. Ruler of Earth and its creatures. Associated with the Earth.

311

Keldes (kel-deez) A member of the pantheon of gods of Sorana. Ruler of the domain of the dead. Associated with a large planet.

Monzapel A member of the pantheon of gods of Sorana. Ruler of intuition. Associated with the moon.

Sendral A director (male) of an aspect of Temple life; e.g., there is a Sendral of Acolytes, a Sendral of Horses, a Sendral of the Vineyard.

Sendrata A director (female) of an aspect of Temple life; e.g., there is a Sendrata of Handmaids, a Sendrata of the Dairy, a Sendrata of Kitchens.

Solz A member of the pantheon of gods of Sorana. Ruler of light and life. Associated with the sun.

Vernelda A member of the pantheon of gods of Sorana. Ruler of justice and love. Associated with a very bright planet often seen on the horizon in the morning and evening.

Winjessen A member of the pantheon of gods of Sorana. Ruler of thought, learning, and travel. Associated with the planet closest to the sun.